HOLES FOR FACES

Ramsey Campbell

Dark Regions Press
ભ 2013 ભ

FOR JACK AND ROBIN—

YOUR KIND OF TALES, I HOPE!

CONTENTS

Passing through Peacehaven

"Wait," Marsden shouted as he floundered off his seat. His vision was so overcast with sleep that it was little better than opaque, but so far as he could see through the carriages the entire train was deserted. "Terminate" was the only word he retained from the announcement that had wakened him. He blundered to the nearest door and leaned on the window to slide it further open while he groped beyond it for the handle. The door swung wide so readily that he almost sprawled on the platform. In staggering dangerously backwards to compensate he slammed the door, which seemed to be the driver's cue. The train was heading into the night before Marsden realised he had never seen the station in his life.

"Wait," he cried, but it was mostly a cough as the smell of some October fire caught in his throat. His eyes felt blackened by smoke and stung when he blinked, so that he could barely see where he was going as he lurched after the train. He succeeded in clearing his vision just in time to glimpse distance or a bend in the track extinguish the last light of the train like an ember. He panted coughing to a halt and stared red-eyed around him.

Two signs named the station Peacehaven. The grudging glow of half a dozen lamps that put him in mind of streetlights in an old photograph illuminated stretches of both platforms but seemed shy of the interior of the enclosed bridge that led across the pair of tracks. A brick wall twice his height extended into the dark beyond the ends of the platform he was on. The exit from the station was on the far side of the tracks, through a passage where he could just distinguish a pay phone in the gloom. Above the wall of that platform, and at some distance, towered an object that he wasted seconds in identifying as a factory chimney. He should be looking for the times of any trains to Manchester, but the timetable among the vintage posters alongside the platform was blackened by more than the dark. As he squinted at it, someone spoke behind him.

It was the voice that had wakened him. Apart from an apology for a delay, the message was a blur. "I can't hear much at the best of times," Marsden grumbled. At least the station hadn't closed for the night, and a timetable on the other platform was beside a lamp. He made for the bridge and climbed the wooden stairs to the elevated corridor, where narrow grimy windows above head height and criss-crossed by wire mesh admitted virtually no illumination. He needn't shuffle through the dark; his mobile phone could light the way. He reached in his overcoat pocket, and dug deeper to find extra emptiness.

Marjorie wouldn't have approved of the words that escaped his lips. He wasn't fond of them himself, especially when he heard them from children in the street. He and Marjorie would have done their best to keep their grandchildren innocent of such language and of a good deal else that was in vogue, but they would need to have had a son or daughter first. He ran out of curses as he trudged back across the bridge, which felt narrowed by darkness piled against the walls. The platform was utterly bare. Did he remember hearing or perhaps only feeling the faintest thump as he'd left his seat? There was no doubt that he'd left the mobile on the train.

He was repeating himself when he wondered if he could be heard. His outburst helped the passage to muffle the announcer's unctuous voice, which apparently had information about a signal failure. Marsden wasn't going to feel like one. He marched out of darkness into dimness, which lightened somewhat as he reached the platform.

2

Had vandals tried to set fire to the timetable? A blackened corner was peeling away from the bricks. Marsden pushed his watch higher on his wizened wrist until the strap took hold. Theoretically the last train—for Bury and Oldham and Manchester—was due in less than twenty minutes. "What's the hold-up again? Say it clearly this time," Marsden invited not quite at the top of his voice. When there was no response he made for the phone on the wall.

Was it opposite some kind of memorial? No, the plaque was a ticket window boarded up behind cracked glass. Surely the gap beneath the window couldn't be occupied by a cobweb, since the place was staffed. He stood with his back to the exit from the station and fumbled coins into the slot beside the receiver before groping for the dial that he could barely see in the glimmer from the platform.

"Ray and Marjorie Marsden must be engaged elsewhere. Please don't let us wonder who you were or when you tried to contact us or where we can return the compliment..." His answering message had amused them when he recorded it—at least, Marjorie had made the face that meant she appreciated his wit—but now it left him feeling more alone than he liked. "Are you there?" he asked the tape. "You'll have gone up, will you? You'll have gone up, of course. Just to let you know I'm stranded by an unexpected change of trains. If you play me back don't worry, I'll be home as soon as practicable. Oh, and the specialist couldn't find anything wrong. I know, you'll say it shows I can hear when I want to. Not true, and shall I tell you why? I'd give a lot to hear you at this very moment. Never mind. I will soon."

Even saying so much in so many words earned him no response, and yet he didn't feel unheard. His audience could be the station announcer, who was presumably beyond one of the doors that faced each other across the corridor, although neither betrayed the faintest trace of light. "I nearly didn't say I love you," he added in a murmur that sounded trapped inside his skull. "Mind you, you'll know that, won't you? If you don't after all these years you never will. I suppose that had better be it for

3

now as long as you're fast asleep."

He still felt overheard. Once he'd hung up he yielded to a ridiculous urge to poke his head out of the corridor. The platforms were deserted, and the tracks led to unrelieved darkness. He might as well learn where he'd ended up while there was no sign of a train. "Just stepping outside," he informed anyone who should know.

The corridor didn't seem long enough to contain so much blackness. He only just managed to refrain from rubbing his eyes as he emerged onto an unpromising road. The front of the station gave it no light, but the pavements on either side of the cracked weedy tarmac were visibly uneven. Beyond high railings across the road the grounds of the factory bristled with tall grass, which appeared to shift, although he couldn't feel a wind. Here and there a flagstone showed pale through the vegetation. A sign beside the open gates had to do with motors or motor components, and Marsden was considering a closer look to pass the time when the announcer spoke again. "Going to attract effect" might have been part of the proclamation, and all that Marsden was able to catch.

Some delay must be owing to a track defect, of course. Much of the voice had ended up as echoes beyond the railings or simply dissipated in the night, but he also blamed its tone for confusing him. It had grown so oily that it sounded more like a parody of a priest than any kind of railway official. Marsden tramped into the passage and knocked on the door beside the ticket window. "Will you repeat that, please?"

If this sounded like an invitation to an argument, it wasn't taken up. He found the doorknob, which felt flaky with age, but the door refused to budge. He rubbed his finger and thumb together as he crossed to the other door, which tottered open at his knock, revealing only a storeroom. It was scattered with brushes and mops, or rather their remains, just distinguishable in the meagre light through a window so nearly opaque that on the platform he'd mistaken it for an empty poster frame. Vandals must have been in the room; the dimness smelled as ashen as it looked, while the tangles of sticks that would once have been handles seemed blackened by more than the dark. That was all he managed to discern before the voice spoke to him.

Was the fellow too close to the microphone? If he was trying to be clearer, it achieved the opposite. Of course nobody was next to alive; a train was the next to arrive. "Speak clearly, not up," Marsden shouted as he slammed the door and hurried to the bridge, where he did his best to maintain his pace by keeping to the middle of the passage. If an object or objects were being dragged somewhere behind him, he wanted to see what was happening. He clumped breathlessly down the stairs and limped onto the platform. How could he have thought the windows were poster frames? There was one on either side of the exit, and although both rooms were unlit, a figure was peering through the window of the office.

Or was it a shadow? It was thin and black enough. There was no light inside the room to cast it, and yet it must be a shadow, since it had nothing for a face. Marsden was still trying to identify its source when he noticed that the door he'd slammed was wide open. It had felt unsteady on its hinges, and at least he had an explanation for the dragging sound he'd heard. He set about laughing at his own unease, and then the laugh snagged in his throat like another cough. The silhouette was no longer pressed against the window.

Had it left traces of its shape on the discoloured glass? As he paced back and forth, trying either to confirm or shake off the impression, he felt like an animal trapped in a cage and watched by spectators. He'd met with no success by the time the voice that might belong to the owner of the shadow had more to say. "Where's the party?" Marsden was provoked to mutter. "What's departing?" he demanded several times as loud. "It's supposed to arrive first," he pointed out, glaring along the tracks at the unrelieved night. The few words he'd managed to recognise or at least to guess had sounded oilier than ever, close to a joke. Why couldn't the fellow simply come and tell him what to expect? Was he amusing himself by spying on the solitary passenger? "Yes, you've got a customer," Marsden declared. "He's the chap who has to stand out here in the cold because you can't be bothered to provide a waiting-room."

The complaint left him more aware of the storeroom, so that he could have imagined he was being observed from there too. He would much rather fancy his return home to the bed that he hoped Marjorie was keeping warm for him. As he hugged himself to fend off the late October chill he wasn't too far from experiencing how her arms would feel when she turned in her sleep to embrace him. He couldn't help wishing that the tape had brought him her voice.

The only one he was likely to hear was the announcer's, and he needed to ensure he did. He lowered himself onto a bench opposite the exit and planted his hands on his knees. Though the seat felt unwelcomingly moist if not actually rotten, he concentrated on staying alert for the next message. His ears were throbbing with the strain, and his skin felt as if his sense of being watched were gathering on it, by the time his attention was rewarded.

Was someone clinking glasses? Had the staff found an excuse to celebrate? Marsden had begun to wonder if they were deriding his predicament when he identified the noise of bricks knocking together. The factory was more dilapidated than he'd been able to make out, then, and there was movement in the rubble. Perhaps an animal was at large—more than one, by the sound of it—or else people were up to no good. Suppose they were the vandals who'd tried to set fire to the station? Would the announcer deign to emerge from hiding if they or others like them trespassed on railway property, or was he capable of leaving his solitary customer to deal with them? Marsden could hear nothing now except his own heart, amplified by his concentration if not pumped up by stress. He wasn't sure if he glimpsed surreptitious movement at the exit, where he could easily imagine that the dark was growing crowded; indeed, the passage was so nearly lightless that any number of intruders might sneak into it unseen. He was gripping his knees and crouching forward like a competitor at the start of some pensioners' event while he strained to see whether anyone was sidling through the gloom when his heart jumped, and he did.

The voice was louder than ever, and its meaning more blurred. Even the odd relatively clear phrase amid the magnified mumbling left much to be desired. Marsden could have thought he was being warned about some further decay and informed that he had a hearing problem. The latter comment must refer to engineering, but wasn't this unreasonable too? How many hindrances was the train going to encounter? The reports of its progress were beginning to seem little better than jokes. But here was a final one, however inefficiently pronounced. It meant that the train was imminent, not that anything would shortly be alive.

Perhaps the man was slurring his words from drunkenness, and the clinking had indeed been glass, unless the contrivance of equality had reached such a pitch that the station was obliged to employ an announcer with a speech impediment. On that basis Marsden might seek a job as a telephone operator, but he and Marjorie were resigned to leaving the world to the young and aggressive. He peered along the railway, where the view stayed as black as the depths of the corridor opposite. All that his strained senses brought him besides a charred smell and a crawling of the skin was, eventually, another message.

"You won't be burying this old man," he retorted under his clogged breath. While the announcement must have referred to the train to Bury and Oldham, the voice had resembled a priest's more than ever. "And where's this train that's supposed to be arriving?" he demanded loud enough to rouse an echo in the exit corridor.

The next message was no answer. Presumably he was being told that unattended luggage would be removed without warning, but since he had no luggage, what was the point? Couldn't the fellow see him? Perhaps some legislation allowed him to be blind as well as largely incomprehensible. Still, here were another few words Marsden understood, even if he couldn't grasp where passengers were being told to change. "What was that?" he shouted, but the announcer hadn't finished. His tone was so ecclesiastical that for

7

the space of an exaggerated heartbeat Marsden fancied he was being offered some kind of service, and then he recognised the phrase. It was "out of service".

He sucked in a breath that he had to replace once he'd finished coughing. "What's out?" he spluttered. "Where's my train?"

The only reply was an echo, all the more derisive for sounding more like "Where's my Ray?" He levered himself to his feet, muttering an impolite word at having somehow blackened the knee of his trousers, and hobbled to the bridge. An arthritic pang set him staggering like an old drunk, but he succeeded in gaining the top of the stairs without recourse to the banisters. He preferred to keep to the middle of the bridge, especially along the passage over the tracks. It was too easy to imagine that the darkness beneath the obscured windows was peopled with supine figures. Surely the humped mounds consisted simply of litter, despite the marks on a window about halfway along, five elongated trails that might have been left by a sooty hand as its owner tried to haul his body up. That afternoon Marsden had given a few coins to a woman lying in a railway underpass, but he hoped not to encounter anyone of the kind just now. He faltered and then stumbled fast to the end of the passage, mumbling "No change" as he clattered down to the platform.

"Here's your customer," he said at several times the volume, "and what are you going to do about it?" The question trailed away, however, and not only because the office was so thoroughly unlit from within. The imprint on the window had silenced him. He might still have taken it for a shadow if it weren't so incomplete. Just the top half of a face with holes for eyes was recognisable, and the bones of a pair of hands.

Some grimy vandal must have been trying to see into the room. Of course the marks weren't on the inside of the glass, or if they were, that was no reason to think that the figure at the window had stood in the same place. Nevertheless Marsden wasn't anxious to look closer, although he'd managed to distinguish nothing in the office. He made for the door with all the confidence he could summon up.

The storeroom distracted him. Even if his stinging eyes had adjusted to the dimness, he couldn't understand how he'd failed to see that the room was more than untidy. It was full of burned sticks and bits of stick, some of which were thin as twigs. One charred tangle that, to judge by the blackened lump at the nearer end, consisted partly of a mop or brush came close to blocking the door. When he lurched to shut away the sight the edge of the door caught the object, and he glimpsed it crumbling into restless fragments before the slam resounded through the passage. He limped to the office door and, having rapped on a scaly panel, shouted "Will you come and tell me to my face what's happening?"

As far as he could determine, silence was the answer. He could have fancied that the station and its surroundings were eager for his next outburst. "You're meant to make yourself plain," he yelled. "I couldn't understand half of what you said."

If he was hoping to provoke a response, it didn't work. Had he offended the man? "I need to know where I'm going," he insisted. "I don't think that's unreasonable, do you?"

Perhaps the fellow thought he could behave as he liked while he was in charge. Perhaps he felt too important to descend to meeting the public, an attitude that would explain his tone of voice. Or might he not be on the premises? If he was beyond the door, what could he expect to gain by lying low? Surely not even the worst employee would act that way—and then Marsden wondered if he'd strayed on the truth. Suppose it wasn't a railway employee who was skulking in the office?

The kind of person who'd tried to set fire to the station would certainly be amused by Marsden's plight and think it even more of a joke to confuse him. Perhaps the indistinctness of the announcements was the result of suppressed mirth. Marsden shouldn't waste any more time if the information was false. He hurried to the phone and glared at the dim wall, which didn't bear a single notice.

No doubt vandals had removed any advertisements for taxis. At least the phone wasn't disabled. He fumbled the receiver off its hook and leaned almost close enough to kiss the blackened dial as he clawed at an enquiry number. He could have thought his hearing had improved when the bell began to ring; it sounded close as the next room. The voice it roused was keeping its distance, however. "Can you speak up?" Marsden urged.

"Where are you calling, please?"

This was sharp enough for a warning. Presumably the speaker was ensuring he was heard. "Peacehaven," Marsden said. "Taxis."

"Where is that, please?"

"Peacehaven," Marsden pronounced loud enough for it to grow blurred against his ear before he realised that he wasn't being asked to repeat the name. "Somewhere near Manchester."

In the pause that ensued he might have heard movement outside the passage. His hectic pulse obscured the noise, which must have been the tall grass scraping in a wind, even if he couldn't feel it. He was relieved when the voice returned until he grasped its message. "Not listed," it said.

"Forgive me, I wasn't asking for Peacehaven Taxis. Any cab firm here will do."

"There is no listing."

Was the fellow pleased to say so? He sounded as smug as the worst sort of priest. "The nearest one, then," Marsden persisted. "I think that might be—"

"There are no listings for Peacehaven."

"No, that can't be right. I'm in it. I'm at the railway station. You must have a number for that at least."

"There is none."

Marsden was aware of the dark all around him and how many unheard lurkers it could hide. "Is there anything more I can do for you?" the voice said.

It sounded so fulsome that Marsden was convinced he was being mocked. "You've done quite enough," he blurted and slammed the receiver on its hook.

He could try another enquiry number, or might he call the police? What could he say that would bring them to his aid yet avoid seeming as pathetic as he was determined not to feel? There was one voice he yearned to hear in the midst of all the darkness, but the chance of this at so late an hour seemed little better than infinitesimal. Nevertheless he was groping for change and for the receiver. He scrabbled at the slot with coins and dragged the indistinct holes around the dial. The bell measured the seconds and at last made way for a human voice. It was his own. "Ray and Marjorie Marsden must be engaged elsewhere…"

"I am. I wish you weren't," he murmured and felt all the more helpless for failing to interrupt his mechanical self. Then his distant muffled voice fell silent, and Marjorie said "Who is it?"

"It's me, love."

"Is that Ray?" She sounded sleepy enough not to know. "I can hardly hear you," she protested. "Where have you gone?"

"You'd wonder." He was straining to hear another sound besides her voice—a noise that might have been the shuffling of feet in rubble. "I'm stuck somewhere," he said. "I'll be late. I can't say how late."

"Did you call before?"

"That was me. Didn't you get me?"

"The tape must be stuck like you. I'll need to get a new one."

"Not a new husband, I hope." He wouldn't have minded being rewarded with the laugh he'd lived with for the best part of fifty years, even though the joke felt as old as him, but perhaps she was wearied by the hour. "Anyway," he said, "if you didn't hear me last time I'll sign off the same way, which as if you didn't know—"

"What was that?"

For too many seconds he wasn't sure. He'd been talking over it, and then she had. Surely it had said that a train was about to arrive; indeed, wasn't the noise he'd mistaken for thin footsteps the distant clicking of wheels? "It's here now," he tried to tell her through a fit of coughing. By the time he would be able to speak clearer, the train might have pulled in. Dropping the receiver on the hook, he dashed for the platform. He hadn't reached it when he heard a scraping behind him.

The storeroom was open again, but that wasn't enough

in itself to delay him. His eyes had grown all too equal to the gloom in the passage, so that he was just able to discern marks on the floor, leading from outside the station to the room. Could someone not be bothered to pick up their dirty feet? The trails looked as if several objects had been dragged into the room. He didn't believe they had just been left; that wasn't why they made him uneasy. He had to squint to see that they were blurred by more than the dark. Whatever had left them—not anybody shuffling along, he hoped, since their feet would have been worse than thin—had crumbled in transit, scattering fragments along the route. He thought he could smell the charred evidence, and swallowed in order not to recommence coughing, suddenly fearful of being heard. What was he afraid of? Was he growing senile? Thank heaven Marjorie wasn't there to see him. The only reason for haste was that he had a train to catch. He tramped out of the passage and might have maintained his defiant pace all the way to the bridge if a shape hadn't reared up at the window of the storeroom.

Was the object that surmounted it the misshapen head of a mop? He couldn't distinguish much through the grimy pane, but the idea was almost reassuring until he acknowledged that somebody would still have had to lift up the scrawny excuse for a figure. It hadn't simply risen or been raised, however. A process that the grime couldn't entirely obscure was continuing to take place. The silhouette—the blackened form, rather—was taking on more substance, though it remained alarmingly emaciated. It was putting itself back together.

The spectacle was so nightmarishly fascinating that Marsden might have been unable to stir except for the clatter of wheels along the tracks. He staggered around to see dim lights a few hundred yards short of the station. "Stop," he coughed, terrified that the driver mightn't notice him and speed straight through. Waving his arms wildly, he sprinted for the bridge.

He'd panted up the stairs and was blundering along the middle of the wooden corridor when he thought he heard a noise besides the approach of the train. Was he desperate to hear it or afraid to? He might have tried to persist in mistaking it for wind in the grass if it weren't so close. He did his utmost to fix his shaky gaze on the far end of the corridor as he fled past shadow after crouching shadow. He almost plunged headlong down the further stairs, and only a grab at the slippery discoloured banister saved him. As he dashed onto the platform he saw that both doors in the passage out of the station were open. The sight brought him even closer to panic, and he began to wave his shivering arms once more as he tottered to the edge of the platform. "Don't leave me here," he cried.

The squeal of brakes seemed to slice through the dark. The engine blotted out the view across the tracks, and then a carriage sped past him. Another followed, but the third was slower. Its last door halted almost in front of him. Though the train was by no means the newest he'd ridden that day, and far from the cleanest, it seemed the next thing to paradise. He clutched the rusty handle and heaved the door open and clambered aboard. "You can go now. Go," he pleaded.

Who was the driver waiting for? Did he think the noises on the bridge were promising more passengers? There was such a volume of eager shuffling and scraping that Marsden almost wished his ears would fail him. He hauled at the door, which some obstruction had wedged open. He was practically deaf with his frantic heartbeat by the time the door gave, slamming with such force that it seemed to be echoed in another carriage. At once the train jerked forward, flinging him onto the nearest musty seat. He was attempting to recover his breath when the announcer spoke.

Was a window open in the carriage? The voice sounded close enough to be on the train, yet no more comprehensible. It was no longer simply unctuous; it could have been mocking a priest out of distaste for the vocation. Its only recognisable words were "train now departing", except that the first one was more like Ray—perhaps not just on this occasion, Marsden thought he recalled. He craned towards the window and was able to glimpse that both doors in the exit corridor were shut. Before he had time to ponder any of this, if indeed he wanted to, the train veered off the main line.

"Where are you taking me?" he blurted, but all too soon he knew. The train was heading for the property behind the station, a turn of events celebrated by a short announcement. There was no question that the speaker was on board, though the blurring of the words left Marsden unsure if they were "Ray is shortly alive." The swerve of the train had thrown open the doors between the carriages, allowing him to hear a chorused hiss that might have signified resentment or have been an enthusiastic "Yes" or, possibly even worse, the collapse of many burned objects into the ash he could smell. As the train sped through a gateway in the railings, he read the name on the sign: not Peacehaven Motors at all, or anything to do with cars. Perhaps the route was only a diversion, he tried to think, or a short tour. Perhaps whoever was on the train just wanted somebody to visit the neglected memorials and the crematorium.

Peep

I'm labouring up the steepest section of the hill above the promenade when the twins run ahead. At least we're past the main road by the railway station. "Don't cross—" I shout or rather gasp. Perhaps each of them thinks or pretends to think I'm addressing the other, because they don't slow down until they reach the first side street and dodge around the corner.

"Stay there," I pant. They're already out of sight, having crouched below the garden wall. I wonder if they're angry with me by association with their parents, since Geraldine wasn't bought a kite to replace the one she trampled to bits when yesterday's weather let her down. They did appear to relish watching teenage drivers speed along the promenade for at least a few minutes, which may mean they aren't punishing me for their boredom. In any case I ought to join in the game. "Where are those children?" I wonder as loudly as my climb leaves breath for. "Where can they be?"

I seem to glimpse an answering movement beyond a bush at the far end of the wall. No doubt a bird is hiding in the foliage, since the twins pop their heads up much closer. Their small plump eight-year-old faces are gleeful, but there's no need for me to feel they're sharing a joke only with each other. Then Geraldine cries "Peep."

Like a chick coming out of its shell, as Auntie Beryl used to say. I can do without remembering what else she said, but where has Geraldine learned this trick? Despite the August sunshine, a wind across the bay traces my backbone with a shiver. Before questioning Geraldine I should usher the children across the junction, and as I plod to the corner I wheeze "Hold my—"

There's no traffic up here. Nevertheless I'm dismayed that the twins dash across the side street and the next one to the road that begins on the summit, opposite the Catholic church with its green skullcap and giant hatpin of a cross. They stop outside my house, where they could be enjoying the view of the bay planted with turbines to farm the wind. Though I follow as fast as I'm able, Gerald is dealing the marble bellpush a series of pokes by the time I step onto the mossy path. Catching my breath makes me sound harsh as I ask "Geraldine, who taught you that game?"

She giggles, and so does Gerald. "The old woman," he says.

I'm about to pursue this when Paula opens my front door. "Don't say that," she rebukes him.

Her face reddens, emphasising how her cropped hair has done the reverse. It's even paler by comparison with the twins' mops, so that I wonder if they're to blame. Before I can put my reluctant question, Gerald greets the aromas from the kitchen by demanding "What's for dinner?"

"We've made you lots of good things while you've been looking after grandpa."

The twins don't think much of at least some of this, although I presume the reference to me was intended to make them feel grown-up. They push past their mother and race into the lounge, jangling all the ornaments. "Careful," Paula calls less forcefully than I would prefer. "Share," she adds as I follow her to the kitchen, where she murmurs "What game were you quizzing them about?"

"You used to play it with babies. I'm not saying you. People did." I have a sudden image of Beryl thrusting her white face over the side of my cot, though if that ever happened, surely I wouldn't remember. "Peep," I explain and demonstrate by covering my eyes before raising my face above my hand.

Paula's husband Bertie glances up from vigorously stirring

vegetables in the wok he and Paula brought with them. "And what was your issue with that?"

Surely I misunderstood Gerald, which can be cleared up later. "Your two were playing it," I say. "A bit babyish at their age, do you think?"

"Good Lord, they're only children. Let them have their fun till they have to get serious like the rest of us," he says and cocks his head towards a squabble over television channels. "Any chance you could restore some balance in there? Everything's under control in here."

I'm perfectly capable of cooking a decent meal. I've had to be since Jo died. I feel as if I'm being told where to go and how to act in my own house. Still, I should help my remaining family, and so I bustle to the lounge, where the instant disappearance of a channel leaves the impression that a face dropped out of sight as I entered. Gerald has captured the remote control and is riffling through broadcasts. "Stop that now," I urge. "Settle on something."

They haven't even on the furniture. They're bouncing from chair to chair by way of the equally venerable sofa in their fight over the control. "I think someone older had better take charge," I say and hold out my hand until Gerald flings the control beside me on the sofa. The disagreement appears to be over two indistinguishably similar programmes in which vaguely Oriental cartoon animals batter one another with multicoloured explosions and other garish displays of power. I propose watching real animals and offer a show set in a zoo for endangered species, but the response makes me feel like a member of one. My suggestion of alternating scenes from each chosen programme brings agreement, though only on dismissing the idea, and Geraldine capitulates to watching her brother's choice.

The onscreen clamour gives me no chance to repeat my question. When I try to sneak the volume down, the objections are deafening. I don't want Paula and her husband to conclude I'm useless—I mustn't give them any excuse to visit even less often—and so I hold my peace, if there can be said to be any in the room. The cartoon is still going off when we're summoned to dinner.

I do my best to act as I feel expected to behave. I consume every grain and shoot and chunk of my meal, however much it reminds me of the cartoon. When my example falls short of the twins I'm compelled to encourage them aloud—"Have a bit more or you won't get any bigger" and "That's lovely, just try it" and in some desperation "Eat up, it's good for you." Perhaps they're sick of hearing about healthy food at home. I feel clownishly false and even more observed than I did over the television. I'm quite relieved when the plates are scraped clean and consigned to the dishwasher.

I'd hoped the twins might have grown up sufficiently since Christmas to be prepared to go to bed before the adults, but apparently holidays rule, and the table is cleared for one of the games Gerald has insisted on bringing. Players take turns to insert plastic sticks in the base of a casket, and the loser is the one whose stick releases the lid and the contents, a wagging head that I suppose is meant to be a clown's, given its whiteness and shock of red hair and enlarged eyes and wide grin just as fixed. I almost knock the game to the floor when one of my shaky attempts to take care lets out the gleeful head, and then I have to feign amusement for the children's sake. At first I'm glad when Gerald is prevailed upon to let his sister choose a game.

It's Monopoly. I think only its potential length daunts me until the children's behaviour reminds me how my aunt would play. They sulk whenever a move goes against them and crow if one fails to benefit their twin, whereas Beryl would change any move she didn't like and say "Oh, let me have it" or simply watch to see whether anyone noticed. "Peep," she would say and lower her hand in front of her eyes if she caught us watching. My parents pretended that she didn't cheat, and so I kept quiet, even though she was more than alert to anyone else's mistakes. Eventually I try conceding tonight's game in the hope the other adults will, but it seems Paula's husband is too much of a stockbroker to relinquish even toy money. The late hour enlivens the twins or at any rate makes them more active, celebrating favourable moves by bouncing on the chairs. "Careful of my poor old furniture," I say, though I'm more dismayed by the reflection of their antics in the mirror that backs the dresser, just the top of one tousled red head or the other springing up among the doubled plates. I'm tired enough to fancy that an unkempt scalp rendered dusty by the glass keeps straying into view even while the twins are still or at least seated. Its owner would be at my back, but since nobody else looks, I won't. Somewhat earlier than midnight Bertie wins the game and sits back satisfied as the twins start sweeping hotels off the board in vexation. "I think someone's ready for bed," I remark.

"You go, then," says Gerald, and his sister giggles in agreement.

"Let grandpa have the bathroom first," says their mother.

Does she honestly believe I was referring to myself? "I won't be long," I promise, not least because I've had enough of mirrors. Having found my toothbrush amid the visiting clutter, I close my eyes while wielding it. "Empty now," I announce on the way to my room. In due course a squabble migrates from the bathroom to the bunks next door and eventually trails into silence. Once I've heard Paula and her husband share the bathroom, which is more than her mother and I ever did, there are just my thoughts to keep me awake.

I don't want to think about the last time I saw Beryl, but I can't help remembering when her playfulness turned unpleasant. It was Christmas Eve, and she'd helped or overseen my mother in making dozens of mince pies, which may have been why my mother was sharper than usual with me. She told me not to touch the pies after she gave me one to taste. I was the twins' age and unable to resist. Halfway through a comedy show full of jokes I didn't understand I sneaked back to the kitchen. I'd taken just one surreptitious bite when I saw Beryl's face leaning around the night outside the window. She was at the door behind me, and I hid the pie in my mouth before turning to her. Her puffy whitish porous face that always put me in mind of dough seemed to widen with a grin that for a moment I imagined was affectionate. "Peep," she said.

Though it sounded almost playful, it was a warning or a threat of worse. Why did it daunt me so much when my offence had been so trivial? Perhaps I was simply aware that my parents had to put up with my mother's sister while wishing she didn't live so close. She always came to us on Christmas Day, and that year I spent it fearing that she might surprise me at some other crime, which made me feel in danger of committing one out of sheer nervousness. "Remember," she said that night, having delivered a doughy kiss that smeared me with lipstick and face powder. "Peep."

Either my parents found this amusing or they felt compelled to pretend. I tried to take refuge in bed and forget about Beryl, and so it seems little has changed in more than sixty years. At least I'm no longer walking to school past her house, apprehensive that she may peer around the spidery net curtains or inch the front door open like a lid. If I didn't see her in the house I grew afraid that she was hiding somewhere else, so that even encountering her in the street felt like a trap she'd set. Surely all this is too childish to bother me now, and when sleep abandons me to daylight I don't immediately know why I'm nervous.

It's the family, of course. I've been wakened by the twins quarrelling outside my room over who should waken me for breakfast. "You both did," I call and hurry to the bathroom to speed through my ablutions. Once the twins have begun to toy with the extravagant remains of their food I risk giving them an excuse to finish. "What shall we do today?" I ask, and meet their expectant gazes by adding "You used to like the beach."

That's phrased to let them claim to have outgrown it, but Gerald says "I've got no spade or bucket."

"I haven't," Geraldine competes.

"I'm sure replacements can be obtained if you're both going to make me proud to be seen out with you," I say and tell their parents "I'll be in charge if you've better things to do."

Bertie purses his thin prim lips and raises his pale eyebrows.

"Nothing's better than bringing up your children."

I'm not sure how many rebukes this incorporates. Too often the way he and Paula are raising the twins seems designed to reprove how she was brought up. "I know my dad wouldn't have meant it like that," she says. "We could go and look at some properties, Bertie."

"You're thinking of moving closer," I urge.

Her husband seems surprised to have to donate even a word of explanation. "Investments."

"Just say if you don't see enough of us," says Paula.

Since I suspect she isn't speaking for all of them, I revert to silence. Once the twins have been prevailed upon to take turns loading the dishwasher so that nothing is broken, I usher them out of the house. "Be good for grandpa," Paula says, which earns her a husbandly frown. "Text if you need to," he tells them.

I should have thought mobile phones were too expensive for young children to take to the beach. I don't want to begin the outing with an argument, and so I lead them downhill by their impatient hands. I see the scrawny windmills twirling on the bay until we turn down the road that slopes to the beach. If I don't revive my question now I may never have the opportunity or the nerve. "You were going to tell me who taught you that game."

Gerald's small hot sticky hand wriggles in my fist. "What game?"

"You know." I'm not about to release their hands while we're passing a supermarket car park. I raise one shoulder and then the other to peer above them at the twins. "Peep," I remind them.

Once they've had enough of giggling Geraldine splutters "Mummy said we mustn't say."

"I don't think she quite meant that, do you? I'm sure she won't mind if you just say it to me when I've asked."

"I'll tell if you tell," Gerald informs his sister.

"That's a good idea, then you'll each just have done half. Do it in chorus if you like."

He gives me a derisive look of the kind I've too often seen his father turn on Paula. "I'll tell mummy if you say," he warns

Geraldine.

I mustn't cause any more strife. I'm only reviving an issue that will surely go away if it's ignored. I escort the twins into a newsagent's shop hung with buckets and spades and associated paraphernalia, the sole establishment to preserve any sense of the seaside among the pubs and wine bars and charity shops. Once we've agreed on items the twins can bear to own I lead them to the beach.

The expanse of sand at the foot of the slipway from the promenade borders the mouth of the river. Except for us it's deserted, but not for long. The twins are seeing who can dump the most castles on the sand when it starts to grow populated. Bald youths tapestried with tattoos let their bullish dogs roam while children not much older than the twins drink cans of lager or roll some kind of cigarette to share, and boys who are barely teenage if even that race motorcycles along the muddy edge of the water. As the twins begin to argue over who's winning the sandcastle competition I reflect that at least they're behaving better than anybody else in sight. I feel as if I'm directing the thought at someone who's judging them, but nobody is peering over or under the railings on the promenade or out of the apartments across it. Nevertheless I feel overheard in declaring "I think you've both done very well. I couldn't choose between you."

I've assumed the principle must be to treat them as equally as possible—even their names seem to try—but just now dissatisfaction is all they're sharing. "I'm bored of this," Gerald says and demolishes several of his rickety castles. "I want to swim."

"Have you brought your costumes?"

"They're in our room," says Geraldine. "I want to swim in a pool, not a mucky river."

"We haven't got a pool here any more. We'd have to go on the train."

"You can take us," Gerald says. "Dad and mum won't mind."

I'm undismayed to give up sitting on the insidiously damp

sand or indeed to leave the loudly peopled beach once I've persuaded the twins not to abandon their buckets and spades. I feel as if the children are straining to lug me uphill except when they mime more exhaustion than I can afford to admit. They drop the beach toys in my hall together with a generous bounty of sand on the way to thundering upstairs. After a brief altercation they reappear and I lead them down to the train.

Before it leaves the two-platformed terminus we're joined by half a dozen rudely pubertal drinkers. At least they're at the far end of the carriage, but their uproar might as well not be. They're fondest of a terse all-purpose word. I ignore the performance as an example to the twins, but when they continue giggling I attempt to distract them with a game of I Spy: s for the sea on the bare horizon, though they're so tardy in participating that I let it stand for the next station; f for a field behind a suburban school, even if I'm fleetingly afraid that Gerald will reveal it represents the teenagers' favourite word; c for cars in their thousands occupying a retail park beside a motorway, because surely Geraldine could never have been thinking of the other syllable the drinkers favour; b for the banks that rise up on both sides of the train as it begins to burrow into Birkenhead... I don't mean it for Beryl, but here is her house.

Just one window is visible above the embankment on our side of the carriage: her bedroom window. I don't know if I'm more disturbed by this glimpse of the room where she died or by having forgotten that we would pass the house. Of course it's someone else's room now—I imagine that the house has been converted into flats—and the room has acquired a window box; the reddish tuft that sprouts above the sill must belong to a plant, however dusty it looks. That's all I've time to see through the grimy window before the bridge I used to cross on the way to school blocks the view. Soon a station lets the drinkers loose, and a tunnel conducts us to our stop.

The lift to the street is open at both ends. It shuts them when Geraldine pushes the button, her brother having been promised that he can operate the lift on our return, and then it gapes afresh.

Since nobody appears I suspect Gerald, but he's too far from the controls. "Must have been having a yawn," I say, and the twins gaze at me as if I'm the cause. No wonder I'm relieved when the doors close and we're hoisted into daylight.

As we turn the corner that brings the swimming pool into view the twins are diverted by a cinema. "I want to see a film," Gerald announces.

"You'll have to make your minds up. I can't be in two places at once. I'm just me."

Once she and her brother have done giggling at some element of this Geraldine says "Grumpo."

I'm saddened to think she means me, especially since Gerald agrees, until I see it's the title of a film that's showing in the complex. "You need to be twelve to go in."

"No we don't," they duet, and Gerald adds "You can take us."

Because they're so insistent I seek support from the girl in the pay booth, only to be told I'm mistaken. She watches me ask "What would your parents say?"

"They'd let us," Geraldine assures me, and Gerald says "We watch fifteens at home."

Wouldn't the girl advise me if the film weren't suitable? I buy tickets and lead the way into a large dark auditorium. We're just in time to see the screen exhort the audience to switch off mobile phones, and I have the twins do so once they've used theirs to light the way along a row in the absence of an usherette. The certificate that precedes the film doesn't tell me why it bears that rating, but that's apparent soon enough. An irascible grandfather embarrasses his offspring with his forgetfulness and the class of his behaviour and especially his language, which even features two appearances of the word I ignored most often on the train. The twins find him hilarious, as do all the children in the cinema except for one that keeps poking its head over the back of a seat several rows ahead. Or is it a child? It doesn't seem to be with anyone, and now it has stopped trying to surprise me with its antics and settles on peering at me over the seat. Just its pale fat face above the nose is visible, crowned and surrounded by an unkempt mass of hair. The flickering of the dimness makes it look eager to jerk up and reveal more of its features, though the light is insufficient to touch off the slightest glimmer in the eyes, which I can't distinguish. At last the oldster in the film saves his children from robbers with a display of martial arts, and his family accepts that he's as loveable as I presume we're expected to have found him. The lights go up as the credits start to climb the screen, and I crane forward for a good look at the child who's been troubling me. It has ducked into hiding, and I sidle past Geraldine to find it. "You're going the wrong way, grandpa," she calls, but neither this nor Gerald's mirth can distract me from the sight of the row, which is deserted.

Members of the audience stare at me as I trudge to the end of the aisle, where words rise up to tower over me, and plod back along the auditorium. By this time it's empty except for the twins and me, and it's ridiculous to fancy that if I glance over my shoulder I'll catch a head in the act of taking cover. "Nothing," I say like Grumpo, if less coarsely, when Gerald asks what I'm looking for. I bustle the twins out of the cinema, and as soon as they revive their phones Gerald's goes off like an alarm.

In a moment Geraldine's restores equality. They read their messages, which consist of less than words, and return their calls. "Hello, mummy," Geraldine says. "We were in a film."

Her brother conveys the information and hands me the mobile. "Dad wants to speak to you."

"Bertie. Forgive me, should we have—"

"I hope you know we came to find you on the beach."

"Gerald didn't say. I do apologise if you—"

"I trust you're bringing them home now. To your house."

I don't understand why he thinks the addition is necessary. "I'm afraid we're in trouble," I inform the twins as Geraldine ends her call. I have to be reminded that it's Gerald's turn to control the lift at the railway station. At least our train reaches the platform as we do, and soon it emerges into the open, at which point I recall how close we are to Beryl's house. As the train passes it I turn to look. There's nothing at her window.

The tenant must have moved the window box. It does no good to wonder where the item that I glimpsed is now. I'm nervous enough by the time we arrive at the end of the line and I lead the twins or am led by them uphill. They seem more eager than I feel, perhaps because they've me to blame. I'm fumbling to extract my keys when Paula's husband opens the front door as if it's his. Having given each of us a stare that settles on me, Bertie says "Dinner won't be long."

It sounds so much like a rebuke, and is backed up by so many trespassing smells, that I retort "I could have made it, you know."

"Could you?" Before I can rise to this challenge he adds "Don't you appreciate my cuisine and Paula's?"

"Your children don't seem to all that much," I'm provoked to respond and quote a favourite saying of Jo's. "It isn't seaside without fish and chips."

"I'm afraid we believe in raising them more healthily."

"Do you, Paula? In other words, not how your mother and I treated you?" When she only gazes sadly at me from the kitchen I say "It can't be very healthy if they hardly touch their food."

"It isn't very healthy for them to hear this kind of thing."

"Find something to watch for a few minutes," her husband tells them. "Maybe your grandfather can choose something suitable."

I feel silenced and dismissed. I follow the children into the lounge and insist on selecting the wildlife show. "I've got to watch as well," I say, even if it sounds like acknowledging a punishment. They greet the announcement of dinner without concealing their relief, although their enthusiasm falls short of the meal itself. When at last they've finished sprinkling cheese on their spaghetti they eat just the sauce, and hardly a leaf of their salad. Though I perform relishing all of mine, I have a sense of being held responsible for their abstinence. I try not to glance at the mirror of the dresser, but whenever I fail there appear to be only the reflections of the family and me.

Once the twins have filled up with chocolate dessert, it's time for games. I vote against reviving the one in which the pallid head pops up, which means that Gerald vetoes his sister's choice of Monopoly. Eventually I remember the games stored in the cupboard under the stairs. The dark shape that rears up beyond the door is my shadow. As I take Snakes and Ladders off the pile I'm reminded of playing it with Paula and her mother, who would smile whenever Paula clapped her hands at having climbed a ladder. I've brought the game into the dining-room before I recall playing it with Beryl.

Was it our last game with her? It feels as if it should have been. Every time she cast a losing throw she moved one space ahead of it. "Can't get me," she would taunt the snakes. "You stay away from me, nasty squirmy things." I thought she was forbidding them to gobble her up as if she were one of her snacks between meals, the powdered sponge cakes that she'd grown more and more to resemble. Whenever she avoided a snake by expanding a move she peered at me out of the concealment of her puffed-up face. I felt challenged to react, and eventually I stopped my counter short of a snake. "Can't he count?" my aunt cried at once. "Go in the next box."

Once I'd descended the snake I complained "Auntie Beryl keeps going where she shouldn't."

"Don't you dare say I can't count. They knew how to teach us when I was at school." This was the start of a diatribe that left her panting and clutching her chest while her face tried on a range of shades of grey. "Look what you've done," my father muttered in my ear while my mother tried to calm her down. When Beryl recaptured her wheezing breath she insisted on finishing the game, staring hard at me every time she was forced to land on a snake. She lost, and glared at me as she said "Better never do anything wrong, even the tiniest thing. You don't know who'll be watching."

Of course I knew or feared I did. I wish I'd chosen another game to play with Paula and her family. Before long Gerald pretends one of his throws hasn't landed on a snake. "Fair play, now," I exhort, earning a scowl from Gerald and a look from his father that manages to be both disapproving and blank. Perhaps Geraldine misinterprets my comment, because soon she cheats too. "If we aren't going to play properly," I say without regarding anyone, "there's no point to the game." Not addressing somebody specific gives me a sense of including more people than are seated at the table, and no amount of glancing at the mirror can rid me of the impression. I've never been so glad to lose a game. "Will you excuse me?" I blurt as my chair stumbles backwards. "I've had quite a day. Time for bed."

My struggles to sleep only hold me awake. When at last the twins are coaxed up to their room and the adults retreat to theirs, I'm still attempting to fend off the memory of my final visit to my aunt's house. She was ill in bed, so shortly after the game of Snakes and Ladders that I felt responsible. She sent my mother out for cakes, though the remains of several were going stale in a box by her bed. There were crumbs on the coverlet and around her mouth, which looked swollen almost bloodlessly pale. I thought there was too much of her to be able to move until she dug her fingers into the bed and, having quivered into a sitting position that dislodged a musty shawl from her distended shoulders, reached for me. I took her hand as a preamble to begging forgiveness, but her cold spongy grasp felt as if it was on the way to becoming a substance other than flesh, which overwhelmed me with such panic that I couldn't speak. Perhaps she was aware of dying of her overloaded heart, since she fixed me with eyes that were practically buried in her face. "I'll be watching," she said and expelled a breath that sounded close to a word. It was almost too loose to include consonants—it seemed as soft as her hand—but it could have been "Peep." I was terrified that it might also be her last breath, since it had intensified her grip on me. Eventually she drew another rattling breath but gave no sign of relaxing her clutch. Her eyes held me as a time even longer than a nightmare seemed to ooze by before I heard my mother letting herself into the house, when I was able to snatch my hand free and dash for the stairs. In less than a week my aunt was dead.

If I didn't see her again, being afraid to was almost as bad. Now that she was gone I thought she could be anywhere and capable of reading all my thoughts, especially the ones I was ashamed to have. I believed that thinking of her might bring her, perhaps in yet worse a form. I'd gathered that the dead lost weight, but I wasn't anxious to imagine how. Wouldn't it let her move faster? All these fears kept me company at night into my adolescence, when for a while I was even more nervous of seeing her face over the end of my bed. That never happened, but when at last I fall uneasily asleep I wake to see a shock of red hair duck below the footboard.

I'm almost quick enough to disguise my shriek as mirth once I realise that the glimpse included two small heads. "Good God," Bertie shouts from downstairs, "who was that?"

"Only me," I call. "Just a dream."

The twins can't hide their giggles. "No, it was us," cries Geraldine.

At least I've headed them off from greeting me with Beryl's word. Their father and to a lesser extent Paula give me such probing looks over breakfast that I feel bound to regain some credibility as an adult by enquiring "How was your search for investments?"

"Unfinished business," Bertie says.

"We were too busy wondering where you could have got to," Paula says.

"I hope I'm allowed to redeem myself. Where would you two like to go today?"

"Shopping," Geraldine says at once.

"Yes, shopping," Gerald agrees louder.

"Make sure you keep your phones switched on," their father says and frowns at me. "Do you still not own one?"

"There aren't that many people for me to call."

Paula offers to lend me hers, but the handful of unfamiliar technology would just be another cause for concern. At least we don't need to pass my aunt's house—we can take a bus. The twins insist on sitting upstairs to watch the parade of small shops interrupted by derelict properties. Wreaths on a lamppost enshrine a teenage car thief before we cross a bridge into the docks. I won't let the flowers remind me of my aunt, whose house is the best part of a mile away. The heads I see ducking behind the reflection in the window of the back seats belong to children. However little good they're up to, I ignore them, and they remain entirely hidden as we make for the stairs at our stop.

The pedestrian precinct appears to lead to a cathedral on the far side of the foreshortened river. The street enclosed by shops is crowded, largely with young girls pushing their siblings in buggies, if the toddlers aren't their offspring. The twins bypass discount stores on the way to a shopping mall, where the tiled floor slopes up to a food court flanked by clothes shops. Twin marts called Boyz and Girlz face each other across tables occupied by pensioners eking out cups of tea and families demolishing the contents of polystyrene cartons. "I'll be in there," Geraldine declares and runs across to Girlz.

"Wait and we'll come—" I might as well not have commenced, since as I turn to Gerald he dodges into Boyz. "Stay in the shops. Call me when you need me," I shout so loud that a little girl at a table renders her mouth clownish with a misaimed cream cake. Geraldine doesn't falter, and I'm not sure if she heard. As she vanishes into the shop beyond the diners I hurry after her brother.

Boyz is full of parents indulging or haranguing their children. When I can't immediately locate Gerald in the noisy aisles I feel convicted of negligence. He's at the rear of the shop, removing fat shoes from boxy alcoves on the wall. "Don't go out whatever you do. I'm just going to see your sister doesn't either," I tell him.

I can't see her in the other shop. I'm sidling between the tables when I grasp that I could have had Gerald phone for me to speak to her. It's just as far to go back now, and so I find my way through an untidy maze of abandoned chairs to Girlz. Any number of those, correctly spelled, are jangling racks of hangers and my nerves while selecting clothes to dispute with their parents, but none of them is Geraldine. I flurry up and down the aisles, back and forth to another catacomb of footwear, but she's nowhere to be seen.

"Geraldine," I plead in the faded voice my exertions have left me. Perhaps it's best that I can't raise it, since she must be in another shop. I didn't actually see her entering this one. As I dash outside I'm seized by a panic that tastes like all the food in the court turned stale. I need to borrow Gerald's mobile, but the thought makes me wonder if the twins could be using their phones to play a game at my expense—to coordinate how they'll keep hiding from me. I stare about in a desperate attempt to locate Geraldine, and catch sight of the top of her head in the clothes store next to Girlz.

"Just you stay there," I pant as I flounder through the entrance. It's clear that she's playing a trick, because it's a shop for adults; indeed, all the dresses that flap on racks in the breeze of my haste seem designed for the older woman. She's crouching behind a waist-high cabinet close to the wall. The cabinet quivers a little at my approach, and she stirs as if she's preparing to bolt for some other cover. "That's enough, Geraldine," I say and make, I hope, not too ungentle a grab. My foot catches on an edge of carpet, however, and I sprawl across the cabinet. Before I can regain any balance my fingers lodge in the dusty reddish hair.

Is it a wig on a dummy head? It comes away in my hand, but it isn't all that does. I manage not to distinguish any features of the tattered whitish item that dangles from it, clinging to my fingers until I hurl the tangled mass at the wall. I'm struggling to back away when the head jerks up to confront me with its eyes and the holes into which they've sunk. I shut mine as I thrust myself away from the cabinet, emitting a noise I would never have expected to make other than in the worst dream.

I'm quiet by the time the rescuers arrive to collect their children and me. It turns out that Geraldine was in a fitting room in Girlz. The twins forgot most of their differences so as to take charge, leading me out to a table where there seems to be an insistent smell of stale sponge cake. Nobody appears to have noticed anything wrong in the clothes shop except me. I'm

31

given the front passenger seat in Bertie's car, which makes me feel like an overgrown child or put in a place of shame. The twins used their phones to communicate about me, having heard my cries, and to summon their parents. I gather that I'm especially to blame for refusing the loan of a mobile that would have prevented my losing the children and succumbing to panic.

I do my best to go along with this version of events. I apologise all the way home for being insufficiently advanced and hope the driver will decide this is enough. I help Paula make a salad, and eat up every slice of cold meat at dinner while I struggle to avoid thinking of another food. I let the children raid the cupboard under the stairs for games, although these keep us in the dining-room. Sitting with my back to the mirror doesn't convince me we're alone, and perhaps my efforts to behave normally are too evident. I've dropped the dice several times to check that nobody is lurking under the table when Paula suggests an early night for all.

As I lie in bed, striving to fend off thoughts that feel capable of bringing their subject to me in the dark, I hear fragments of an argument. The twins are asleep or at any rate quiet. I'm wondering whether to intervene as diplomatically as possible when Paula's husband says "It's one thing your father being such an old woman—"

"I've told you not to call him that."

"—but today breaks the deal. I won't have him acting like that with my children."

There's more, not least about how they aren't just his, but the disagreements grow more muted, and I'm still hearing what he called me. It makes me feel alone, not only in the bed that's twice the size I need but also in the room. Somehow I sleep, and look for the twins at the foot of the bed when I waken, but perhaps they've been advised to stay away. They're so subdued at breakfast that I'm not entirely surprised when Paula says "Dad, we're truly sorry but we have to go home. I'll come and see you again soon, I promise."

I refrain from asking Bertie whether he'll be returning in

search of investments. Once all the suitcases have been wedged into the boot of the Jaguar I give the twins all the kisses they can stand, along with twenty pounds each that feels like buying affection, and deliver a token handshake to Paula's husband before competing with her for the longest hug. As I wave the car downhill while the children's faces dwindle in the rear window, I could imagine that the windmills on the bay are mimicking my gesture. I turn back to the house and am halted by the view into the dining-room.

The family didn't clear away their last game. It's Snakes and Ladders, and I could imagine they left it for me to play with a companion. I slam the front door and hurry into the room. I'm not anxious to share the house with the reminder that the game brings. I stoop so fast to pick up the box from the floor that an ache tweaks my spine. As I straighten, it's almost enough to distract me from the sight of my head bobbing up in the mirror.

But it isn't in the mirror, nor is it my head. It's on the far side of the table, though it has left even more of its face elsewhere. It still has eyes, glinting deep in their holes. Perhaps it is indeed here for a game, and if I join in it may eventually tire of playing. I can think of no other way to deal with it. I drop the box and crouch painfully, and once my playmate imitates me I poke my head above the table as it does. "Peep," I cry, though I'm terrified to hear an answer. "Peep."

Getting It Wrong

Edgeworth was listening to a reminiscence of the bus ride in Hitchcock's *Lucky Jim* when the phone rang. He switched off the deluxe anniversary special collector's edition of *Family Plot* and raised the back of his armchair to vertical. As he grabbed the receiver he saw the time on his watch jerk even closer to midnight. "Hello?" he said and in less than a second "Hello?"

"Is this Mr Edgeworth?"

He didn't recognise the woman's voice, not that he knew any women he could imagine ringing him. "That's who you've got," he said.

"Mr Eric Edgeworth?"

"You're not wrong yet."

"Have you a few minutes, Mr Edgeworth?"

"I don't want anybody fixing my computer. I haven't had an accident at work or anywhere else either. I'm not buying anything and I'm not going to tell you where I shop or what I shop for. My politics are my affair and so's the rest of what I think right now. I've never won a competition, so don't bother saying I have. I don't go on holiday abroad, so you needn't try to sell me anything over there. I don't go away here either, not that it's any of your business. Anything else you want to know?"

"That isn't why we're calling, Mr Edgeworth." In the same brisk efficient tone she said "Will you be a friend of Mary Barton?"

At first Edgeworth couldn't place the name, and then it brought him an image from work—a woman heaping cardboard tubs of popcorn while she kept up a smile no doubt designed to look bright but more symptomatic of bravery. "I wouldn't go that far," he said, although the call had engaged his interest now: it might be the police. "Is she in trouble?"

"She's in inquisition." This might well have meant yes until the woman added "She'd like you to be her expert friend."

"Never heard of it." Having deduced that they were talking about a quiz show, Edgeworth said "Why me?"

"She says she's never met anyone who knows so much about films."

"I don't suppose she has at that." All the same, he was growing suspicious. Could this be a joke played by some of his workmates? "When's she going to want me?" Edgeworth said.

"Immediately if you're agreeable."

"Pretty late for a quiz, isn't it?"

"It's not a show for children, Mr Edgeworth."

"Aren't I supposed to be asked first?"

"We're doing that now."

If all this was indeed a joke, he'd turn it on them. "Fair enough, put her on," he said as he stood up, retrieving his dinner container and its equally plastic fork from beside the chair.

"Please stay on the line."

As Edgeworth used his elbow to switch on the light in the boxy kitchen off the main room of the apartment, a man spoke in his ear. "Eric? Good to have you on. Terry Rice of *Inquisition* here."

He sounded smug and amused, and Edgeworth had no doubt he was a fake. The kitchen bin released a stagnant tang of last night's Chinese takeaway while Edgeworth shoved the new container down hard enough to splinter it and snap the fork in half. "Mary's hoping you'll give her an edge," the man said. "Do you know the rules?"

"Remind me."

"There's only one you should bother about. You're allowed to get three answers wrong."

"If we're talking about films I'm not bothered at all."

"You don't need any more from me, then. Mary, talk to your friend."

"Eric? I'm sorry to trouble you like this so late. I couldn't think of anybody else."

That was a laugh when she'd hardly ever spoken to him. It was the first time she'd even used his name, at least to him. From her tone he could tell she was wearing her plucky smile. "What channel are you on?" he said.

He was hoping to throw her, but she barely hesitated. "Night Owl."

The hoaxers must have thought this up in advance. Edgeworth would have asked how he could watch the channel, but he didn't want to end the game too soon. He'd begun to enjoy pretending to be fooled, and so he said "What have you brought me on for?"

"Because I don't know what a film is."

He thought this was true of just about all his workmates—a good film, at any rate. He'd imagined a job in a cinema would mean working with people who loved films as much as he did. Had she tried to put a tremble in her voice just now? She'd got that wrong; contestants on quiz shows weren't supposed to sound like that. "Give me a go, then," he said.

"What's the film where James Dean has a milkshake?"

Edgeworth waited, but that was all. She ought to be telling him how little time he had, and shouldn't there be some kind of urgent music? "*East of Eden*," he said.

"That's a twist," said whoever was calling himself Terry Rice.

"Mr Rice is saying you're not right, Eric."

It was a funny way of saying so, even by the standards of a prank. Perhaps that was why she sounded nervous. "Then it'll be *Rebel without a Cause*," Edgeworth said with a grin but no mirth.

"That's another."

"Mr Rice says that's not right either."

She sounded close to desperation. However far they took the pretence, Edgeworth could go further. "It's *Giant* for sure, then," he said. "They're the only films he starred in."

"That's one more."

Did Edgeworth hear a faint suppressed shriek? Perhaps one of Mary Barton's accomplices had poked her to prompt her to speak. "That can't be right, Eric," she said high enough to irritate his ear.

"Give up," the supposed quizmaster said or asked, though Edgeworth wasn't sure who was being addressed. "Eric can't have heard of *Has Anyone Seen My Gal?*"

"Of course I have. I've seen it. James Dean has a milkshake at the soda fountain." In case this failed to restore his own reputation Edgeworth added "I knew it was the answer."

"Were you fancying a bit of fun? You should play seriously even if you think it's just a game." To Edgeworth's disbelief, this sounded like a rebuke. "I expect your friend has something to say about it," the man said.

"She's not my friend and none of you are." Edgeworth confined himself to mouthing this, if only to hear what comment she would have to manufacture. He heard her draw an unsteady breath and say "Thanks for coming on, Eric. I wish—"

"No point in wishing here. You know that isn't how we play. Thank you for entering into the spirit, Eric," the man said and, along with Mary and the girl who'd called, was gone.

Surely his last words contradicted his rebuke, which had to mean he couldn't even keep the hoax up. Of course the number he'd called from had been withheld. It was too late for Edgeworth to go back to the commentary on the disc, and he returned the film to the shelf before tramping to the bathroom and then to bed.

With all his films he didn't need to dream. In the morning he ate off a tray in front of *Third Time Sucky,* a Stooges short just the right length for breakfast. "I wish I knew what to wish for." "I wish I had one of your wishes." "I wish you two would shut up," Moe retorted, the effects of which made Edgeworth splutter a mouthful of Sticky Rotters over his dressing-gown. He showered and donned his uniform, which said Frugotomovies on the sweater, and headed for the Frugoplex.

The cinema was an extensive concrete block that resembled the one where he lived. The February sky was just as flat and white. He'd chosen the apartment because he could walk to the cinema, but there were increasingly fewer new films that he wanted to watch; he hardly used his free pass any more. At least he didn't have to enthuse about them to the public. He was gazing with disfavour at the titles outside when the manager let him in. "Any problem?" Mr Gittins said, and his plump smooth face displayed a smile too swift and sketchy to be identified as such. "I hope you can leave it at home."

Rather than retort that some of his workmates were to blame, Edgeworth made for the anonymous concrete staffroom. Soon the rest of the staff began to show up, some of them not far from late. Without exception they were decades younger than he was. As he took his place behind a ticket desk Larry Rivers came over. "What were you watching last night, Eric?" Larry said with a grin as scrawny as his face.

Had he called himself Terry Rice last night? His name was similar, and he liked quizzing Edgeworth, who said "I was listening."

"What were you listening to, Eric?"

He was using the name like a quizmaster. Edgeworth was tempted to confront him, but perhaps that was exactly what he and the rest of them wanted. "The man who wrote *North by Northwest*," Edgeworth said.

"Don't know it. Is it a film?"

Edgeworth suspected this wasn't even meant as a joke. "Cary Grant," he said. "James Mason."

"Don't know them either."

"Hitch, for heaven's sake."

"Is that the film with Will Smith?" one of the girls seemed to feel it would be helpful to suggest.

"Hitchcock, love."

"Sounds a bit mucky to me."

"Sounds a bit like sexual harassment," another girl warned

Edgeworth.

"Alfred Hitchcock," he said in desperation. "*Psycho.*"

"Was that the one with Vince Vaughn?" Larry said.

Did they all think the past—anything older than them—was a joke? No wonder Timeless Video had failed when there were so many people like them. Edgeworth had lost all the money he'd sunk in the video library, which was why he'd been glad of the job at the Frugoplex. Some old things wouldn't go away, not least him. He was about to say at least some of this when Mr Gittins opened the door once again. "Only just in time," he said like a head teacher at a school gate.

Mary Barton ducked as if her apologetic smile had dragged her head down. Did she glance at Edgeworth or just towards all the staff around the ticket counter? She seemed wary of being seen to look. She hurried to the staffroom and scampered back to the lobby as Mr Gittins addressed the staff. "Let's keep the public happy and coming back for more."

Edgeworth might have wished to be a projectionist if the job wouldn't have involved watching too many films that bored him if not worse. He was reduced to noticing which film attracted the most customers, a dispiriting observation. Today it was the latest 3-D film, *Get Outta My Face*. Whenever there was a lull he watched Mary Barton at the refreshments counter opposite. Had her left little finger been bandaged yesterday? It looked significantly bigger than its twin. Her smile was if possible braver than ever, especially if she caught him watching, though then he stared at her until her eyes flinched aside. At times he thought her thin prematurely lined face was trying to look even older than it was, almost as old as him. He wasn't going to accuse her and give everyone a chance to scoff at him; he wouldn't put it past them to accuse him of harassing her. Instead he made sure she never had an opportunity to speak to him away from the public— she clearly didn't have the courage or the gall to approach him in front of anyone who wasn't privy to last night's witless joke.

When he left for home she was besieged by a queue, but as she filled a popcorn tub that she was holding gingerly with her left hand she sent him an apologetic look. If they'd been alone it might well have goaded him to respond. He had to be content with stalking next door to Pieca Pizza, where he bought a Massive Mighty Meat that would do for tomorrow's dinner as well.

He downed two slices in the kitchen and took another three into the main room, one for each version of *Touch of Evil.* He was halfway through Orson Welles' preferred cut when the phone rang. He paused the manic gangling hotel clerk and prepared to say a very few short words to the uninvited caller. "It's that time again, Eric," said a voice he could hardly believe he was hearing.

"My God, you're worse than a joke." Edgeworth almost cut him off, but he wanted to learn how long they could keep up the pretence. "Can't you even get your own rules right?" he jeered.

"Which rules are those, Eric?"

"Three mistakes and I was supposed to be out of your game."

"You haven't quite got it, my friend. Last night was just one question you couldn't answer."

"Trust me, I could. I was having a laugh just like you."

"Please don't, Eric."

Mary Barton sounded so apologetic it was painful, which he hoped it was for her. He could almost have thought she'd been forced against her will to participate in the hoax, but any sympathy he might have felt she lost by adding "Don't make any more mistakes. It's serious."

"He sounds it."

"We get this problem sometimes." The man's amusement was still plain. "Listen to your friend," he said. "See how she sounds."

"I'm truly sorry to be pestering you again, Eric. Hand on heart, you're my only hope."

Edgeworth didn't know which of them angered him more. Her pathetic attempt to convince him she was desperate made her sound as though she was trying to suppress the emotion, and he was provoked to demand "Where are you on the television? I want to watch."

"We're on the radio." With a giggle all the more unpleasant because it had to be affected the man said "You wouldn't want to, trust me."

Edgeworth agreed, having left out the comma. What radio show would have inflicted this kind of conversation on its audience? All that interested him now, though not much, was learning what question they'd come up with this time. They must have been reading a film guide to have thought of last night's. "Go on then, Mr Terry Rice," he said, baring his teeth in a substitute for a grin. "Terrorise me again."

"Do your best, Mary."

"What's the Alfred Hitchcock film where you see him miss a bus?"

Someone stupider than Edgeworth might have imagined she was pleading with him. Did they genuinely expect him not to realise they were mocking what he'd said today to Larry Rivers? "*Strangers on a Train*," he said at once.

"Have a closer look."

He didn't know if this was meant for him or the Barton woman, but her voice grew shrill and not entirely firm. "Not that one, Eric."

"Must have been *The Birds*, then."

"Closer."

"Please, Eric," Mary Barton blurted, and he was disgusted to hear her attempting to sound close to tears. "You must know. It's your kind of thing."

"I know," Edgeworth said with a vicious grin. "I'll give it to you. *Rope.*"

"Not close enough yet."

"Please!"

Edgeworth jerked the receiver away from his aching ear. "What are you supposed to be doing?"

"It's my eye."

Was he also meant to hear a stifled sob? "That's what my grandma used to say," he retorted. "She'd say it to anyone talking rubbish." Nevertheless he wasn't going to seem ignorant. "Here's your answer since you're making such a fuss about it, as if you didn't know. It's—"

"Too late, Eric," the man said without concealing his delight. "You've had your second chance."

"Please…"

Edgeworth could only just hear Mary Barton's voice, as if it was no longer directed at him. He was right to hold the phone at arm's length to protect his eardrum from any surprises they had in mind, because he heard a shrill metallic sound before the line went dead. It was ridiculous even to think of searching the airwaves for Night Owl. He did his best to pick up the Welles film where he'd left off, but the twitching maniac in charge of the motel disturbed him more than he liked. He put the film back in its place among the dozens of Ts before tramping angrily to bed.

He lurched awake so often, imagining he'd heard the phone, that not just his eyes were prickly with irritation by the time he had to get up for work. He was going to let Mary Barton know he'd had more than enough, and he wouldn't give the rest of them the chance to enjoy the show. "Eager to get going?" the manager said by way of greeting.

"I'm eager all right," Eric said and grinned as well.

He clocked on and hurried to the ticket counter, hoping Mary Barton would be first to arrive so that he could follow her to the staffroom. She'd been warned yesterday about timekeeping, after all. He watched the manager let in their workmates and grew more frustrated every time the newcomer wasn't her. Larry Rivers was among the last to join Edgeworth at the counter. "What were you up to last night, Eric?" he said.

Edgeworth almost turned on him, but he could play too. "Nothing you've ever seemed interested in."

Somebody more gullible than Edgeworth might have thought the fellow felt rebuffed. No doubt he was disappointed that Edgeworth hadn't taken the bait, and some of their audience looked as if they were. There was still no sign of Mary Barton by opening time. "Meet the public with a smile," Mr Gittins said.

Perhaps the woman had stayed home because she was too embarrassed to face Edgeworth, unless it was her day off. "Isn't Mary Barton coming in?" he said before he knew he meant to.

"She's called in sick." Mr Gittins seemed surprised if not disapproving that Edgeworth felt entitled to ask. As he made for the doors he added "Some trouble with her eye."

Edgeworth struggled to think of a question. "She'll have had it for a while, won't she?"

"She's never said so." Mr Gittins stopped short of the doors to say "Her mother hasn't either."

"What's she got to do with anything?"

"She's looking after Mary's children while Mary's at the hospital. Happy now, Eric? Then I hope we can crack on with the job."

As Mr Gittins let the public in, one of the girls alongside Edgeworth murmured "You'll have to send her a Valentine, Eric. She isn't married any longer."

"Keep your gossiping tongues to yourselves." He glared at her and her friends who'd giggled, and then past them at Rivers. "I'm putting you on your honour," he said as his grandmother often had. "You and your friends have been ringing me up at night, haven't you?"

"What?" Once Rivers finished the laugh that underlined the word he said "We get more of you here than we want as it is, Eric."

After that nobody except the public spoke to Edgeworth, and he couldn't even interest himself in which films they were unwise enough to pay for. Of course there was no reason to believe Rivers was as ignorant as he'd pretended—not about the late-night calls, at any rate. Edgeworth felt as if the long slow uneventful day were a curtain that would soon be raised on a performance he had no appetite for. At last he was able to leave behind everyone's contemptuous amusement, which felt like a threat of worse to come. When he shut himself in his apartment he found that he hoped he was waiting for nothing at all.

The pizza tasted stale and stodgy, an unsuccessful attempt to live up to itself. He tried watching classic comedies, but even his favourites seemed unbearably forced, like jokes cracked in the midst of a disaster or anticipating one. They hardly even passed the time, never mind distracting him from it. He was gazing in undefined dismay at the collapse of a dinosaur skeleton under Cary Grant and Katherine Hepburn when the phone went off like an alarm.

He killed the film and stared at the blank screen while the phone rang and rang again. He left it unanswered until a surge of irrational guilt made him grab it. "What is it now?" he demanded.

"Someone was scared you weren't playing any more, Eric."

"I thought your friend was meant to be in hospital," Edgeworth said in triumph.

"She's your friend, Eric, only yours. You're the only one she can turn to about films."

"Can't she even speak for herself now?"

"I'm here, Eric." Mary Barton's voice had lost some strength or was designed to sound as feeble as the prank. "They've fixed me up for now," she said. "I had to come back tonight or I'd have lost everything."

"Trying to make a bit extra for your children, are you?"

"I'm trying to win as much as we need."

Was she too preoccupied to notice his sarcasm, or wouldn't that fit in with her game? Could she really be so heartless that she would use her children to prolong a spiteful joke? His grandmother never would have—not even his mother, though she'd had plenty to say about any of Edgeworth's shortcomings that reminded her of his unidentified father. "Ready to help?" the man with Mary Barton said.

"What will you do if I don't?"

Edgeworth heard a suppressed moan that must be meant to sound as terrified as pained. "Up to you if you want to find out," the man said.

"Go on then, do your worst." At once Edgeworth was overtaken by more panic than he understood. "I mean," he said hastily, "ask me about films."

"Be careful, Mary. See he understands."

The man seemed more amused than ever. Did he plan to ask about some detail in the kind of recent film they knew Edgeworth never watched? Edgeworth was ready with a furious rejoinder by the time Mary Barton faltered "Which was the film where Elisha Cook played a gangster?"

There were three possibilities; that was the trick. If she and Rivers hoped to make Edgeworth nervous of giving the wrong answer, they had no chance. "*The Maltese Falcon,*" he said.

"Wider, Mary."

"That's not right, Eric."

Her voice had grown shriller and shakier too, and Edgeworth was enraged to find this disturbed him. "He was a gangster in that," he objected.

"It isn't what they want."

"Then I expect they're thinking of *The Killing.*"

"Wider again," the man said as if he could hardly bear to put off the end of the joke.

"No, Eric, no."

It occurred to Edgeworth that the actor had played a criminal rather than a gangster in the Kubrick film. The piercing harshness of the woman's ragged voice made it hard for him to think. "Just one left, eh?" he said.

"Please, Eric. Please be right this time."

She might almost have been praying. Far from winning Edgeworth over, it embarrassed him, but he wasn't going to give a wrong answer. "No question," he said. "It's *Baby Face Nelson.*"

"Wider still."

"What are you playing at?" Edgeworth protested. "He was a gangster in that."

"No, it was his son," the man said. "It was Elisha Cook Junior."

"That's what you've been working up to all along, is it?" Edgeworth wiped his mouth, having inadvertently spat with rage. "What a stupid trick," he said, "even for you." He would have added a great deal if Mary Barton hadn't cried "No."

It was scarcely a word. It went on for some time with interruptions and rose considerably higher. Before it had to pause for breath Edgeworth shouted "What are you doing?"

"It's a good thing we aren't on television." By the sound of it, the man had moved the phone away from her. "We couldn't show it," he said gleefully, "and I don't think you'd want to see."

"Stop it," Edgeworth yelled but failed to drown out the cry.

"Relax, Eric. That's all for you for now," Terry Rice said and left silence aching in Edgeworth's ear.

The number was withheld again. Edgeworth thought of calling the police, but what could that achieve? Perhaps it would just prove he'd fallen for a joke after all. Perhaps everything had been recorded for his workmates to hear. He grabbed the remote control and set about searching the audio channels on the television. He thought he'd scanned through every available radio station, since the identifications on the screen had run out, when a voice he very much wished he couldn't recognise came out of the blank monitor. "This is Night Owl signing off," Terry Rice said, and Edgeworth thought he heard a muffled sobbing. "Another night, another game."

Edgeworth gazed at the silent screen until he seemed to glimpse a vague pale movement like a frantic attempt to escape. He turned off the set, nearly breaking the switch in his haste, and sought refuge in bed. Very occasionally his thoughts grew so exhausted that they almost let him doze. He did without breakfast—he couldn't have borne to watch a film. Once the shower had made him as clean as he had any chance of feeling he dressed and hurried to work.

He had to ring the bell twice at length to bring Mr Gittins out of his office. The manager's plump smooth face set not much less hard than marble as he saw Edgeworth. He was plainly unimpressed by Edgeworth's timeliness; perhaps he thought it was a ruse to gain his favour. "I hope you'll be doing your best to get on with your colleagues," he said.

"Why, who's said what?"

Mr Gittins didn't deign to answer. He was turning away until Edgeworth blurted "Do we know if Mary Barton's coming in today?"

"What concern is it of yours?" Having gazed at Edgeworth,

Mr Gittins said "She won't be in for some time. I'm told she can't walk."

Edgeworth swallowed, but his voice still emerged as a croak. "Do we know why?"

"It really isn't something I'm prepared to discuss further."

Mr Gittins looked disgusted by Edgeworth's interest and whatever it revived in his mind. Edgeworth gave him a grimace that felt nothing like apologetic and dashed to the staffroom. For once the list of staff and their phone numbers on the notice board was of some use. He keyed Mary Barton's number on his mobile and made the call before he had time to grow any more fearful. Well ahead of any preparation he could make for it a woman's tightened weary voice said "Hello, yes?"

"I'm one of Mary's friends at work. I was wondering how she is." With more of an effort he managed to add "Just wondering what's wrong with her."

"Has it got something to do with you?"

The woman's voice was loud and harsh enough to start two children crying, and Edgeworth felt as if the sounds were impaling his brain. "I wouldn't say it has exactly, but—"

"If I thought you were the man who did that to Mary I'd find you and make sure you never went near a woman again. Just you tell me your name or I'll—"

Edgeworth jabbed the key to terminate the call and shoved the mobile in his pocket. As soon as it began to ring he switched it off. He couldn't loiter in the staffroom in case Mr Gittins wondered why, and so he ventured into the lobby, where a stray lump of popcorn squeaked piteously underfoot and then splintered like an insect. He'd hardly reached the ticket counter when the phones on it began to ring in chorus. "See who it is," Mr Gittins said.

Edgeworth clutched at the nearest receiver and hoisted it towards his face. "Frugoplex Cinemas," he said, trying not to sound like himself.

When he heard the woman's voice he turned his back on the manager. While she wasn't the caller he'd been afraid to hear or the one he might have hoped for, she was all too familiar. "Congratulations, Eric," she said. "Three wrong means you're our next contestant. Someone will pick you up tonight."

He dropped the phone, not quite missing its holder, and turned to find Mr Gittins frowning at him. "Was that a personal call?"

"It was wrong. Wrong number," Edgeworth said and wished he could believe. Mr Gittins frowned again before making for the doors as some of Edgeworth's workmates gathered outside. Edgeworth searched their faces through the glass and struggled to think what he could say to them. Just a few words were repeating themselves in his head like a silent prayer. "You're my friend, aren't you?" he would have to say to someone. "Be my friend."

THE ROOM BEYOND

As soon as Todd drove off the motorway it vanished from the mirror, and so did the sun across the moor. On both sides of the street the slender terraced houses huddled together like old folk afraid of descending the precipitous slope. Most of the shops in the town at the foot of the street were illuminated, but the streetlamps seemed oblivious of the September dusk. As he braked and braked again he saw the hotel sign across the maze of roofs.

The middle was blocked by the spire of a church, but **BEL** and the final **E** were visible. He hadn't realised that the hotel was on the far side of town. Whenever he stayed with his uncle and aunt he'd come by train, from which they had escorted him through the back streets to their house, interrogating him and talking at him so incessantly that he'd had little chance to learn the route. It had been the same on Sundays, when they'd walked to the Bellevue for a dauntingly formal lunch. Now the town hardly seemed large enough to accommodate either route.

More than this had changed in fifty years. While the clock from beneath which figures emerged on the hour was still outside the jewellers on the High Street, the road was one way only now. It turned away from the hotel, and all the side streets leading there displayed No Entry signs. Most of the shops were either new or disused, and the Apollo, where he'd once seen an airman climbing steps to heaven, had become the Valley Bottom pub.

51

In a few minutes Todd found himself back at the clock, which hadn't moved on from twenty-five to six. The tarnished figures were paralysed on their track, and one stood in a miniature doorway as if he were loath to venture beyond. Shops were being shuttered, and at last the streetlamps came on, illuminating virtually deserted streets. This time Todd left the High Street ahead of the bend, but the lane he followed returned to the clock. He glimpsed Christ the Redeemer down a narrow alley, though the church was dark. He had to drive along the High Street yet again to discover that a road around the outside of the town led towards the hotel.

Was the park beside the road the one where his relatives had taken him to hear a brass band? He wouldn't have placed it so close to the hotel. The doctor's surgery must have been in one of the derelict houses facing the park, but Todd couldn't identify which. He hadn't thought of it for all these years, and he would have been happy to forget it now. He hadn't passed a single inhabited house by the time the road brought him to the hotel.

He had to laugh, as his uncle liked him to. The long black building was less than half the size he seemed to remember. While it might have been designed to resemble a mansion, he could have taken it for some kind of institution now. A wind blundered off the moor and flapped a torn section of the canvas awning across most of the unilluminated name. A couple of cars were parked on the forecourt, under a solitary orange floodlight that turned his blue Passat as black as they appeared to be. Dead windblown vegetation splintered beneath the wheels as he parked in front of a tall window blacked out by heavy curtains. His boxy suitcase was resting on the back seat, and he trundled it to the hotel.

No uniformed doorman was waiting to sweep the massive glass door wide, and Todd might have imagined that the door itself had shrunk. Its metal corner scraped over the tiled floor with an excruciating screech that made the receptionist glower. She was a brawny broad-shouldered woman with gilded spectacles as narrow as her eyes. Her grey hair was severely waved, and the glasses seemed to pinch her features small and sharp. She kept up her frown as Todd crossed the lobby, which was lit to some extent by a few bulbs of the dusty chandelier. More than just her attitude reminded him of someone else, so that he blurted "Excuse me, did you have a mother?"

She pursed her lips so hard that the surrounding skin turned grey along with them. "I beg your pardon," she said while doing nothing of the kind.

Her voice was hoarse and blurred, like a smoker's who was also somewhat drunk. "Sorry," Todd said and risked a laugh, only to wish he'd kept it to himself. "Does it run in the family, I meant to say."

"I'm sure I don't know what you mean."

"What you do. Admitting. Admission." Todd's words seemed to be straying out of his control, an unwelcome reminder of his age. "What I'm trying to say," he said, "was she a receptionist? The one in the practice by the park round the corner."

"That's a graveyard, not a park."

He could only assume she had somewhere else in mind. "Anyway," he said, "can I have my room?"

"Have you booked?"

"I rang," Todd said and wondered if the woman who'd taken the call had been her in a more hospitable mood. "Jacob Todd."

"Todd." His uncle used to greet him with a cry of "Now it's all jake," but Todd felt as if the receptionist had dropped his name with a dull thud. She dragged a ledger bound in black from under the counter and plucked at the pages before repeating "Todd" like an accusation. He might have thought the pages at the back were loose with age until he realised they were registration forms, one of which she laid before him on the counter. "Fill yourself in," she said.

Discolouration had lent the form a dark border. The print was both small and smudged, and squinting at it only left Todd more frustrated with the task it set him. "Who needs all this?"

The receptionist raised her spectacles to train her gaze on him. Her fingertips looked as earthy as the edges of the form. "You might be taken ill," she said.

53

"Suppose I am, who'll want all this information?"

"The authorities," she said and stared unblinkingly at him.

The solitary writing instrument on the counter was a ballpoint splintered like a bone and bandaged with sticky plastic tape. As Todd strove to fit his details into narrow boxes on the form, the inky tip stumbled about like a senile limb. Last name, first name, address, date of birth, place of birth... "What's your business in our town?" the receptionist said.

"A funeral."

"You'll be just round the corner."

Even if that was indeed a graveyard, it needn't be the only one in town. Christ the Redeemer hadn't appeared to be anywhere near the hotel. Todd could go for a walk and find his way to the church once he'd checked into his room. Profession, driving licence number, car registration number, telephone number, email... "Will you be taking the dinner?" the receptionist said.

Todd was distracted by someone's attempts to enter the hotel or even to locate the handle of the door. He turned to see that the door was shaking just with rain, which was surging across the moor. "When do you need to know?" he said.

"As soon as you like." This plainly meant as soon as she did. "Cook wants to get away."

Perhaps at least the meal would be up to the standard Todd remembered, and he could save his walk in case the rain ceased. "Put me down, then," he said.

The receptionist vanished like a shadow into a small office behind the counter. Presumably the dim light from the lobby was all she required, for Todd heard the rattle of a telephone receiver. "One for dinner," she said, and somewhere in the building a distant version of her voice joined in. Another hollow rattle was succeeded by a metallic one, and she reappeared with a key attached to a tarnished baton. "Are you written up yet?" she said.

Towards the bottom of the form the print was almost too indistinct to read. Method of payment, onward destination, next of kin... "That's a blank, I'm afraid," Todd said. He scrawled his signature, in which age had reduced the first name to resembling

Jab, and unstuck his discoloured fingers from the pen while the receptionist pored over the form.

He'd had more than enough of the sight of her greyish scalp through her irregular parting—it put him in mind of a crack in weedy stone—by the time she raised her head. "Retired from what?" she apparently felt entitled to learn.

"Education." When this didn't lessen her scrutiny Todd added "Teaching them their sums."

This failed to earn him even a blink. "Will you be dressing?" she said.

"For dinner, you mean?" She'd begun to remind him of his aunt, who had always found some element of his appearance to improve—a collar to tug higher on his neck, a tie to yank tighter, a handkerchief that was either lying too low in his breast pocket or standing too impolitely erect. "I'll be changing," he said.

"Better look alive, then. It's nearly eight, you know."

"Nowhere near," said Todd, shaking the cuff of his heavy sweater back from his thin wrist. He was about to brandish the time—not much after half past five—when he saw his watch had stopped. His aunt and uncle had sent it for his twenty-first, and it had never let him down before. He drew his cuff over its battered face and found the receptionist frowning at him as if he'd betrayed some innumeracy. "Let's have my key, then," he said, "and I'll be down as soon as I'm fit to kill."

Whenever she'd finished sprucing him Todd's aunt used to say that was how he was dressed, but perhaps the receptionist didn't know the phrase. "You're number one," she informed him, planting the brass club on the counter with a blow like the stroke of a hammer. "You'll have to work the lift yourself."

Todd couldn't tell whether she was apologising for the attendant's absence or reminiscing about the hotel's better days. As he headed for the gloomy alcove that housed the entrance to the single lift, a wheel of his suitcase dislodged a loose tile. The receptionist watched with disfavour while he replaced it in its gritty niche, and he didn't linger over deciphering the blurred letters on the underside of the tile—presumably some firm's trademark. Once he dragged open both latticed doors of the lift he struggled over shutting them. The wall of the lift shaft inched past the rusty mesh, and at last the floor of a grudgingly illuminated corridor sank into view, although the lift fell short of aligning with it. Todd had to clamber up and haul his suitcase after him before he could make for his room.

It was at the far end of the left-hand stretch of corridor, where a window above a fire escape showed the town reduced to runny mud by the rain on the glass. The feeble lamps on the corridor walls resembled glazed flames, all the more by flickering. The number on Todd's door was dangling head down from its one remaining screw. He twisted the key in the aged shaky lock and pushed the leaden door open, to be met by a smell of old fabric. It made Todd feel enclosed, invisibly and impalpably but oppressively, even after he switched on the miniature chandelier.

The small room was darkened by the furniture—a black wardrobe with a full-length mirror in its narrow door, an ebony dressing-table, a squat chest of drawers that looked stunted by age, a bed that wasn't quite single or double, with a hint of an indentation underneath a shaggy blanket as brown as turned earth. A door led to a shower and toilet, while another would have communicated with the next bedroom but was blocked by a luggage stand. Behind the heavy curtains at the foot of the bed Todd found a window that showed him darkness raging above the moor. He was unpacking his case when he heard what could have been the fall of several pans in the kitchen. As he changed into his dark suit—the only one he'd brought—a phone rang.

At first he thought it was in the next room. It shrilled at least a dozen times before he traced the dusty wire from the skirting board to the upper compartment of the wardrobe. When he swung the door open, the receiver toppled off the hook, starting to speak as he fumbled it towards his face. "The gong's gone, Mr Todd."

The receptionist's tone seemed capable of stripping Todd of all the years since his last visit. "Oh, is that what it was?" he retorted. "I'll be with you as soon as I can."

He would have liked to shower and shave, but the hotel could take the blame, even if the man in the black frame of the mirror would never have passed his aunt's inspection. Todd had always felt on probation, never quite knowing if his visits were treats or punishments. "If you won't behave you can go to your aunt's," his mother used to say, and he'd suspected she was a little afraid of her older sister. His uncle hadn't seemed to be, and made a joke wherever he could find one, but then he'd done so at the surgery as well. Todd didn't need to be alone with those memories, and hurried out of the room.

If he'd been able to locate the stairs he would have used them, but the corridor offered him just the silent doors, bearing numbers like steps in a child's first arithmetic lesson. He was close to hearing them chanted in his skull. He stepped gingerly down into the lift and pushed the marble button, only to leave a blotchy print on it. He hadn't even washed his hands. "Not my fault," he muttered, feeling threatened by a second childhood.

The lobby was deserted except for a sign on a stand outside a room Todd hadn't previously noticed. The plastic numbers separated by a hyphen weren't years, they were hours with just sixty minutes between them. The words above them would have said **DINING ROOM** if they hadn't lost a letter. Todd found the N on the carpet in the doorway—carpet trampled as flat and black as soil. As he attempted to replace the letter between the I and its twin he felt as if he were playing an infantile game. He hadn't succeeded when he grew aware of being watched from the room beyond the sign. "Just putting you together," he said.

The waiter was dressed even more sombrely than Todd. He stepped back a silent pace and indicated the room with a sweep of one white-gloved hand. The room was nowhere near as daunting as Todd recalled. While the tables were still draped like altars, and the place was certainly as hushed as a church, it was scarcely big enough for a chapel. Even if it had always sported chandeliers, he didn't remember them as being so ineffectual. He had to squint to be sure of the burly waiter's small sharp face, the eyes narrowed as though in need of spectacles, the brow that he could have imagined had been tugged unnaturally smooth by the removal of a wig from the clipped grey hair. He was disconcerted enough to blurt "Has your sister gone off?"

The waiter paced to the farthest table and drew back its solitary chair. "Who was that, sir?"

His voice was as unctuously slow as a priest's at a pulpit, and might have been striving for hoarseness and depth. "Aren't you related to the lady at reception?" Todd said.

"They say we're all related, don't they?" Before Todd could give this whatever response it deserved, the waiter said "Will you be taking the buffet?"

Todd sat down as the waiter slipped the chilly leather seat beneath him. "Can I see the menu?" he said.

He never had while he was visiting—he'd only watched his aunt and uncle leafing through leather-bound volumes and then ordering for him. "I wouldn't recommend it, sir," the waiter said.

Todd was starting to feel as he'd felt as a child—that everyone around him knew a secret he wouldn't learn until he was older. "Why not?" he demanded.

"We're just providing the buffet option on this occasion. Chef had to leave us."

"Then I haven't much choice, have I?"

"We always have while we're alive."

The waiter sounded more priestly than ever, and his pace was deliberate enough for a ritual as he approached the lengthy table that stood along the left side of the room. He uncovered every salver and tureen before extending a hand towards them. "Enough for a large party, sir."

When waiters used to say things like that, Todd had expected his uncle to respond with a witticism. The hotel seemed to be turning into a joke Todd didn't understand. As he crossed the shiny blackened carpet to the buffet, the waiter raised a cloth from an elongated heap at the end of the table and handed him a plate. The buffet offered chicken legs and slices of cold meat, potatoes above which a fog hovered or at least a stagnant cloud of steam, a mound of chips that reminded him of extracting sticks from a haphazard pile in a game for which his aunt had never had the patience. Last came salads, and as he loaded his plate a lettuce leaf attempted a feeble crawl before subsiding on the salver. The movement might have betrayed the presence of an insect, but it was the work of a wind that had moved the floor-length curtain away from a window behind the table as though somebody was lurking there. As a child Todd had somehow been led to believe that God lived behind the curtains above the altar in the church. The curtains on the far side of the table veiled only a vast darkness tossing restlessly as a sleeper in a nightmare. He did his best to ignore the impression while remarking "At least I'm the first one down."

"The only one," the waiter said and found utensils under the cloth for him. "It's all been put on for you, Mr Todd."

Was this meant to shame him into taking more? Todd might have wondered if his fellow guests knew better than to eat at the hotel, but he was more inclined to ask how the waiter knew his name. The man spoke before Todd could. "Will you be having the house?"

"I'll try a bottle. Make it red." In a further attempt to recapture some sense of maintaining control Todd said "And a jug out of the tap."

The waiter gave a priestly bow before gliding through a doorway to the left of the buffet, and Todd heard him droning to himself under his breath. Any response was in the same voice, and monotonous enough to suggest that the man was murmuring a ritual. After some sounds of pouring the waiter reappeared with a tray that bore an unstoppered carafe and a jug. He served Todd water and wine and stepped back. "Can you taste it, sir?" he murmured.

Todd took a mouthful of the wine, which seemed oddly lifeless, like some kind of token drink. "It'll do," he said, if only to make the waiter step back.

The man continued loitering within rather less than arm's length. He'd clasped his hands together on his chest, which put Todd in mind of someone praying beside a bed. When he tried to concentrate on his meal the hands glimmered so much at the edge of his vision that he might have imagined the gloves were plastic. "I'll be fine now," he said as persuasively as he could.

The waiter seemed reluctant to part his hands or otherwise move. At last he retreated, so slowly that he might have felt he didn't exist apart from his job. "Call me if there's anything you need," he said as he replaced the covers on the buffet before withdrawing into the inner room. He began murmuring again at once, which made it hard for Todd to breathe. It reminded him too much of the voice he used to hear beyond the doctor's waiting-room.

"Go to the doctor's with your uncle," his aunt would say, and Todd had never known whether she disliked having him in the house by herself or was providing her husband with company if not distraction, unless it had been her way of making certain that Todd's uncle saw the doctor yet again. Every time he'd filled the wait with jokes at which Todd had felt bound to laugh, although neither the quips nor his mirth had seemed to please the other patients. He'd felt not just embarrassed but increasingly aware that the joking was designed to distract someone—himself or his uncle or both—from the reason they were waiting in the room. He had never ventured to ask, and his uncle hadn't volunteered the information. It had been the secret waiting beyond the door through which his uncle would disappear with a last wry grin at Todd, after which Todd would gaze at the scuffed carpet while he tried to hear the discussion muffled by the wall. Eventually his uncle would return, looking as if he'd never given up his grin. While Todd had seldom managed to distinguish even a word, he'd once overheard his uncle protest "This isn't much of a joke."

Todd knew the secret now, but he preferred not to remember. He was even glad to be distracted by the waiter, who had stolen at some point back into the dining-room. Todd seemed to have been so preoccupied that he might have imagined somebody else had eaten his dinner, which he couldn't recall tasting. The jug and carafe were empty too. He'd barely glanced at his plate when the waiter came swiftly but noiselessly to him. "Do go back, Mr Todd."

60

The subdued light and the oppressive silence, not to mention the buffet, were making Todd feel as if he were already at a wake. "I've finished, thank you," he said. "The doctor says I have to watch my food."

When his uncle used to say that, Todd could never tell if it was a joke. Certainly his uncle had gazed at his food until his wife protested "Don't put ideas in the boy's head, Jack." Since the waiter seemed ready to persist, Todd said "I'll be down in the morning. I have to be ready for a funeral."

The waiter looked lugubriously sympathetic, but Todd was thrown by the notion that the man already had. "Whose is that, sir?"

"I'd rather not talk about it if you don't mind." Todd regretted having brought the subject up. "I'm on my own now," he said as he made his way between the empty tables, which had begun to remind him of furniture covered with dustsheets in an unoccupied house. When he glanced back from the lobby the waiter was nowhere to be seen, and Todd's place was so thoroughly cleared that he might never have been there. A curtain stirred beside the long uneven mound draped from head to foot on the buffet table, and Todd discovered he would rather not see the mound stir too. He made some haste to leave before he realised that he didn't know when breakfast was served. Calling "Hello?" brought him no response, neither from the dining-room nor from the impenetrably dark office beyond the reception counter. He'd arrange to be wakened once he was in his room.

Why did he expect to be met in the lift? He was close to fancying there was no room for anyone but him as soon as he returned to the panelled box. He fumbled the gates shut and watched the wall ooze past them like a mudslide. He was anxious for light to appear above it well before that happened, and as soon as the lift wobbled to a halt he clambered up into the corridor.

It was as silent as ever. The sombre doors between the dim glazed flames could easily have reminded him of a mausoleum. The rain on the window at the end was borrowing colours from the lights of the town. The storm was slackening, and Todd was able to read some of the illuminated signs. Beneath the race of headlamps on the motorway he made out several letters perched on a high roof—ELLE and also U. An unwelcome thought took him to the window, on which he couldn't distinguish his breath from the unravelling skeins of rain. The sign swam into focus as if he were regaining his vision, and he saw it belonged to the Bellevue Hotel.

If anybody heard his gasp of disbelief, they gave no response. For a moment he had no idea where he was going, and then he found his numbered baton and jammed the key into the lock. A few bulbs flared in the dwarfish chandelier—not as many as last time, but they showed him the shabby leather folder on the dressing-table. He threw the folder open on the bed, revealing a few dog-eared sheets of notepaper and a solitary envelope. While he couldn't tell how much of their brownishness the items owed to age, there was no mistaking the name they bore. He was in the Belgrave Hotel.

It might have been yet another element of a joke that somebody was playing on him, unless he was playing it on himself. He was too late to change hotels, whatever time it was—"too late, Kate," as his uncle liked to say even when Todd's aunt wasn't there. Just now Todd wanted nothing more than to lie down, but first he needed to arrange his morning call.

He retrieved the phone from the upper cupboard of the wardrobe, only to find no instructions on the yellowed paper disc in the middle of the dial. When he picked up the bony receiver he heard a sound not unlike a protracted breathless gust of wind, presumably the Belgrave's version of a dialling tone. 9 seemed the likeliest number, but when he tried it Todd heard a phone begin to ring along the corridor. He was tempted to speak to his fellow guest, if only to establish there was one, but the hollow muffled note tolled until he cut it off. Dialling 1 brought him only the empty tone, and so he tried the zero. A bell went off in the depths of the building and was silenced, and a slow hoarse blurred voice in his ear said "Mr Todd."

"Can you get me up for eight?"

"For how many would that be, sir?"

"I'm saying can you see I'm down for breakfast. What time's that?"

"Eight will do it, Mr Todd."

Had the receptionist heard his first question after all? Todd was too weary to say any more—almost too exhausted to stand up. He stumbled to the token bathroom, where he lingered as briefly as seemed polite. The shower cubicle put him in mind of a cramped lift that had somehow acquired plumbing, while the space outside it was so confined it almost forced the toilet under the sink. Another reason for him to leave the windowless room was the mirror, but the wardrobe door showed him more of the same, displaying how age had shrunken and sharpened his face. He switched off the light and clambered into bed.

The indentation in the mattress made it easiest for him to lie on his back, hands crossed on his breastbone. He heard a hollow plop of rain on wood and then an increasingly sluggish repetition of the sound, which put him in mind of heartbeats. The wind was more constant, keeping up an empty drone not unlike the voiceless noise of the receiver. Though he'd remembered one of his uncle's favourite turns of phrase—the comment about lateness—it didn't revive as many jokes as Todd hoped. It only brought back his uncle's response to hearing the doctor's receptionist call his name. "That's me," he would say, "on my tod."

It wasn't even true. His nephew had been with him, sharing the apprehension the man had been anxious if not desperate to conceal. None of these were memories Todd wanted to keep close to him in the dark. With an effort he recalled names his uncle had dug up from history: Addled Hitler, Guiser Wilhelm, Josef Starling, Linoleum Bonypart, Winsome Churchill … For years Todd had believed they had all been alive at the same time. Now the names seemed more like evidence of senility than jokes— blurred versions of the past that put him in mind of the way the rain on the window had twisted the world into a different shape. They left him unsure of himself, so that he was grateful to hear a voice.

It was next door. No, it was beyond the other room, though not far, and apparently calling a name. Presumably the caller wanted to be let in, since Todd heard a door open and shut. For a while there was silence, and then someone came out of the adjoining bathroom—a door opened, at any rate. As Todd tried to use the hint of companionship to help him fall asleep, he grew aware of more sounds in the next room.

His neighbour must be drunk. They seemed to be doing their utmost to speak—to judge by their tone, striving to voice some form of protest—but so unsuccessfully that Todd might have imagined they had no means of pronouncing words. He was struggling to make sense of it, since it was impossible to ignore, when someone else spoke. Was it the voice he'd first heard? Or perhaps the guest in the next room but one was calling for quiet. In a moment a door opened and closed. Todd willed the silence to let him sleep, but he was still awake when he heard the door again, followed by activity in the other room. His neighbour seemed to be in a worse state than ever, and had given up any attempt to speak while bumping into all the furniture. After some time the ungainly antics subsided, letting Todd hope his neighbour had found the bed or at least fallen asleep. But a voice was calling a name, and the door was audible again. By now Todd knew the silence wouldn't last, and he reared up from the trough of the mattress. "What are you doing in there?" he shouted.

The darkness engulfed his protest as somebody came back into the next room. They no longer sounded able to walk. They were crawling about on the floor, so effortfully that Todd fancied he heard them thumping it with their hands if not clawing at it. He'd had enough, and he lurched off the bed, groping at the dark until he found the light-switch. As soon as a couple of bulbs flickered in the chandelier he stumbled along the corridor to knock on the door of his neighbour's room.

The huge indifferent voice of the dark answered him—the wind. He pounded on the door until the number shivered on its loose screw, but nobody responded. The nearest glazed flame lent the digit a vague shadow that came close to transforming it into an 8, although Todd was reminded of a different symbol. It would have needed to be lying down, as he did. He thumped on the door again as a preamble to tramping back to his room. He parted his thin dry lips as he snatched the receiver off the hook and heard its empty sound. It was the wind, and the instrument was dead as a bone.

As he let the receiver drop into its cradle he heard the door in the next room. He couldn't take a breath while he listened to the noises that ensued. His neighbour was crawling about as blindly as before but less accurately than ever. It took them a considerable time to progress across the room. Todd would have preferred them not to find the connecting door, especially once he heard a fumbling at the bottom of it, a rudimentary attempt that sounded too undefined to involve fingers. As the door began to shake, a rage indistinguishable from panic swept away Todd's thoughts. Grabbing the suitcase, he flung it on the bed and dragged the luggage stand aside. He heard a series of confused noises in the other room, as if somebody were floundering across it, retreating in an agony of embarrassment at their own state. The connecting door wasn't locked, and he threw it wide open.

The next room was deserted, and it wasn't a bedroom. By the light from his own room Todd made out two low tables strewn with open books and magazines. Against the walls stood various chairs so decrepit that they seemed to need the dimness to lend them more substance. If the room hadn't been deserted he might not have ventured in, but he felt compelled to examine the items on the tables, like a child determined to learn a secret. He was halfway across the stained damp carpet when he wished he hadn't left his room.

The books were textbooks, in so many pieces that they might have been dismantled by someone's fumbling attempts to read them. There were no magazines, just scattered pages of the oversized books. Despite the dimness, Todd was able to discern more about the illustrations than he even slightly liked. All of them depicted surgical procedures he wanted to believe could never have been put into practice, certainly not on anyone alive or still living afterwards. Mixed up with the pages were sheets of blank paper on which someone had drawn with a ballpoint pen, perhaps the taped-up pen that lay among them. Its unsteadiness might explain the grotesque nature of the drawings, which looked like a child's work or that of someone unusually crippled. In a way Todd was grateful that he couldn't judge whether the drawings were attempts to reproduce the illustrations from the textbooks or to portray something even worse. He was struggling to breathe and to retreat from the sight of all the images, not to mention everything they conjured up, when he heard the door shut behind him.

He whirled around to find he could still see it—could see it had no handle on this side. He only had to push it open, or would have except that it was locked. He was throwing all his weight against it, the very little weight he seemed to have left, when a voice at his back said "Mr Todd."

It was the voice he'd been hearing, as hoarse and practically as blurred as it had sounded through the wall. "You don't want me," he pleaded, "you want someone else," but the silence was so eloquent that he had to turn. He still had one hope—that he could flee into the corridor—but the door to it had no handle either. The only open door was on the far side of the room.

The doorway was admitting the light, such as it was. When he trudged across the waiting-room he saw that the source of the dim glow was a solitary bare bulb on a tattered flex. It illuminated a room as cramped as a trench. The bare rough walls were the colour of earth, which might be the material of the floor. The room was empty apart from a long unlidded box. Surely the box might already contain someone, and Todd ventured forward to see. He had barely crossed the threshold when a voice behind him murmured "He's gone at last." They switched off the power and shut him in, and the light left him so immediately that he had no time to be sure that the room was another antechamber.

HOLES FOR FACES

As Charlie turned away from the breakfast buffet his mother gave a frown like the first line of a sketch of disapproval. "Don't take more than you can eat, please."

He didn't know how much this was meant to be. He put back one of the boiled eggs that chilled his fingers and used the tongs to replace a bread roll in its linen nest, but had to give up several round slices of meat before her look relented. "Come and sit down now, Charles," she said as though it had been his idea to loiter.

His father met him with a grin that might have been the promise of a joke or an apology for not venturing to make one. "Who wants to go to church today, Charlie?"

It wasn't even Sunday. Perhaps in Italy it didn't have to be. "At least we won't be robbed in there," his father said.

"You're safe in Naples, son," the man at the next table contributed. "We've always been."

"How old will you be?" his equally bulky wife said.

"I'm nearly eight." Since the frown looked imminent, Charlie had to say "I'm seven and nine months."

"That's three quarters, isn't it," the man said as if Charlie needed to be told.

"Just you stay close to your mummy and daddy and mind what they say," said his wife, "and you'll come to no harm."

It was Charlie's mother who was fearful of the streets. When they'd arrived last night after dark she'd refused to leave the hotel, even though it didn't serve dinner. His father had brought Charlie a sandwich in the room, and the adults had made do with some in the bar. He'd been too nervous to finish the sandwich, instead throwing it out of the window and hoping birds would carry off the evidence. Going back to the buffet might betray what he'd done, and he did his best to take his time over his plate while the adults introduced themselves. "Don't miss the catacombs," Bobby said as he pushed his chair back.

"Unless anything's going to be too much for someone," his wife Bobbie said.

"Nobody we know," said Charlie's father.

"Teeth," his mother said to send Charlie up to the room, where she inspected herself in the mirror. She'd plaited her long reddish hair in a loop on either side of her face, which was almost as small and sharp as his. His father's hair reminded Charlie of black filings drawn up by a magnet that had tugged his father's face close to rectangular. His mother gave Charlie's unruly curls a further thorough brush and insisted on zipping his cumbersome jacket up, all of which struck him as the last of her excuses to stay in the hotel.

The street was just as wide as it had seemed last night, and many of the buildings were as black, but shops at ground level had brought most of them to life. While the broad pavements were crowded Charlie couldn't see any criminals, unless any if not all of the people chattering on phones were arranging a crime, since even the women sounded like gangsters in cartoons to him. Reaching the opposite pavement was akin to dodging across a racetrack—no traffic lights were to be seen. Charlie's mother tried to hold his father back, but she was already clutching the boy's hand with one of hers and her handbag with the other. "It's how the locals do it," Charlie's father said. "We won't get anywhere if we don't show a bit of pluck."

There were bus stops around the corner near the harbour, and gusts of April wind that made Charlie's mother zip up the last inch of his jacket. On the bus she clung to her bag with both

hands and sat against him. At least he was by the window, and had
fun noticing how many cars were damaged in some way, bumpers
crumpled, wings scraped, side mirrors splintered or wrenched
off. His father looked up from consulting the Frugoguide to say
"Underworld next stop."

Wasn't that where gangsters lived? A pedestrian crossing
proved to lead across the road to a lift beside the pavement. A
face peered through the little window as they reached the lift, and
Charlie's mother didn't quite recoil. "We'll be fine down there,
won't we?" Charlie's father asked the attendant. "You wouldn't
be taking us otherwise."

The man waved his hands extravagantly. "No problem."

When the lift came to rest at the foot of the shaft the doors
opened on a view like a secret the city was sharing with the
visitors—a street of shops and tenements hidden from the road
above. Between the tenements clothes on lines strung across the
alleys flapped like pennants. "Come on, Maur," Charlie's father
urged. "It doesn't get any better than this."

Charlie didn't know if she was frowning at the prospect or at
disliking the version of her name. As they followed his father out
of the lift she took a firmer grip on Charlie's hand. "Is that the
church you brought us to see, Edward?"

Charlie thought his father was trying not to sound let down
by her response. "I expect so."

The stone porch under a tower that poked at the pale grey
sky was at least as tall as their house. Beyond the lumbering door
a marble silence held the flames of dozens of candles still. At
the far end of the high wide space a staircase with carved babies
perched on the ends of the banisters framed the altar. The floor
looked like a puzzle someone must have taken ages to complete,
and Charlie wondered what a puzzle was supposed to have to do
with God. His mother released his hand and seemed content to
stroll through the church, lingering over items he couldn't see
much point in. As he tried to keep his footsteps quiet his father
came back from consulting a timetable. "We need to go down
now," he murmured.

A pointer that didn't quite say **CATACOMBS** sent the family along a corridor. An old woman with a face like a string bag of wrinkles was sitting by a door. "No English," she declared and shook her head at Charlie, who thought she was barring him and perhaps his parents too until he realised she meant they didn't have to pay for him and couldn't expect her to speak their language. As his father counted out some European coins a man rather more than called "Don't go without us."

"Well, look who it never is," his wife Bobbie cried. "We thought we'd take our own advice."

As soon as Bobby handed the guide the notes he was brandishing she stumped to open the door. At the bottom of a gloomy flight of steps a corridor led into darkness. "Will you look after me, son?" Bobbie said. "Don't know if I can trust him."

Charlie wasn't sure whether this was one of those jokes adults made. While the corridor wasn't as dark as it had looked from above—the round arches supporting the brick roof were lit the amber of a traffic light—the illumination didn't reach all the way into the alcoves on both sides of the passage. "You could play hide and seek if nobody was watching," Bobby told him.

Hiding in an alcove didn't appeal much to Charlie. Suppose you found somebody already was? Dead people must be kept down here even if he couldn't see them, and who did Bobby think was watching? Charlie stayed close to his parents as the old woman shuffled along the corridor, jabbing a knuckly finger at plaques and mosaics while she uttered phrases that might have been names or descriptions. The movements in the alcoves were only overlapping shadows, even if they shifted like restless limbs. "You've not seen the best yet, son," Bobby said.

This sounded less like an adventure than some kind of threat, and Charlie was about to ask whether it was in the guidebook when Bobby whispered "Look for the people in the walls." As though the words had brought it to a kind of life, Charlie saw a thin figure beyond the next arch.

It was standing up straight with its hands near its sides. He thought it was squashed like a huge insect and surrounded by a stain until he made out that it seemed to be a human fossil embedded in the plaster. There was more or rather less to it than that, and once he'd peered at the ill-defined roundish blotch above the emaciated neck he had to blurt "Where's its head?"

The old woman emitted a dry wordless stutter, possibly expressing mirth. "Maybe it's hiding in the hole," Bobby said. "Maybe it's waiting for someone to look."

The skeletal shape implanted in the wall had indeed been deprived of its skull. Perched on the scrawny neck was a hole deep enough for a man's head to fit in. "Don't," Bobbie said as if she was both delighted and appalled.

Charlie had to follow his parents under the arch as the old woman poked a finger at the gaping hole and let out a stream of words he might have taken for a curse or an equally fervent prayer. Now he saw bodies in both walls of the passage, and wished he didn't need to ask "Who took all their heads?"

"Maybe it was someone after souvenirs," Bobby said. "I don't suppose this lot were too tickled with losing their noggins. Watch out they don't think we're the ones that did it."

"They can't think. They've got no brains left."

"You tell him, son," Bobbie enthused just as his mother said "Charles."

He'd felt as if his words had robbed the figures in the walls of power until her rebuke gave it back to them. He could imagine the headless bodies peeling themselves loose from their corpse-shaped indentations and the stains that must have been part of them once, to jerk and stagger rapidly towards him. Far too soon some of them were at his back while others surrounded him, and there were surreptitious movements in the holes they had for heads—glimpses like animals retreating into their burrows to hide until people had gone by. Surely those were just the shadows of the visitors, and Charlie was making himself look closer when Bobby said "Don't stick your hand in, son. You never know what's waiting."

"Don't touch, Charles," his mother said at once.

"I wasn't going to."

71

"And," she said, "please don't speak to your mother in that fashion."

"Take no notice, son," Bobbie advised. "He was just having a joke."

"I'd like us to leave now, please," Charlie's mother said. "I think everyone's seen enough."

When Charlie turned to follow her he caught sight of a movement above the neck of the embedded body beside him, as if a face like a featureless stain had swung to watch. She must be causing it, there and in the cavities the other fleshless bodies had in place of heads. He tried not to look, especially back, while he trotted after her. It was only his father who was close behind him. The church was meant to be a refuge, and no footsteps other than the family's were clattering across the stone floor to the exit, however many echoes there might be. Outside all the clothes on the lines might have been miming agitation that his mother was trying to conceal. "I think we've been down here long enough," she said.

Long enough for what? Rather than ask, Charlie hurried after her to the lift, where the sight of a face peering through the small window had lost some of its appeal. As the lift creaked upwards his father consulted the guidebook. "They took the heads somewhere for safety," he said.

As Charlie wondered who was being kept safe and from what, his mother said "I'd like to put them behind us, thank you, Edward."

"How far?" Charlie blurted.

"I've been surprised at you today, Charles. I hope you won't let us down any more."

She strode to poke the button for the traffic lights, and his father hung back to murmur "They thought something might be catching, Charlie. That's why they took the heads off, to protect people."

Who might something catch, and why? As Charlie made to ask, his mother doubled her frown at them. "Come on, Charlie," his father muttered. "We don't want you ending up in more trouble."

72

Once they'd joined the queue at the bus stop Charlie's mother grasped her handbag every time a moped raced through the increasingly gridlocked traffic. The bicycles buzzing like wasps didn't bother Charlie, but he could have done without the face that kept looming at the window of the lift across the road. Very eventually a bus appeared in the distance, and less than ten minutes later it arrived at the stop.

From the bus he watched cars inch past one another, their drivers reaching to pull side mirrors inwards. The ruse would have amused him more if he hadn't seen one reflected face swell up like a worm emerging from a hole as the driver hauled at the mirror. Having leafed through the guidebook, his father said "Who'd like to go up to a park?"

"Let's," Charlie's mother said at once.

The picture in the book showed a railway platform made of steps alongside an equally steep train. When the bus came to an official stop at last and his father led the way to the station, however, Charlie saw an ordinary horizontal platform leading to a tunnel, where he tried to enjoy the sight of a blank-faced train worming its way towards him out of the dark. At first there wasn't much to see when the train moved off, though a toddler in the next carriage kept poking her head up to peer at him. Her breath on the window between the carriages blurred her face and turned it grey. He tried to focus his attention on the tunnel, where he couldn't see any holes in the walls—nowhere that anything could creep or struggle or bulge out from.

A wind boarded the train when, having escaped into the open, it reached the top of a hill, and Charlie's mother tugged his zip under his chin. At a restaurant between the station and a park they had a pizza big enough for the three of them. Plastic sheets around the dining area didn't just obscure the view but made the face of anybody who came near seem to take shape only gradually and not quite enough.

There were views from all sides of the park. The guidebook fluttered like a captured bird while Charlie's father named buildings and piazzas and streets. The boy was more taken with

Vesuvius, a hump the colour of its own dark smoke across the bay. "Would you like to use the telescope, Charles?" his mother said, but the notion of looking through a hole that brought things closer didn't tempt him. As she pocketed the coin for the slot machine he saw a face struggling through a gap in a mass of foliage behind her. Only the leaves were active, and the statue was on the far side of the bush.

"We can take a ferry tomorrow," Charlie's father said on the way back to the hotel, "to somewhere your mother should like." Charlie thought she'd heard more than was intended—perhaps a rebuke. Nobody spoke much until they were up in their room. As soon as his father started looking in the Frugoguide she said "I'd like to eat wherever's nearest."

"I hope that won't be its only merit," said his father.

"I hope some things mean more to you than your stomach." Her glance at Charlie made it plain what should. "Time for a rest before we go out," she said to bring all discussion to an end.

Charlie tried to lie still on his bed while his parents did on theirs beside him. He might have liked to see their faces, which were turned away from him. His father's hand lay slack on top of the side of his mother's waist, and Charlie had a sense that it was inhibited from moving, just like him. He struggled not to think this might be how it would feel to be embedded in a wall. You'd have to move eventually, however you could. He strained to keep his restlessness discreet, but once his bed had creaked several times his mother said wearily "We may as well go for dinner."

The nearest restaurant was just two doors away from the hotel. It was an osteria, which sounded too much like a word for panic. Two mirrors the length of the side walls multiplied the room full of small tables. A waiter set about befriending Charlie, calling him signor and pouring him a sip of lemonade to taste as Charlie's father sampled the wine. He told Charlie that his choice of spaghetti Bolognese was the best dish on the menu, so that the boy felt obliged to finish it, though it wasn't much like his mother's recipe. As his parents drank the liqueur that came with the bill she said "I'll be happy to come here every night."

"Seconded," Charlie's father said, though Charlie didn't think she had been inviting a vote.

The boy might have shared their enthusiasm except for the word for the restaurant. It was engraved on the frosted window, and the O was a transparent oval like a hole a face would have to squash itself through. From the table at the back of the restaurant the letter resembled a hollow full of the darkness outside, and Charlie had glimpsed more than one face in it during the meal. Perhaps they'd belonged to people with an eye to dining, though they hadn't come in. "And I'm sure you'll want to see your friend again, Charles," his mother said.

She hurried him back to the hotel and up to the room, where she said "Face and teeth." Once he'd washed the one and brushed the others she dealt him a kiss so terse it was barely perceptible, and his father squeezed his shoulder. As Charlie lay under the quilt with his eyes shut he heard his mother say "I'm quite tired. You go down to the bar if you want, of course."

"No need for that," his father said before the low voices moved to the bathroom, where Charlie heard him murmur "Don't keep making that face." He imagined putting a face together like a jigsaw, a fancy preferable to the dreams he felt threatened by having. Eventually his parents finished muttering and went to bed. They weren't with him as he tried to find his way home through the town, where all the signs were as incomprehensible as the answers people gave him. In any case he didn't like speaking to anyone he met, however expensively dressed they were; they looked too thin inside their elegant costumes, and he couldn't make much of their faces. Perhaps there were none to be seen—not yet, at any rate. When they began to squirm up from the holes in the collars he stuffed the quilt into his mouth to mute his cries. Having to explain to his parents would be even worse than the dream.

At breakfast the English couple came over. "Bobby has something to say to you," Bobbie said.

"I'm sorry if I caused any upset down below."

"Don't be saying things like that at breakfast. In the

catacombs, he means," Bobbie said as though apologising for a child. "Did he go too far, son?"

"He was joking. You said."

"So long as you don't forget," Bobbie said and turned to Charlie's mother. "We've been putting you down for a teacher."

"We both are," his father said.

At least all this helped distract them from how little the boy ate. After breakfast the family walked down to the harbour, to find the sea had grown so boisterous that the ferries had been cancelled. Now that Charlie saw all the windows in the boats he was happy to stay on land, even though he hadn't noticed any faces at them. "There's always Pompeii," his father said.

Opposite the main railway terminal was a kind of market, men hoping to sell shabby items that cluttered the pavement. One peddler had a dog, presumably not for sale. Its bony piebald face poked out of a discoloured plastic cone around its neck, and it bared uneven yellow teeth in a silent snarl. On the train Charlie tried to forget it and anything it brought to mind. The clocks on the stations were some help, since every one showed a different incorrect time. "They've stopped time," his father said as Charlie imagined he might have told the delinquents he taught creative writing in the unit at the school. Perhaps because modern history was her job, his mother didn't seem to think much of the idea. Charlie wasn't sure how to feel about the notion, but then this was true of much in his life.

Beyond the gates to Pompeii, where a woman's face nodded forward in the ticket booth, was an entire ruined town. Sightseers clustered like flies around the nearest buildings, where the open fronts were covered with wire mesh as if to cage the occupants— figures that Charlie wished he could mistake for statues lying on shelves. "Not more mummies," his mother protested.

"They aren't, Charlie. They're just casts."

Weren't those the husks worms left behind where they crawled out of the earth? "What does that mean?" Charlie had to ask.

"They're plaster." This seemed reassuring until his father added "They're the shape of whoever was there when the volcano caught them. All that was left were hollows where they'd been, and that's what the plaster was put in."

Too many if not all of the contorted figures looked about to writhe and creep towards their audience, and the idea of dead shapes that had grown in holes didn't appeal to Charlie either. He followed his parents into the town, where the streets were the colour of bone—of the shapes in the cages. The face that poked out of an unglazed window belonged to a girl somebody was photographing. After that Charlie kept alert for cameras, which often brought faces out of holes in the walls. He was glad his parents had forgotten to bring their cameras because of disagreeing over what to pack.

Lunch was no excuse to leave, since they'd bought sandwiches and drinks on the way from the station. They picnicked in the amphitheatre, where Charlie's father attempted to entertain him with a speech about someone called Spartacus who'd lived in Vesuvius and set people free. The passing spectators seemed more amused than Charlie's mother did, and Charlie didn't know which of his parents to side with. "Sorry if that was too much like school," his father eventually said.

"Perhaps Charles thinks it hasn't anything to do with him."

"All history does, Charlie. It isn't just behind us, it's part of us."

Charlie didn't care for either of his father's notions, which stayed with him as he trudged through the crumbling skeleton of a town. His father wanted to show him and especially his mother frescoes and mosaics recommended by the Frugoguide, but the boy was distracted by more faces at windows than there were amateur photographers. He wished he'd thought sooner to unzip his jacket, since as soon as he did his mother said "I think that's the best of the day."

He hoped that didn't mean worse was to come. He felt as if the clocks on the stations were holding time back. He couldn't see the dog in the market opposite the terminal, but if it was about, what else might he have overlooked? Despite the gathering dusk, his father made a detour on the way to the hotel.

The inside of this church was high and pallid, with pillars like polished bones. As the twilight blurred the figures outlined in the windows, their blotchy faces seemed poised to nod forward. Did he glimpse a face beyond the door of a confessional? The box made him think of an upright coffin in one of the kinds of film he wasn't allowed to watch. When he peered towards it the face was snatched into the gloom, and he heard a bony rattle. "Have you had enough for one day, Charlie?" his father said.

In a number of ways the boy had, but he confined himself to admitting "I'm a bit tired."

In the hotel room he felt as if his parents were waiting to catch him not just being tired, and he turned his back so that they couldn't see his face. At the restaurant the waiter gave them the same table and asked if the signor wanted his favourite. Charlie thought it safest to say yes, along with please when his mother's frown began to gather. A different dish might have been even harder to finish while he was aware of the O on the window. He kept thinking a face was about to peer in at him, and far too often faces did, retreating into the dark before he could distinguish any features they might have. When he tried to ignore the gaping oval he began to fancy that one face too many was hidden in the repetitive reflections on both sides of him.

"Face and teeth," his mother said upstairs with a toothy grin as a demonstration if not a joke. As well as the mirror on the bathroom wall a round one stood on a shelf above the sink. It magnified Charlie's reflection, and when he lurched to turn it away he saw his face swell up like a balloon, baring its teeth. He couldn't help taking the sight to bed, where he was visited by faces that grew bloated, parts of them bulging out of proportion as the heads struggled to emerge from their lairs. Each time he woke he had to jam the quilt into his mouth.

He might have left his plate at breakfast empty if his parents wouldn't have wanted to know why. When he returned to the table four people were watching him. "Were you disappointed you couldn't go on your boat?" Bobbie said.

He wasn't sure how much of a lie to tell. "A bit," he said.

"It's your last day, Charles." Perhaps his mother didn't mean this to sound ominous, because she added "Would you rather not spend five hours on a ferry? Tell the truth."

"Don't mind."

It was rather that he couldn't think what he would prefer. When his mother raised her hands like a weary victim of a hold-up his father said "Would you like a surprise for your last day, Charlie?"

The boy wished they wouldn't keep using the phrase. "If you like," he couldn't avoid saying.

"Aren't I allowed to know either, Edward?"

"We don't want to give it away, do we, Maur?" Charlie's father covered the side of his face while he mouthed at her, and Charlie hoped she'd winced only at his dropping half of her name. "That'll be a thrill for him," Bobbie said.

Surely the surprise wasn't more of Pompeii, though the family boarded that train. The clocks on the stations made Charlie feel as if time had abandoned him. His father stood up when the train reached Herculaneum. Weren't there supposed to be mummies there too? It was only when his father bought bus tickets from a bar outside the station that Charlie realised his treat was Vesuvius.

As the bus climbed out of the town he saw a fair beside the road and felt guilty for wanting to be there instead. The nearer the volcano came, the less of an adventure it seemed likely to be. It loomed above the road like a storm rendered solid while his father read out from the guidebook that the Romans used to believe volcanoes were entrances to hell. Why would he take Charlie anywhere like that? Did the boy deserve it somehow?

Beyond a ticket booth a man was handing out sticks at the foot of the route to the crater. Much of the track consisted of loose flat stones, which made footsteps sound bony and thin, especially all those at Charlie's back. The path kept promising and failing to grow less steep, and whenever he tried to take more of a breath the wind assailed him with the stench of the volcano. It smelled as if the earth were farting, and if he'd been with other boys he might have been able to laugh.

Near the summit the path led between souvenir stalls. Among the trinkets Charlie noticed skulls, which gave him the unwelcome notion that someone might have brought the heads up from the catacomb to sell. The crater wasn't reassuring—a vast hollow in which fumes crept out of the black earth, he couldn't see exactly where, to crawl about as though groping for their own shapes. Charlie didn't like to wonder what kind of creature Spartacus had been to live here, never mind what he'd set free.

He did his utmost to look pleased with the treat for his father's sake and to give his parents one less reason to disagree. At last his father asked if he'd seen enough. As they passed between the stalls again a cloud like an emanation of the crater massed overhead. Charlie felt walled in by skulls, which were no less ominous for being plainly manufactured. When a wind followed him down from the summit he could have thought more than the stench of rot was after him. Some of the people toiling uphill had tugged hoods around their faces against the wind, which yanked at the material so that their features thrust up at Charlie. More than one of them bared their teeth, surely only at the wind.

The bus had almost reached the station when Charlie's father turned to him. "I know something else you'll like."

He meant the fair. It had a roundabout Charlie went on twice, and a dog with a ruff around its neck, prancing on two legs while its front legs clawed at the air. There was a target gallery where neither Charlie nor his parents could shoot quite straight enough, and a stall where you flung wooden balls to knock grinning faces backwards, leaving dark holes. He didn't want to try that, and he hurried past to an attraction screened by trees. At once he wished he hadn't seen it, but his parents already had.

Two life-size figures were painted on a board taller than his father. No doubt they were meant to be comical. The man sported a clownish costume so baggy it made him look puffed up by gas, while his partner wore a spangled dress that bared her bony hirsute legs. They had no faces, only holes for them, filled just now by the dark swollen sky. Charlie was about to thank his parents for the treat and flee towards the road when a man bustled over, gesticulating with a camera. "Go on, Charles," his mother said. "Put your head through, then at least we'll have one photograph."

The surge of dread was worse for being undefinable. The prospect of causing an argument between his parents dismayed him as well. "You and dad first," he said in desperation.

As soon as they stepped behind the board he felt he'd risked them to save himself. They seemed unconcerned when they put their faces through; they even produced grins, though his mother's resembled her habitual patient expression, while his father's looked hopeful. The boy was able to respond, having thought of an excuse not to go near. "I won't reach."

"Of course you will," his mother said, letting her grin subside now that the camera had whirred twice. "Lift him up, Edward."

She pulled her face out of the hole to watch until he had to venture behind the board, to see only his parents and its unadorned back. His father took Charlie's waist in both hands and raised him like an offering to the hole in front of them. "Gosh, there isn't much of you," he murmured. "We'll have to feed you up."

Charlie saw his mother give them both a resentful look. He kept his head back until the photographer motioned vigorously for him to bring it forward. As the edges of the skull-sized orifice loomed around his face he saw the blurred misshapen body he'd acquired. The camera whirred and whirred again, and he thought the ordeal was over until his mother said "I'll take him, Edward. You deserve a turn."

He couldn't let her see him hesitate to go to her. "You aren't so skinny," she said as she hoisted him with her arms under his armpits, so that he wondered if she'd just wanted an excuse to weigh him. When his head came level with the hole she said "Don't do what you did with your face."

Had she noticed his reluctance? He jerked his head forward and did his best to grin. As he realised that his body had become the scrawny thing in a dress, the camera went off. He struggled to hold his face still while the shutter sounded once more, and then he made himself heavy so that his mother put him down. The photographer beckoned them all to a caravan, where he indicated a printer and moved his hands apart to specify the size of photograph. The machine quivered and rattled and eventually disgorged six large prints. Only the pictures of Charlie's parents were clear. In the rest, presumably because nervousness had made him move without realising, the boy's face was an indistinct bulge with a bony slit for a mouth.

"I think that's quite enough expense," his mother said when the photographer flourished the camera. His father paid and was handed the pictures in an envelope. The way out of the fair led past the painted board, and Charlie almost managed not to look, but couldn't resist glancing over his shoulder. Although nobody had been behind or even near the board, two swollen blotchy faces were dangling through the holes. They looked as if the process of emerging had come close to pulling them apart, given how much of them drooped over the edge of the holes. In the instant before he succeeded in wrenching his gaze away, Charlie saw that the effort had bared not just their teeth.

He clutched both his parents by the hands, apparently to their surprise, and dragged them towards the road. On the train he sat next to his father, away from the window, and couldn't tell where it was safe to look. The walk to the hotel felt like an omen of worse—the pavement market where the dog with its head in a hole might be lurking, the church with the box for faces to peer from, the restaurant where a head ducked towards the O of the engraved sign to grin out at him. He just managed to suppress his cry, having recognised the waiter who'd befriended him.

As his father unlocked the room Bobbie looked out of the one across the corridor. "Having a good last day?"

"I'd say so," Charlie's father said.

"We've an early start tomorrow. If you two want some time to yourselves after dinner we'll be in our room."

"You can ring us if there's any problem, son," Bobby said.

"You don't mind, do you, Charlie?" said his father.

Admitting his fears out loud seemed likely to make them

more real. Perhaps only his silence about them was keeping them away. Besides, he felt responsible for the tension between his parents, especially since they couldn't discuss it in front of him. "I'll be all right," he prayed aloud.

"He'll behave himself, don't worry." He gathered Bobbie meant her husband. To Charlie's parents she said "We'll keep an eye."

He was unwillingly reminded that the faces in the holes hadn't been too good at keeping theirs. Once he was in the room he knew he wouldn't be able to lie still; trying would only make him shiver. "Can I read?" he pleaded.

"I said he ought to have brought some of his books, Edward."

"Can't I read the one about here?"

"I certainly don't see why not," his father said not even mainly to him, and passed him the guidebook.

Charlie was looking for reassurance, but there wasn't much. Spartacus had been a rebel slave who'd set up camp on Vesuvius six years before it erupted. Lot's wife in the Bible had probably been turned into a kind of mummy by a volcano. Charlie could have lived without learning this, never mind that some of the headless remains in the catacomb had been painted on the walls where the bodies used to be. Even if this explained the uneven outlines he'd mistaken for stains, it made the figures far too reminiscent of the ones at the fair, and what had happened to the bodies? The guidebook left that out as if it would do people no good to know. He was gazing at the page rather than read on when his father said "Too much for you, Charlie? Time for a feed."

In the restaurant the task of grinning at the waiter made the boy's face feel as constricted as it had by the board at the fair. He managed to avoid looking whenever anything loomed at the oval in the window. He took all the time he could over the meal the waiter assumed was his favourite, and succeeded in eating some of it as long as he forgot how the mirrors could be hiding an intruder. Eventually his mother said "Time to say goodbye, Charles."

The other couple must have heard them come upstairs, because Bobby called "Ready" as if he were playing hide and seek. Charlie hurried to the bathroom, hoping to outdistance his mother's night-time phrase, but she called through the door "Face and teeth." At the sink he shut his eyes so as not to see his bulbous face in the magnifying mirror. His parents delivered their signs of affection and waited for him to climb into bed. "We won't be any longer than we need to be," his mother said.

As soon as he couldn't hear their footsteps Charlie lurched out of bed to switch on the nearest light and then the rest of them. He tried watching television with the sound turned low, but he couldn't find any programmes in English, which made him feel as if the people on the screen were saying things it was vital for him to understand. They reminded him of his parents and the secrets he suspected were about him. He didn't want to read the guidebook in case it contained more information he wouldn't want to be alone with, and the sight of the photographs from the fair would be worse. He read every word in the folder about the hotel and tried to avoid looking at the spyhole in the door; every glance at it felt too much like inviting a response. He'd lost count of how often he'd read through the folder by the time he heard a fumbling at the door.

Was it one of his parents? Whenever they drank a lot they seemed to have trouble climbing the stairs at home—but the noise was too shapeless, almost not there and yet more present than he liked. With more reluctance than he'd ever previously experienced Charlie tiptoed to the door and stretched up to peer through the spyhole. When he glimpsed a shape so ill-defined it looked incomplete, vanishing from sight like a worm withdrawing into the earth, he managed to stay at the door long enough to jam the end of the chain into the socket. Once he'd shot the bolt as well he retreated to his bed and dragged the quilt over the whole of himself.

He was in a nervous fitful doze when he heard the fumbling again. He pressed the quilt against his ears so hard that he didn't hear the voices and the rapping on the door until they must have gone on for some minutes. He floundered off the bed and ran to let his parents in. Bobbie and her husband were watching from across the corridor. "Who on earth do you think you are, Charles?" his mother demanded. "This is our room."

He thought of an answer he hoped would placate her. "I didn't want any robbers to get in."

She only shook her head as if she had an insect in her hair and gestured him into the room, not even glancing at the other couple as his father murmured to them. From his bed Charlie heard his parents muttering at length in the bathroom. If they'd resolved their differences while they were without him, he'd spoiled that now. He heard his father declare "I'm not saying what I think has made him like this."

Eventually his parents went to bed. Their silence felt as ominous as the cloud above Vesuvius, and weighed on the dark. Charlie listened for signs that they'd fallen asleep, which might relieve at least some of the foreboding even if it left him by himself, but he didn't know whether they'd drifted off by the time he did. He dreamed they were at the door again, although when he managed to unchain it and open all the bolts and locks, the faces that poked at him out of his parents' heads weren't theirs. He clutched at the pillow to blot out his screams as his jolt awake almost flung him off the bed. The quilt dragged the pillowcase back so that the pillow bulged into his face. The pillow was lumpier than he remembered, and the irregular padding that covered the lumps was unhelpfully thin. Feathers must be spilling out of the pillow to make it feel as though fragments were flaking off. Charlie was pulling his head back, disliking the dry sour taste, when his thumbs dug into the contents of the linen sack—into something hinged, where an object stirred like a worm. In the faint light from the corridor he saw that his bed-mate had widened its withered eyes and bared its mottled teeth.

His shrieks brought Bobby to pound on the door while Bobbie blinked across the corridor. "Just a nightmare," Charlie's father said, perhaps with desperate optimism. Charlie's mother rubbed the boy's shoulders with more vigour than affection, not looking at his face. There was nothing in his bed or under it, which only made him wonder where the extra guest had gone. His mother shook the pillow when it was clear that she thought it was time he lay down. He almost hoped some unexpected contents would appear for his parents to see.

Even when he held the end of the pillowcase shut with both hands under the quilt he was afraid something would wriggle forth if he slept. Whenever he jerked awake from a few seconds' forgetful doze he clutched the pillowcase harder. At last it was time for breakfast, where he felt as if Bobby and Bobbie had left early because of him. He took as little from the buffet as he thought he could get away with taking while everyone in the room seemed to be aware of him, but he couldn't even eat that much. "I expect you're eager to be home," his father said, not really as if he believed it himself.

The day was so sunlit Charlie might have thought it was celebrating his departure. The light was pretending there was nowhere anything he dreaded could hide. In the taxi to the airport a face spied on him through the mirror. Knowing that it was the driver didn't comfort him, any more than the way the women at the check-in desk and the boarding gate scrutinised him. Very eventually he and his parents were allowed to shuffle onto the plane, where he stared at everybody seated further down the cabin until his mother said "Sit down, Charles. That isn't how you've been taught to behave."

He watched people filing along the aisle to sit behind him and in front of him. The procession was slow enough for a funeral, and made him feel breathlessly trapped. The face that had followed him out of the catacombs could hide anywhere— wherever his parents wouldn't believe it was. He craned around to peer between the seats at his mother, hoping she'd forgiven him for causing last night's scene, but she met him with a frown. "Turn round, Charles, please. You've shown us up enough."

"Look out of the window," his father urged, and Charlie couldn't let them sense his fear. As he ducked towards the cramped pane a blotch of a face swelled up to meet him—his own. At once he understood everything. His mother kept telling the truth about him, about the face and teeth, and his father didn't want to say what had made him how he was. The past was indeed part of him. The ground began to move before his eyes as the plane headed for the runway, and when he sat back the blurred face retreated into hiding—into him. He closed his eyes in the hope his father wouldn't make him look again, but it didn't help him forget. He couldn't leave behind the horror his parents were bringing home.

THE ROUNDS

As the train arrives at James Street one of the women behind me in the carriage murmurs "They're talking about us again."

"What's somebody saying this time?" her friend protests, but I miss the answer in the midst of a recorded warning not to leave luggage unattended. The amplified voice seems to herd commuters off the underground platform onto the train, and an Asian woman in a headscarf black enough for a funeral takes a seat at the far end of the carriage. Perhaps she's a lawyer from the courts at the top of James Street, since she's carrying a briefcase. The voice falls silent as the train heads into the tunnel.

There's just a solitary track on the loop under Liverpool, where the tunnel shrinks to half its previous width. Lights embedded in the walls flash out of the dark every few seconds like some kind of signal. In about a minute more passengers board at Moorfields; it's the start of the rush hour. I'm at the nearest doors well before the train pulls into Lime Street, where the Muslim woman alights further down the carriage. As I make to step onto the platform I notice she's without her briefcase.

"Excuse me," I call, but she doesn't seem to hear. Several people look up or around and then lose interest as I dash along the carriage. The case is on the floor by the seat she vacated, and I grab it before struggling between the last of the commuters boarding the train. The woman isn't on the platform. She could have used the lift, but the escalators are closer, and I sprint for the exit that leads to them.

Is she late for a main line train? By the time I reach the bank of escalators her strides have taken her almost to the top. I'd try and overtake her on the other upward escalator, but it isn't moving. "Excuse me," I shout, "you dropped this."

She turns with one hand on the banister and smiles, though the expression looks a little automatic. I'm hurrying towards her when she sails out of view. The briefcase is so shabby that I might conclude she meant to dump it if it weren't also heavy with documents. I assume that's what the contents are, but the lock is jammed; it's so distorted that someone might already have tried to force it—perhaps she has lost the key. I admit I'm glad to find her waiting beyond the escalator, this side of the ticket barrier. "Oh, thank you," she says and makes her smile rueful. "I don't know what I could have been thinking of."

I'm at least equally ashamed of having thought she might be up to no good. It shows how prejudiced we've all grown, how inclined to think in today's stereotypes. I pass her the briefcase with both hands, and she grasps the scruffy handle as she shows her ticket at the barrier. I flash my pass and am following her along the passage to the escalators that lead up to the main station when my breast pocket emits a series of piercing clanks that put me in mind of a faulty pacemaker.

I read the message on my mobile as the escalator lifts me into the glare of sunlight through the glass roof. **Have to cancel**, it says. **No train**. Beneath the huge cautionary voice of the station there's the babble of a crowd that's hurrying to the platforms while at least as many people stream out onto the concourse. The Muslim woman has disappeared among them. I pocket the mobile without sending a response and tramp down the descending escalator. As I display my pass the ticket collector says "You look familiar."

"I expect there's plenty more like me."

I'd say that was as witty as her quip, but she doesn't bother laughing. She seems to feel it's her duty to ask "Weren't you here

90

just now?"

"If you say so."

"Did you forget something?"

"That's not me. I thought I was meeting someone but I'm not after all."

"You want to be sure what's happening another time."

The pointless exchange has delayed me so much that as I step on the underground escalator I hear a squeal of wheels—the arrival of the train I meant to catch. I clutch at the unsynchronised banisters and dash down two sinking steps at a time, to reach the platform just as the train sets about shutting its doors. With a leap that leaves me feeling rejuvenated I jam my foot between the nearest pair, which flinch apart, raising an alarm that all the others take up. "I've still got it," I declare as I board the train.

Nobody seems interested. One man lowers his head as though his tweed hat is weighing it down. A younger man is leafing through a cardboard folder full of documents, and a girl is lost in the world of her personal stereo, while a woman in a coat patterned like a chessboard frowns at a Mtogo poster as if she thinks an African restaurant has no right to advertise on the train. I find a seat near the doors as the train heads for Central Station, where it swaps commuters for commuters before following the loop back to James Street. Just one passenger alights there, hurrying behind the crowd on the platform. She's the Muslim with the briefcase.

She must have used the lift at Lime Street while I was held up at the barrier. I've a reason to have caught the first train back, but what's hers? However prejudiced it makes me feel, I can't help lurching to my feet and forcing my way onto the platform. She's already past the nearest exit—she isn't even on the stairs to which it leads. If I find she's returning to the courts, where she could perfectly well have left some item, I hope I'll be cured of making suspicious assumptions. If she sees me I'll be more embarrassed still. I sprint up the boxed-in stairs and reach the top just in time to see her leaving the enclosed bridge across the underground tracks. She isn't bound for the outside world. She's on her way down to the platform for the trains around the loop.

I hear a train approaching, and her running down to meet it. I can't see her as I dash down the steps, and she isn't on the platform scattered with commuters. I'm opposite the last carriage of the train. I could try to reach the driver or attract their attention, but what would I say? All I know is that if the woman plans to abandon the briefcase again, we should all be safe until she's well away from it. The thought sends me onto the train.

This time I don't trigger the alarm, and the train moves off at once. The carriage is crowded, but I can see every head, and there's no sign of a headscarf. Suppose she's so fanatical that she would take it off to be less obvious? I struggle through the crowd, peering at every face and at the floor beside and between and especially under the seats. All the people in the aisle would make a briefcase easier to hide, but it seems the woman wasn't in this carriage, or at least she hasn't left the case here. I haul open the door between the carriages, to see a man leaning against the next door. He's so bulky that he blocks the view into the other carriage, and he doesn't budge when I knock on the window. I make to shove the door at him, and then I'm overwhelmed by a blaze of light. It isn't an explosion, even if my innards wince. The train has emerged from the tunnel.

We're at Moorfields. The doors open to the platform, but I'm nowhere near any of them. When I push at the one between the carriages the man with his wide flabby shoulders against it doesn't shift an inch. More people squeeze onto the train, and I'm near to panicking. As it moves off I crane back to stare through a window at the platform. A woman is striding fast along a passage to the escalators. She's the headscarved Mohammedan, and she doesn't have her briefcase.

My guts clench like a helpless fist, and a sour taste surges into my mouth. Until this moment I can't really have believed my own suspicions—I might as well have been enacting a scene from a cheap thriller based on the news. As the tunnel closes around the carriage I kick the connecting door and pound on it with both fists. When the hulking man turns his big stupid head to stare at me I flash my pass, too quickly for him to take issue with it. "Let me through," I shout and mime as well.

Even he must realise we all need to be concerned about security, though he makes it clear that he's doing me a favour by stepping aside. I brush past him and shoulder my way through the swaying crowd. The lights on the walls of the tunnel are hurtling towards me like the future. There's a bag of shopping between two seats, and there's another carrier bag on the floor, but where's the briefcase? Is it even in this carriage? How much distance may the woman want to put between herself and the case, or how little? I'm nearly at the first set of doors, and I'm shamefully tempted to make my escape, but we're still in the tunnel. The train lurches as if it has been derailed, and its hollow roar seems to grow louder. I seize the metal pole above the partition that separates the seats from the crowded space in front of a pair of doors. The carriage steadies, and as I grasp there was no explosion I see a briefcase on the floor, almost hidden by the legs of passengers. "Sir," I say urgently, "is that your case?"

The man who's closest to it glances down and then just as indifferently at my face. "Nothing to do with me."

His neighbours shake their heads, and I stoop to retrieve the case. I recognise it at once—recognise the warped lock, which I'm beginning to think might have been deliberately forced out of shape so that nobody can open it. I close my fist around the ragged handle and lift the case.

At once light flares all around me. I'm back at Lime Street. All along the carriage matrix signs spell it out, and a woman's amplified voice pronounces the words for anyone who can't read. As I make for the doors I'm frantically trying to decide where to take the briefcase. The train is coasting to a halt, and I'm still trapped by all the bodies pressing close around me, when someone taps me on the shoulder hard enough for a knock on a door. "That yours?" a man says in my ear.

"It isn't," I declare and struggle around to face him. He's a cleaner in a yellow jerkin. Usually the cleaners don't collect the rubbish from the trains during the rush hour, and his appearance is as unexpected as it's reassuring—even the Union Jack badge just visible on the lapel of his jacket. "It was left before," I murmur for only him to hear. "I think—"

"We saw," he says just as low and reaches for the briefcase. "Give it here."

However grateful I am to let it go, I want to be sure he understands. "You saw who left it," I mutter.

"We know all about those."

This could be prejudice symbolised by the badge. Under the circumstances I can't be choosy, and I hand him the briefcase. "Be careful with it," I whisper. "Whatever's inside—"

"It's seen to, granddad," he says and steps onto the platform.

As he strides towards the nearest exit a young woman offers me a seat. Perhaps I look shaken by having to deal with the briefcase, unless she heard what the cleaner called me. I sink onto the seat, but I can't begin to relax until the train leaves the station and is safely in the tunnel. "Thank God that's over," I say aloud.

I oughtn't to have spoken. At least nobody seems to want to enquire into my remark. One man clasps his hands and bows his head as if to dazzle everyone with the shine of his bald scalp. A girl in a sweater striped like a wasp stares out of the window at the repetition of the lights. A young businessman reads a magazine, and the woman next to him might almost be hypnotised by the swaying of her earrings, which are shaped like inverted question marks although she doesn't look remotely Spanish. More passengers manage to find room when we reach Central Station, and soon the voice of the train reads out the illuminated announcement about James Street. In a very few moments I'll be out of the loop at last. Just one person leaves the train and heads for the exit. He's wearing a yellow jerkin, and he's carrying a briefcase.

He's the man who spoke to me. It needn't be the same case, except that I can see the warped lock. Didn't he understand my warning? How could he risk bringing the case back on the train? The explanation makes my nerves yank me to my feet. "It's him as well," I gasp. "He's part of it."

Nobody appears to want to understand or to let me off the train. I have to shout in one man's ear before he gives an inch, followed by hardly any more as I struggle past him. I've barely staggered onto the platform when the train shuts its doors. I could shout to the driver, but if anyone else hears me, won't that cause a panic or worse? My heart thumps like a frenzied drum as I dash up the steps to the underground bridge.

I can't see the man in the yellow jerkin or the briefcase. Has he used one of the lifts up to street level? I could—there are always staff at the top—but that might take longer than it's safe to take. There's a more immediate way of communicating with the staff, and I sprint across the bridge to leap down two steps at a time to the other platform.

Passengers are waiting for a train around the loop, but I can't see what I'm afraid to see. An intercom is embedded in the wall. A blue button offers **Information**, but I jab the green one that says **Emergency**. My heart deals me a couple of irregular thumps that I hear as well as feel before the grille above the buttons speaks. "Hello?"

"I'm at James Street." Lurching close to the grille, I cup my hands around my mouth to murmur "I think—"

"Can't hear you."

"You won't want anybody else hearing." All the same, the man's voice is coarse with static, and suppose mine is even more distorted? I press the sides of my hands around the grille and shove my mouth closer. "Someone's up to something down here," I say as loud as I dare. "They keep trying to leave a case on the train."

"Who does?"

"I think they're Muslims, or they may not be. Maybe they're people who're against Muslims and trying to make it look as if it's them." The speaker has begun to remind me of a grille in the door of a cell. I strain my eyes as far to the side as their aching muscles will drag them. I can't see the man or the briefcase, but everyone nearby seems to be watching me until they look away. I'm the last person they ought to suspect, and they wouldn't find my behaviour odd if they knew I was acting on their behalf. "The one who's got the case now," I say urgently, "he's one of your cleaners or he's pretending to be."

"Where are you saying he is?"

"He just got off the train at James Street. I'm not sure where he went." I have to raise my voice to compete with the sounds of the latest train. Most of the people around me converge on the doors, and I'm so confused by nervousness that for a moment I think I'm about to miss the train. Of course I don't want to return to the loop, and I'm about to demand how the railway will be dealing with my information when a man darts off the stairs and onto the train.

He's wearing an unobtrusively dark suit. It's no longer hidden by the yellow jerkin, and I might not have recognised him except for the flag pinned to his lapel and the briefcase in his hand. "He's here," I shout, and my hands sprawl away from the grille. "He's got back on the train."

The only response from the grille is a blurred metallic clatter. I didn't say that the man has the case, and now I'm sure it's too late. My instincts send me to the train before I have a chance to think, and I dodge between the closing doors. "Let me through," I say at once.

I didn't have time to reach the carriage the man boarded. Nobody ahead of me seems to believe my mission is urgent. I have to thrust my pass over people's shoulders to flash it in their faces, just long enough to leave them with an impression of officialdom. I'm crawling with sweat from the closeness of so many bodies, whose softness feels horribly vulnerable, ready to be blown apart. The carriage seems little better than airless, and I feel walled in by the tunnel, not to mention my own scarcely rational decision to pursue the man onto the train. Now I'm at the door to the next carriage, and someone is lounging against it. As I pound on the glass my heart mimics the rhythm. At last the loafer turns his sluggish apathetic head. He stares at my pass and then at me as if I might be a patient posing as a nurse, and then he slouches aside just far enough to let me sidle around the door.

I can't see the man with the briefcase. His badge is too small to show up in the crowd, and what else is there to distinguish him? Mousy hair, bland nondescript face, dark suit—none of these stands out. My heart counts the seconds like a clock or some more lethal mechanism as I force my way along the carriage. I peer at the floor but see only people's legs—bones that could shatter in a moment, flesh and muscles that would fill the air. I'm nearly at the first set of doors, and I crane around the partition behind the seats. There indeed is the briefcase.

I feel as though I've rehearsed the moment. I stoop and grab the handle, and I'm lifting the case when the train shudders in the midst of a burst of light. I'm almost used to that, because I know it means we've reached Moorfields. I still haven't located the man with the flag in his lapel, but it can't matter just now. The moment the door opens I struggle through the crowd and its reinforcements onto the platform. Where can I take the briefcase? I'm fleeing to the nearest exit when a hand grasps my shoulder. "Where do you think you're going with that?" says a voice.

It belongs to a tall man in an unobtrusively expensive suit. The lines on his high forehead and the hint of grey in his cropped black hair may be raising his apparent age, but he seems reassuringly official. "Where's safe?" I blurt.

"I'm asking what you're doing with it," he says and keeps hold of my shoulder.

"Trying to get rid of it, to dispose of it, I mean. Someone deliberately left it on the train, and not just once either. Don't you know what that means?" I'm so desperate that I shake the case at him, and it emits an ominous metallic rattle. "Just let me—"

"You made the call."

I don't see how this can be an accusation, and so I say "It was me, yes."

"Thank you, Mr Conrad."

I'm bemused by this, even though his grip on my shoulder has begun to feel more appreciative than custodial. "How do you know my name?"

97

"We know everything we have to know."

His eyes have grown so professionally blank that I say "You're not with the railway, are you?"

"We're responsible for this kind of situation. That's all I can tell you." He lets go of my shoulder and repeats "Thank you, Mr Conrad."

Even when he holds out his hand I don't immediately see he's asking for the briefcase. Its reappearances have left me wary, and I say "I wonder if you've got some identification."

"Don't you think we would have?" he says and produces a wallet almost as thin as a wafer. It contains a single card with his name and his likeness and some abbreviated information. "Is that good enough for you?" he wants to know.

"Thank you, Mr Joseph," I say and hand over the briefcase.

He doesn't move away at once. He has to know what he's about, which is why I didn't panic when he lingered over questioning me—he would hardly have been putting himself at risk. There may be a trace of doubt in my eyes, since he says "Are you sure that settles it? Would you like to be there when it's disposed of?"

"I'm sure." Indeed, I'm growing anxious for him and the case to be gone. "You're the authority," I tell him. "It's in safe hands now."

As he heads for the nearest stairway I hear a train. I'm eager to board, and more eager for it to leave any danger behind. The doors close as I find a seat and give in to expressing relief—shaking my head, mopping my brow, letting out a loud sigh that shudders with my heartbeat. "I've really done it this time," I declare.

Nobody responds except for glancing at me as if I might be a mental patient on the loose. I don't care what they think of me; I know I've kept them safe. A young man in a business suit returns to reading a comic book, and a girl gazes at her extravagantly large wristwatch, which shows seven minutes to six. A woman who pushed her thin spectacles high with a forefinger lets them subside, and a man lifts one foot after the other to rub the toecaps of his shoes even shinier on his trouser cuffs. None of the passengers might be able to do any of this without me. The idea accompanies me around the loop, past Lime Street and Central Station, and prompts me to stare along the James Street platform. I see nobody with a briefcase, but the absence isn't quite reassuring enough. As the doors start to close I jump off the train and run up the stairs to the underground bridge.

I still seem to have a task. When a train appears I stay on the platform until the doors begin to close, but I can't see anyone suspicious. As soon as I step aboard a girl gives me a seat, and everything seems settled as the train sets off around the loop. A bald man with a tweed hat on his lap gazes at the polished toecaps of his shoes before turning over his newspaper. A bespectacled woman in a checked overcoat and with queries dangling from her earlobes is reading another copy of the paper. A young man dressed for business takes a comic book from among the documents in a cardboard folder, and a young woman in a waspishly striped sweater pushes a headphone away from one ear while she consults her considerable wristwatch. As blackness closes around the train I see the time is seven minutes to six.

I could imagine the lights on the tunnel walls are signalling to me, and I search for some distraction inside the carriage. The headline on the front page of the bald man's newspaper says **ISLAMIC PANIC**, but I'm not sure if that's the name of a terrorist group. The bespectacled woman's paper has its letters page facing me. One letter is entitled **NO ASYLUM**, which seems to be the slogan of a party called Pure Brit, and the correspondent has suggested that the party is planting bombs so as to blame Muslims and provoke a backlash against immigrants. I grow aware of a voice too small to belong to any of the passengers. It isn't in my head; it's on the young woman's headphones—a recorded radio phone-in, where somebody is arguing that the bombs are the work not of Muslims or their foes but the first stages of a plan by the secret service to force the country to accept dictatorship. Another caller on the phone-in accuses the man who was credited with trying to save his fellow passengers of having planted the bomb himself. All these idle theories make me feel as if nothing is to be trusted, and I focus my attention on the young man's comic book. The cover shows a boffin grimacing in disbelief while he tells his colleagues "It's not that kind of time bomb. It's a bomb that destroys time. It'll blow the past to bits."

"It's nothing like that." The idea has gone too far, and I can't keep quiet any longer, especially since I've seen the truth at last. I can hear the women murmuring behind me like nurses, and I should have listened to them sooner. "That's right, someone's talking about us again," I tell everyone. "But don't you see, if they can keep changing it we can change it too."

Nobody appears to want to listen. They're all gazing at the floor, even those who've turned towards me. "It needn't be what any of them say happened to us," I insist—I feel as if a voice is speaking through me. "It needn't even be what did."

Everyone is staring at the floor beside me. I look at last and see the briefcase. "We don't have to be what people say just because of where we are," I vow as I take hold of the handle. A thunderous rumble swells in my ears, and brightness flares in my eyes, but it's on the wall of the tunnel. I mustn't be distracted by the absence of my shadow—of anyone's. I have to get my task right this time, and then we can head for the light, out of the tunnel.

THE DECORATIONS

Here they are at last," David's grandmother cried, and her face lit up: green from the luminous plastic holly that bordered the front door and then, as she took a plump step to hug David's mother, red with the glow from the costume of the Santa in the sleigh beneath the window. "Was the traffic that bad, Jane?"

"I still don't drive, mummy. One of the trains was held up and we missed a connection."

"You want to get yourself another man. Never mind, you'll always have Davy," his grandmother panted as she waddled to embrace him.

Her clasp was even fatter than last time. It smelled of clothes he thought could be as old as she was, and of perfume that didn't quite disguise a further staleness he was afraid was her. His embarrassment was aggravated by a car that slowed outside the house, though the driver was only admiring the Christmas display. When his grandmother abruptly released him he thought she'd noticed his reaction, but she was peering at the sleigh. "Has he got down?" she whispered.

David understood before his mother seemed to. He retreated along the path between the flower-beds full of grass to squint past the lights that flashed **MERRY CHRISTMAS** above the bedroom windows. The second Santa was still perched on the roof; a wind set the illuminated figure rocking back and forth as if with silent laughter. "He's there," David said.

"I expect he has to be in lots of places at once."

Now that he was nearly eight, David knew that his father had always been Santa. Before he could say as much, his grandmother plodded to gaze at the roof. "Do you like him?"

"I like coming to see all your Christmas things."

"I'm not so fond of him. He looks too empty for my liking." As the figure shifted in another wind she shouted "You stay up there where you belong. Never mind thinking of jumping on us."

David's grandfather hurried out to her, his slippers flapping on his thin feet, his reduced face wincing. "Come inside, Dora. You'll have the neighbours looking."

"I don't care about the fat old thing," she said loud enough to be heard on the roof and tramped into the house. "You can take your mummy's case up, can't you, David? You're a big strong boy now."

He enjoyed hauling the wheeled suitcase on its leash—it was like having a dog he could talk to, sometimes not only in his head—but bumping the luggage upstairs risked snagging the already threadbare carpet, and so his mother supported the burden. "I'll just unpack quickly," she told him. "Go down and see if anyone needs help."

He used the frilly toilet in the equally pink bathroom and lingered until his mother asked if he was all right. He was trying to stay clear of the argument he could just hear through the salmon carpet. As he ventured downstairs his grandmother pounced on some remark so muted it was almost silent. "You do better, then. Let's see you cook."

He could smell the subject of the disagreement. Once he'd finished setting the table from the tray with which his grandfather sent him out of the kitchen, he and his mother saw it too: a casserole encrusted with gravy and containing a shrivelled lump of beef. Potatoes roasted close to impenetrability came with it, and green beans from which someone had tried to scrape the worst of the charring. "It's not as bad as it looks, is it?" David's grandmother said through her first mouthful. "I expect it's like having a barbecue, Davy."

"I don't know," he confessed, never having had one.

"They've no idea, these men, have they, Jane? They don't have to keep dinner waiting for people. I expect your hubby's the same."

"Was, but can we not talk about him?"

"He's learned his lesson, then. No call to make that face at me, Tom. I'm only saying Davy's father—Oh, you've split up, Jane, haven't you. Sorry about my big fat trap. Sorry Davy too."

"Just eat what you want," his grandfather advised him, "and then you'd best be scampering off to bed so Santa can make his deliveries."

"We all want to be tucked up before he's on the move," said his grandmother before remembering to smile.

Santa had gone away like David's father, and David was too old to miss either of them. He managed to breach the carapace of a second potato and chewed several forkfuls of dried-up beef, but the burned remains of beans defeated him. All the same, he thanked his grandmother as he stood up. "There's a good boy," she said rather too loudly, as if interceding with someone on his behalf. "Do your best to go to sleep."

That sounded like an inexplicit warning, and was one of the elements that kept him awake in his bedroom, which was no larger than his room in the flat he'd moved to with his mother. Despite their heaviness, the curtains admitted a repetitive flicker from the letters ERR above the window, and a buzz that suggested an insect was hovering over the bed. He could just hear voices downstairs, which gave him the impression that they didn't want him to know what they were saying. He was most troubled by a hollow creaking that reminded him of someone in a rocking chair, but overhead. The Santa figure must be swaying in the wind, not doing its best to heave itself free. David was too old for stories: while real ones didn't always stay true, that wasn't an excuse to make any up. Still, he was glad to hear his mother and her parents coming upstairs at last, lowering their voices to compensate. He heard doors shutting for the night, and then a nervous question from his grandmother through the wall between their rooms. "What's he doing? Is he loose?"

"If he falls he falls," his grandfather said barely audibly, "and good riddance to him if he's getting on your nerves. For pity's sake come to bed."

David tried not to find this more disturbing than the notion that his parents had shared one. Rather than hear the mattress sag under the weight his grandmother had put on, he tugged the quilt over his head. His grasp must have slackened when he drifted off to sleep, because he was roused by a voice. It was outside the house but too close to the window.

It was his grandfather's. David was disconcerted by the notion that the old man had clambered onto the roof until he realised his grandfather was calling out of the adjacent window. "What do you think you're doing, Dora? Come in before you catch your death."

"I'm seeing he's stayed where he's meant to be," David's grandmother responded from below. "Yes, you know I'm talking about you, don't you. Never mind pretending you didn't nod."

"Get in for the Lord's sake," his grandfather urged, underlining his words with a rumble of the sash. David heard him pad across the room and as rapidly, if more stealthily, down the stairs. A bated argument grew increasingly stifled as it ascended to the bedroom. David had refrained from looking out of the window for fear of embarrassing his grandparents, but now he was nervous that his mother would be drawn to find out what was happening. He mustn't go to her; he had to be a man, as she kept telling him, and not one like his father, who ran off to women because there was so little to him. In time the muttering beyond the wall subsided, and David was alone with the insistence of electricity and the restlessness on the roof.

When he opened his eyes the curtains had acquired a hem of daylight. It was Christmas Day. Last year he'd run downstairs to handle all the packages addressed to him under the tree and guess at their contents, but now he was wary of encountering his grandparents by himself in case he betrayed he was concealing their secret. As he lay hoping that his grandmother had slept off her condition, he heard his mother in the kitchen. "Let me make breakfast, mummy. It can be a little extra present for you."

He didn't venture down until she called him. "Here's the Christmas boy," his grandmother shouted as if he was responsible for the occasion, and dealt him such a hug that he struggled within himself. "Eat up or you won't grow."

Her onslaught had dislodged a taste of last night's food. He did his best to bury it under his breakfast, then volunteered to wash up the plates and utensils and dry them as well. Before he finished she was crying "Hurry up so we can see what Santa's brought. I'm as excited as you, Davy."

He hoped she was only making these remarks on his behalf, not somehow growing younger than he was. In the front room his grandfather distributed the presents while the bulbs on the tree flashed patterns that made David think of secret messages. His grandparents had wrapped him up puzzle books and tales of heroic boys, his mother's gifts to him were games for his home computer. "Thank you," he said, sometimes dutifully.

It was the last computer game that prompted his grandmother to ask "Who are you thanking?" At once, as if she feared she'd spoiled the day for him, she added "I expect he's listening."

"Nobody's listening," his grandfather objected. "Nobody's there."

"Don't say things like that, Tom, not in front of Davy."

"That isn't necessary, mummy. You know the truth, don't you, David? Tell your grandmother."

"Santa's just a fairy tale," David said, although it felt like robbing a younger child of an illusion. "Really people have to save up to buy presents."

"He had to know when we've so much less coming in this Christmas," said his mother. "You see how good he's being. I believe he's taken it better than I did."

"I'm sorry if I upset you, Davy."

"You didn't," David said, not least because his grandmother's eyes looked dangerously moist. "I'm sorry if I upset you."

Her face was already quivering as if there was too much of it to hold still. When she shook her head her cheeks wobbled like a whitish rubber mask that was about to fall loose. He didn't know whether she meant to answer him or had strayed onto another subject as she peered towards the window. "There's nothing to him at all then, is there? He's just an empty old shell. Can't we get him down now?"

"Better wait till the new year," David's grandfather said, and with sudden bitterness "We don't want any more bad luck."

Her faded sunken armchair creaked with relief as she levered herself to her feet. "Where are you going?" her husband protested and limped after her, out of the front door. He murmured at her while she stared up at the roof. At least she didn't shout, but she began to talk not much less quietly as she returned to the house. "I don't like him moving about with nothing inside him," she said before she appeared to recollect David's presence. "Maybe he's like one of those beans with a worm inside, Davy, that used to jig about all the time."

While David didn't understand and was unsure he wanted to, his mother's hasty intervention wasn't reassuring either. "Shall we play some games? What would you like to play, mummy?"

"What do you call it, Lollopy. The one with all the little houses. Too little for any big fat things to climb on. Lollopy."

"Monopoly."

"Lollopy," David's grandmother maintained, only to continue "I don't want to play that. Too many sums. What's your favourite, Davy?"

Monopoly was, but he didn't want to add to all the tensions that he sensed rather than comprehended. "Whatever yours is."

"Ludo," she cried and clapped her hands. "I'd play it every Sunday with your granny and grandpa when I was Davy's age, Jane."

He wondered if she wasn't just remembering but behaving as she used to. She pleaded to be allowed to move her counters whenever she failed to throw a six, and kept trying to move more than she threw. David would have let her win, but his grandfather persisted in reminding her that she had to cast the precise amount to guide her counters home. After several games in which his grandmother squinted with increasingly less comical suspicion at her opponents' moves, David's mother said "Who'd like to go out for a walk?"

Apparently everyone did, which meant they couldn't go fast or far. David felt out of place compared with the boys he saw riding their Christmas bicycles or brandishing their Christmas weapons. Beneath a sky frosty with cloud, all the decorations in the duplicated streets looked deadened by the pale sunlight, though they were still among the very few elements that distinguished one squat boxy house from another. "They're not as good as ours, are they?" his grandmother kept remarking when she wasn't frowning at the roofs. "He's not there either," he heard her mutter more than once, and as her house came in sight "See, he didn't follow us. We'd have heard him."

She was saying that nothing had moved or could move, David tried to think, but he was nervous of returning to the house. The preparation of Christmas dinner proved to be reason enough. "Too many women in this kitchen," his mother was told when she offered to help, but his grandmother had to be reminded to turn the oven on, and she made to take the turkey out too soon more than once. Between these incidents she disagreed with her husband and her daughter about various memories of theirs while David tried to stay low in a book of mazes he had to trace with a pencil. At dinner he could tell that his mother was willing him to clean his plate so as not to distress his grandmother. He did his best, and struggled to ignore pangs of indigestion as he washed up, and then as his grandmother kept talking about if not to every television programme her husband put on. "Not very Christmassy," she commented on all of them, and followed the remark with at least a glance towards the curtained window. Waiting for her to say worse, and his impression that his mother and grandfather were too, kept clenching David's stomach well before his mother declared "I think it's time someone was in bed."

As his grandmother's lips searched for an expression he wondered if she assumed that her daughter meant her. "I'm going," he said and had to be called back to be hugged and kissed and wished happy Christmas thrice.

He used the toilet, having pulled the chain to cover up his noises, and huddled in bed. He had a sense of hiding behind the scenes, the way he'd waited offstage at school to perform a line about Jesus last year, when his parents had held hands at the sight of him. The flickers and the buzzing that the bedroom curtains failed to exclude could have been stage effects, while over the mumbling of the television downstairs he heard sounds of imminent drama. At least there was no creaking on the roof. He did his best to remember last Christmas as a sharp stale taste of this one continued its antics inside him, until the memories blurred into the beginnings of a dream and let him sleep.

Movements above his head wakened him. Something soft but determined was groping at the window—a wind so vigorous that its onslaughts made the light from the sign flare like a fire someone was breathing on. The wind must be swinging the bulbs closer to his window. He hadn't time to wonder how dangerous that might be, because the creaking overhead was different: more prolonged, more purposeful. He was mostly nervous that his grandmother would hear, but there was no sign of awareness in the next room, and silence downstairs. He pressed the quilt around his ears, and then he heard sounds too loud for it to fend off—a hollow slithering followed by a thump at the window, and another. Whatever was outside seemed eager to break the glass.

David scrambled onto all fours and backed away until the quilt slipped off his body, but then he had to reach out to part the curtains at arms' length. He might have screamed if a taste hadn't choked him. Two eyes as dead as pebbles were level with his. They didn't blink, but sputtered as if they were trying to come to a kind of life, as did the rest of the swollen face. Worse still, the nose and mouth surrounded by a dirty whitish fungus of beard were above the eyes. The inversion lent the unnecessarily crimson lips a clown's ambiguous grimace.

The mask dealt the window another blundering thump before a savage gust of wind seized the puffed-up figure. As the face sailed away from the glass, it was extinguished as though the wind had blown it out. David heard wires rip loose and saw the shape fly like a greyish vaguely human balloon over the garden wall to land on its back in the road.

It sounded as if someone had thrown away a used plastic bottle or an empty hamburger carton. Was the noise enough to bring his grandmother to her window? He wasn't sure if he would prefer not to be alone to see the grinning object flounder and begin to edge towards the house. As it twitched several inches he regretted ever having tipped an insect over to watch it struggle on its back. Then another squall of wind took possession of the dim figure, sweeping it leftwards out of sight along the middle of the road. David heard a car speed across an intersection, its progress hardly interrupted by a hollow thump and a crunch that made him think of a beetle crushed underfoot.

Once the engine dwindled into silence, nothing moved on the roads except the wind. David let the curtains fall together and slipped under the quilt. The drama had ended, even if some of its lighting effects were still operating outside the window. He didn't dream, and wakened late, remembering at once that there was nothing on the roof to worry his grandmother. Only how would she react to the absence?

He stole to the bathroom and then retreated to his bedroom. The muffled conversations downstairs felt like a pretence that all was well until his grandmother called "What are you doing up there?"

She meant David. He knew that when she warned him that his breakfast would go cold. She sounded untroubled, but for how long? "Eat up all the lovely food your mother's made," she cried, and he complied for fear of letting her suspect he was nervous, even when his stomach threatened to throw his efforts back at him. As he downed the last mouthful she said "I do believe that's the biggest breakfast I've ever had in my life. I think we all need a walk."

David swallowed too soon in order to blurt "I've got to wash up."

"What a good boy he is to his poor old granny. Don't worry, we'll wait for you. We won't run away and leave you," she said and stared at her husband for sighing.

David took all the time he could over each plate and utensil. He was considering feigning illness if that would keep his grandmother inside the house when he saw the door at the end of the back garden start to shake as if someone was fumbling at it. The grass shivered too, and he would have except for seeing why it did. "It'll be too windy to go for a walk," he told his grandmother. "It's like grandad said, you'll catch cold."

His mouth stayed open as he realised his mistake, but that wasn't the connection she made. "How windy is it?" she said, standing up with a groan to tramp along the hall. "What's it going to do to that empty old thing?"

David couldn't look away from the quivering expanse of grass while he heard her open the front door and step onto the path. His shoulders rose as if he fancied they could block his ears, but even sticking his fingers in mightn't have deafened him to her cry. "He's got down. Where's he hidden himself?"

David turned to find his mother rubbing her forehead as though to erase her thoughts. His grandfather had lifted his hands towards his wife, but they drooped beneath an invisible weight. David's grandmother was pivoting around and around on the path, and David was reminded of ballet classes until he saw her dismayed face. He felt that all the adults were performing, as adults so often seemed compelled to do, and that he ought to stop them if he could. "It fell down," he called. "It blew away."

His grandmother pirouetted to a clumsy halt and peered along the hall at him. "Why didn't you say? What are you trying to do?"

"Don't stand out there, Dora," his grandfather protested. "You can see he only wants—"

"Never mind what Davy wants. It can be what I want for a change. It's meant to be my Christmas too. Where is he, Davy? Show me if you think you know so much."

Her voice was growing louder and more petulant. David

felt as if he'd been given the job of rescuing his mother and his grandfather from further embarrassment or argument. He dodged past them and the stranded sleigh to run to the end of the path. "It went along there," he said, pointing. "A car ran it over."

"You didn't say that before. Are you just saying so I won't be frightened?"

Until that moment he hadn't grasped how much she was. He strained his gaze at the intersection, but it looked as deserted as the rest of the street. "Show me where," she urged.

Might there be some trace? David was beginning to wish he hadn't spoken. He couldn't use her pace as an excuse for delay; she was waddling so fast to the intersection that her entire body wobbled. He ran into the middle of the crossroads, but there was no sign of last night's accident. He was even more disconcerted to realise that she was so frightened she hadn't even warned him to be careful on the road. He straightened up and swung around to look for fragments, and saw the remains heaped at the foot of a garden wall.

Someone must have tidied them into the side road. Most of the body was a shattered pile of red and white, but the head and half the left shoulder formed a single item propped on top. David was about to point around the corner when the object shifted. Still grinning, it toppled sideways as if the vanished neck had snapped. The wind was moving it, he told himself, but he wasn't sure that his grandmother ought to see. Before he could think how to prevent her, she followed his gaze. "It is him," she cried. "Someone else mustn't have liked him."

David was reaching to grab her hand and lead her away when the head shifted again. It tilted awry with a slowness that made its grin appear increasingly mocking, and slithered off the rest of the debris to inch along the pavement, scraping like a skull. "He's coming for me," David's grandmother babbled. "There's something inside him. It's the worm."

David's mother was hurrying along the street ahead of his grandfather. Before they could join his grandmother, the grinning object skittered at her. She recoiled a step, and then she lurched to trample her tormentor to bits. "That'll stop you laughing," she cried as the eyes shattered. "It's all right now, Davy. He's gone."

Was the pretence of acting on his behalf aimed at him or at the others? They seemed to accept it when at last she finished stamping and let them usher her back to the house, unless they were pretending as well. Though the adults had reverted to behaving as they were supposed to, it was too sudden. It felt like a performance they were staging to reassure him.

He must be expected to take part. He had to, or he wouldn't be a man. He pretended not to want to go home, and did his best to simulate enjoyment of the television programmes and the games that the others were anxious his grandmother should like. He feigned an appetite when the remnants of Christmas dinner were revived, accompanied by vegetables that his mother succeeded in rescuing from his grandmother's ambitions for them.

While the day had felt far too protracted, he would have preferred it to take more time over growing dark. The wind had dropped, but not so much that he didn't have to struggle to ignore how his grandmother's eyes fluttered whenever a window shook. He made for bed as soon as he thought he wouldn't be drawing attention to his earliness. "That's right, Davy, we all need our sleep," his grandmother said as if he might be denying them theirs. He suffered another round of happy Christmases and hugs that felt more strenuous than last night's, and then he fled to his room.

The night was still except for the occasional car that slowed outside the house—not, David had to remember, because there was anything on the roof. When he switched off the light the room took on a surreptitious flicker, as if his surroundings were nervous. Surely he had no reason to be, although he could have imagined that the irritable buzz was adding an edge to the voices downstairs. He hid under the quilt and pretended he was about to sleep until the sham overtook him.

A change in the lighting roused him. He was pushing the quilt away from his face so as to greet the day that would take him home when he noticed that the illumination was too fitful to be sunlight. As it glared under the curtains again he heard uncoordinated movement through the window. The wind must have returned to play with the lit sign. He was hoping that it wouldn't awaken his grandmother, or that she would at least know what was really there, when he realised with a shock that paralysed his breath how wrong he was. He hadn't heard the wind. The clumsy noises outside were more solid and more localised. Light stained the wall above his bed, and an object blundered as if it was limbless against the front door.

If this hadn't robbed David of the ability to move, the thought of his grandmother's reaction would have. It was even worse than the prospect of looking himself. He hadn't succeeded in breathing when he heard her say "Who's that? Has he come back?"

David would have blocked his ears if he had been capable of lifting his fists from beside him. He must have breathed, but he was otherwise helpless. The pause in the next room was almost as ominous as the sounds that brought it to an end: the rumble of the window, another series of light but impatient thumps at the front door, his grandmother's loose unsteady voice. "He's here for me. He's all lit up, his eyes are. The worm's put him back together. I should have squashed the worm."

"Stop wandering for God's sake," said David's grandfather. "I can't take much more of this, I'm telling you."

"Look how he's been put back together," she said with such a mixture of dismay and pleading that David was terrified it would compel him to obey. Instead his panic wakened him.

He was lying inert, his thoughts as tangled as the quilt, when he heard his grandmother insist "He was there."

"Just get back in bed," his grandfather told her.

David didn't know how long he lay waiting for her to shut the window. After that there seemed to be nothing to hear once her bed acknowledged her with an outburst of creaking. He stayed uneasily alert until he managed to think of a way to make sense of events: he'd overheard her in his sleep and had dreamed the rest. Having resolved this let him feel manly enough to regain his slumber.

This time daylight found him. It seemed to render the night irrelevant, at least to him. He wasn't sure about his grandmother, who looked uncertain of something. She insisted on cooking breakfast, rather more than aided by her husband. Once David and his mother had done their duty by their portions it was time to call a taxi. David manhandled the suitcase downstairs by himself and wheeled it to the car, past the decorations that appeared dusty with sunlight. His grandparents hugged him at the gate, and his grandmother repeated the gesture as if she'd already forgotten it. "Come and see us again soon," she said without too much conviction, perhaps because she was distracted by glancing along the street and at the roof.

David thought he saw his chance to demonstrate how much of a man he was. "It wasn't there, granny. It was just a dream."

Her face quivered, and her eyes. "What was, Davy? What are you talking about?"

He had a sudden awful sense of having miscalculated, but all he could do was answer. "There wasn't anything out here last night."

Her mouth was too nervous to hold onto a smile that might have been triumphant. "You heard him as well."

"No," David protested, but his mother grabbed his arm. "That's enough," she said in a tone he'd never heard her use before. "We'll miss the train. Look after each other," she blurted at her parents, and shoved David into the taxi. All the way through the streets full of lifeless decorations, and for some time on the train, she had no more to say to him than "Just leave me alone for a while."

He thought she blamed him for frightening his grandmother. He remembered that two months later, when his grandmother died. At the funeral he imagined how heavy the box with her inside it must be on the shoulders of the four gloomy men. He succeeded in withholding his guilty tears, since his grandfather left crying to David's mother. When David tried to sprinkle earth on the coffin in the hole, a fierce wind carried off his handful as if his grandmother had blown it away with an angry breath. Eventually all the cars paraded back to the house that was only his grandfather's now, where a crowd of people David hadn't met before ate the sandwiches his mother had made and kept telling him how grown-up he was. He felt required to pretend, and wished his mother hadn't taken two days off from working at the nursery so that they could stay overnight. Once the guests left he felt more isolated still. His grandfather broke one of many silences by saying "You look as if you'd like to ask a question, Davy. Don't be shy."

David wasn't sure he wanted to be heard, but he had to be polite and answer. "What happened to granny?"

"People change when they get old, son. You'll find that out, well, you have. She was still your grandmother really."

Too much of this was more ominous than reassuring. David was loath to ask how she'd died, and almost to say "I meant where's she gone."

"I can't tell you that, son. All of us are going to have to wait and see."

Perhaps David's mother sensed this was the opposite of comforting, for she said "I think it's like turning into a butterfly, David. Our body's just the chrysalis we leave behind."

He had to affect to be happy with that, despite the memory it threatened to revive, because he was afraid he might otherwise hear worse. He apparently convinced his mother, who turned to his grandfather. "I wish I'd seen mummy one last time."

"She looked like a doll."

"No, while she was alive."

"I don't think you'd have liked it, Jane. Try and remember her how she used to be and I will. You will, won't you, Davy?"

David didn't want to imagine the consequences of giving or even thinking the wrong answer. "I'll try," he said.

This appeared to be less than was expected of him. He was desperate to change the subject, but all he could think of was how bare the house seemed without its Christmas finery. Rather than say so he enquired "Where do all the decorations go?"

"They've gone as well, son. They were always Dora's."

David was beginning to feel that nothing was safe to ask or say. He could tell that the adults wanted him to leave them alone to talk. At least they oughtn't to be arguing, not like his parents used to as soon as he was out of the way, making him think that the low hostile remarks he could never quite hear were blaming him for the trouble with the marriage. At least he wouldn't be distracted by the buzzing and the insistent light while he tried to sleep or hear. The wind helped blur the voices below him, so that although he gathered that they were agreeing, he only suspected they were discussing him. Were they saying how he'd scared his grandmother to death? "I'm sorry," he kept whispering like a prayer, which belatedly lulled him to sleep.

A siren wakened him—an ambulance. The pair of notes might have been crying "Davy" through the streets. He wondered if an ambulance had carried off his grandmother. The braying faded into the distance, leaving silence except for the wind. His mother and his grandfather must be in their beds, unless they had decided David was sufficiently grown-up to be left by himself in the house. He hoped not, because the wind sounded like a loose voice repeating his name. The noises on the stairs might be doing so as well, except that they were shuffling footsteps or, as he was able to make out before long, rather less than footsteps. Another sound was approaching. It was indeed a version of his name, pronounced by an exhalation that was just about a voice, by no means entirely like his grandmother's but too much so. It and the slow determined unformed paces halted outside his room.

He couldn't cry out for his mother, not because he wouldn't be a man but for fear of drawing attention to himself. He was offstage, he tried to think. He only had to listen, he needn't see more than the lurid light that flared across the carpet. Then his visitor set about opening the door.

It made a good deal of locating the doorknob, and attempting to take hold of it, and fumbling to turn it, so that David had far more time than he wanted to imagine what was there. If his grandmother had gone away, had whatever remained come to find him? Was something of her still inside her to move it, or was that a worm? The door shuddered and edged open, admitting a grotesquely festive glow, and David tried to shut his eyes. But he was even more afraid not to see the shape that floundered into the room.

He saw at once that she'd become what she was afraid of. She was draped with a necklace of fairy lights, and two guttering bulbs had taken the place of her eyes. Dim green light spilled like slimy water down her cheeks. She wore a long white dress, if the vague pale mass wasn't part of her, for her face looked inflated to hollowness, close to bursting. Perhaps that was why her mouth was stretched so wide, but her grin was terrified. He had a sudden dreadful thought that both she and the worm were inside the shape.

It blundered forward and then fell against the door. Either it had very little control of its movements or it intended to trap him in the room. It lurched at him as if it was as helpless as he was, and David sprawled out of bed. He grabbed one of his shoes from the floor and hurled it at the swollen flickering mass. It was only a doll, he thought, because the grin didn't falter. Perhaps it was less than a doll, since it vanished like a bubble. As his shoe struck the door the room went dark.

He might almost have believed that nothing had been there if he hadn't heard more than his shoe drop to the floor. When he tore the curtains open he saw fairy lights strewn across the carpet. They weren't what he was certain he'd heard slithering into some part of the room. All the same, once he'd put on his shoes he trampled the bulbs into fragments, and then he fell to his hands and knees. He was still crawling about the floor when his mother hurried in and peered unhappily at him. "Help me find it," he pleaded. "We've got to kill the worm."

THE ADDRESS

Fraith did his best to stay amused as long as he could. At the car park into which he wandered almost before realising he had, nobody even knew there was a railway station. Presumably this meant it wasn't along the road, and he tramped back into the forest, where the rusty colours were starting to lose their appeal. An October wind cold enough for winter met him, and then a muddy couple tugged by two Labradors did. They disagreed over directions while the dogs joined in, and eventually the man tried to send Fraith back to the road. Further down the path that was restless with leaves, the mother of two children about the ages of his daughter's daughters took pity on him. "Out by yourself today?" she said.

"I very often am. I'm just giving the family a breather."

"They look after you, do they?"

Fraith wasn't sure how much of her sympathy was reserved for him. "More like the other way round," he retorted.

"I know."

Her tone had turned more soothing, not unlike a nurse's by a bed. Fraith managed to say only "Can you tell me where the station is?"

"Was that the big place, mummy?" the boy said at once.

"That was a school," his sister informed him with all the disdain earned by her age or gender.

"There hasn't been a school for a long time. Be quiet about

119

it." Since the woman was still gazing at Fraith, he could have thought this was addressed to him. "I'm sure I saw the sign you want," she said. "Carry on where we've come from and I think it's the next side path."

"I don't suppose either of you two saw a train."

"They haven't. Not today." With enough force to be rebuking Fraith the woman added "Just do as I said and you'll find what you asked for."

"I hope so." Fraith could sound like that too. "I need to get back to my daughter," he said. "She hasn't anybody else."

He hoped his return would be as welcome as his decision to go walking by himself had seemed to be. Were there really no walks closer to the house than a train ride away? Perhaps Carla had wanted a few hours by herself with the girls. He was doing all he could to help—enough for two people now her mother wasn't with them—but perhaps he seemed too interfering. He would ask Carla once the girls were in bed, though she disliked admitting to feelings like those, just as her mother had. Before he knew he meant to speak he said "Have you anyone like me?"

"We had," the woman said.

"He went to live with all the other granddads," the boy informed him.

Fraith could do without knowing what this might be a euphemism for. "I won't be doing that just yet," he said and strode into the woods.

He must have overlooked the sign she'd mentioned. Though the sun was lying low behind the trees, it wouldn't be dark for hours. The light transformed foliage into masses of orange flame and spilled between the trees to lend leaves on the path a tinfoil glare. The concrete path wasn't admitting to its destination; every few hundred yards another curve obscured the way ahead. While he hadn't counted the bends, it took more of them than he remembered to bring him back to the next junction, where nothing like a signpost was to be seen.

The woman must have mistaken the place, which surely ought to mean the next path wasn't far. He knew the station wasn't to the left—he'd come that way earlier—and the trail ahead curved rightwards. He zipped up the last inches of his padded jacket against the wind despite starting to sweat with exertion. "Best feet forward. You've a pair each," he would have said if Carla's daughters had been with him.

Soon the path straightened out, levelling the sunlight at him. For minutes he was as bad as blind. At last the path strewn with leaves like shards of mirrors veered to the right again, and he blinked his patchy vision clear, to be rewarded by the sight of a junction ahead. Or were those only gaps between the trees on both sides of the track? No, there was a transverse path, but it was entirely unmarked.

He halted at the crossing and stared around him. His skin was as clammy as his mouth was dry, and at first the reverberations of his heart wouldn't let him think. Where had he gone wrong? He'd set out to follow a circular route from the station, but one of the bridges across the railway had been fenced off, and since then he'd lost the main path. If only Carla had reminded him to take his mobile phone, except that even if he hadn't left it by his bed he didn't suppose it would have helped him now. Should he return to the car park while he still knew where it was, in case someone could direct him? He was turning back when he heard voices on the right-hand path.

They weren't speaking English. Like many people in the street these days—sometimes enough to make him feel he was losing his grasp of his own language—the young men were from somewhere in the heart of Europe. They looked friendly enough, and stopped at the junction when Fraith held up a hand. "Did you come by the railway?" he said.

Two of them smiled while their companions frowned, and all four shook their heads. "Railway," Fraith repeated to the same effect and pumped his arms like pistons while puffing as hard as he could, only to realise that he could have been portraying an exhausted athlete. "Choo choo," he tried hooting and shoved his fists out hard enough to pummel an opponent. "Choo choo."

The men gazed at him as if they wondered where he'd been

121

let out from—as Carla's daughters did too often while he was exerting himself to amuse them. "Station," he urged, shading his eyes to peer along each path in turn. "Station."

Three men shrugged. Their companion, the oldest, sketched a cross on himself before kissing his thumb, and Fraith wondered if this was a gesture to greet the deranged. He'd thought of nothing more to say by the time the men turned along the path he had been following. As he hesitated the oldest man looked back and waved him away. "No," he said and jabbed a finger at the path to Fraith's left. "Station."

He pronounced it so deliberately it might have been two separate words. Surely that could be the right path—if the men had passed the railway they would have figured out Fraith's performance. All the same, as he turned that way he felt as if he were being dragged by his shadow. His heart sounded like a cheap effect in a film, and his mouth was growing parched again. He'd reached a bend that showed him more path and trees with their tips ablaze—his crooked silhouette was jerking along the unkempt verge, putting him in mind of the second hand of a decrepit clock—when he heard another voice.

Though it was blurred, not just by distance, he knew where the woman was. The man's voice that had greeted the train at the station had been distorted too. "Keep talking," Fraith urged and tramped faster along the path.

She fell silent at once. He could almost have fancied she was as contrary as Carla's girls. His shadow was veering around a bend as if in search of the direction by the time she spoke again. As far as he could make out she was publicising a special service, which seemed unlikely to concern him. Straining his ears only turned his heartbeat up, and he did his best to breathe more evenly as the bend showed him another deserted stretch of path. Wasn't that the red-brick station beyond the furthest trees? He was halfway to it before he could be sure it was a mass of autumn foliage.

He'd seen no other path since meeting the four men, but he'd begun to wonder if he was still right for the station until he heard the voice apparently announcing the first train due and the next ones. The wind threw the words about like a young animal worrying some kind of toy, so that Fraith couldn't locate the voice. At least he was closer to it. Surely that wasn't just an effect of the wind.

He'd passed another extended bend before she spoke again—something about the track and a delay. At least that should give him more of a chance to catch the train, but he kept on almost fast enough to lose his footing on the sodden leaves. As the wind flung the words away from him he could have imagined the treetops were groping to retrieve the message, not necessarily on his behalf. All at once a phrase made him falter. Could she just have announced the last train?

It shouldn't be due for hours yet. There was still enough light to trap his silhouette among the glistening shadows of trees. He made for the voice almost fast enough to leave his breath behind, though not the uneven drumbeat of his heart. Was he hearing about a mail train now—one that carried sacks? Presumably the public was being advised that it didn't take passengers. Fraith could see the building through the trees at the next bend, at least until he came close enough to realise it wasn't solid enough. The distant shape wasn't overgrown with leaves, it was composed of them. He was almost at the bend by the time the voice spoke again. It was behind him.

It was to his left as well, among the trees. As he strained his eyes to find a path he'd overlooked, he heard a rhythmic clatter and a brief high sound. The mail train must be racing through the station, whistling to warn commuters. He'd thought the voice had just mentioned relaying the track, but this couldn't be affecting the trains. He was facing the sounds now, and he shouldn't waste any more time looking for a path.

The way through the trees wasn't as straightforward as he hoped. The forest was humpy with mounds of earth much taller than he was. None of the trails leading over or between them looked manmade, even inadvertently. The first route he followed brought him into a muddy hollow full of stagnant pools disguised by leaves, and he was on his knees by the time he clambered out of it. After that he did his best to stay on the mounds, no matter how treacherous they proved to be. Would they never let him glimpse the station? He might have thought its voice was mocking his progress, not least since it had grown even less comprehensible. Perhaps the bits of it that reached him on the wind were talking about prices and the next train, but what had it said about some form of support? "Doesn't matter," Fraith panted, "just don't shut up," and almost lost his balance on a scree of leaves as he laboured up a slope. He grabbed a scaly tree-trunk to haul himself onto the top of the mound, and a soggy lump of bark crumbled in his grasp. He sucked in a breath so as to release it, letting out a sound he would have preferred not to make. He could see where he'd been hearing from, and it had no connection with the railway. The building obscured by trees was a school.

The main building was long and wide and red. Two wings extended from it to enclose a schoolyard, beyond which distant figures stood around the edges of a field, watching others run. At once a great deal made sense. It was a sports day, nothing to do with support. The voice had been talking about prizes, not prices—about a sack race and a relay, and announcing the winners in numerical order.

For an irrational moment Fraith was tempted to retreat to the main path. He'd already begun to feel like a child lost in a maze, and besides, he had loathed sports at school. "Don't blubber, Blubber," the gym master took delight in saying, though Fraith hadn't been especially overweight and had never let anyone see him weep. Only sweat had trickled down his face, not to mention down the rest of him, as he'd panted to the finish in everybody else's wake, urged on by the teacher's ironic cheers that too many spectators had emulated. They surely weren't allowed to treat children like that now, even in a school as remote as this one. If the way Carla's girls behaved was any indication, there were no longer many rules at all.

Someone at the school would be able to direct him to the railway, and he slithered down the mound. Now he couldn't see

the building, but the announcer—no doubt the games mistress—
was still audible with some words about the head. If the organiser
of the games was anything like Carla, the competitors would
be having an easy time. She could very well be firmer with his
grandchildren, but perhaps she thought he'd been too strict with
her at their age.

He wasn't going to risk the shortest route to the school—
he couldn't afford a broken bone or even a sprain just now, if
ever—and so he settled for the least hazardous. From the top of a
mound the school blocked his view of the playing field. The next
time it rose into sight, only the roof was visible above the high
thick hedge that boxed the grounds in. He had to find his way
around a copse webbed with ivy before he was able to reach the
hedge.

A track led beside it, or at least a penumbra of mud that
fringed the shadow of the forest. The hedge was several times
Fraith's height and at least twice as thick as the width of his
rotund stomach. It was far too thoroughly entangled for even
the smallest child to squeeze through, and not just full of vicious
thorns but bristling with them. Surely nothing like it would be
allowed on school property these days, and he wondered how
long ago it had been planted to have grown so much.

Since he couldn't see the school gates, he made his way along
the soggy track towards the field. The windows he glimpsed
through the hedge were as dark as the depths of the woods.
Either the woman with the microphone hadn't often used one
or her shrillness was distorting the transmission. Perhaps she was
pretending to be excited, because Fraith couldn't see much to
inspire her as he came in sight of the field.

The sack race was over. Several man-sized bags were propped
against the schoolyard wall. Fraith's head was swimming with
exertion, and he might have imagined that the contestants had
stayed in their sacks, which were jerking with the wind. In fact
the bags couldn't have been used in the race—they must be full
of rubbish, given how stained they were. He was glad to see that
the sports day wasn't too rigorously organised; some of the young

spectators on the far side of the field were playing a game of their own, throwing a ragged rugby ball or baseball to one another. Perhaps the amplified voice had grown shrill in a bid to reclaim their attention for the official event, such as it was. Fraith could see just one runner on the field, dashing along a track composed of muddy footprints in the not especially neat grass. Whatever kind of competition this might be, Fraith hadn't time to wait for it to finish. "Excuse me," he shouted through the widest gap—thinner than his thumb—he could find in the hedge. "Can you help?"

Perhaps nobody could see him, but none of the spectators facing away from him turned to look. Surely the hedge couldn't have made him inaudible. Perhaps the children had been told to ignore anyone outside the grounds. In any case he would do better talking to an adult, and he advanced along the unofficial track. He hadn't identified a single grown-up, not even the one with the microphone or loudhailer, when he caught sight of the gates past the front of the school.

They were open, though not fully. He would have to make his way around two sides of the grounds to them, but at least he wouldn't be yelling through the hedge. As he turned away he glimpsed the solitary runner stumble and fall. Half a dozen spectators ran to help him up, quite the opposite of how Fraith would have been treated at school. Fraith was alongside the brick wing that enclosed the schoolyard when he thought he heard the amplified voice calling him back.

It was saying somebody was back at school, although surely not the competitors. Now that Fraith thought about it, the lone runner hadn't looked too youthful. Might that explain what Fraith had heard earlier? Perhaps this was a special day, the kind schools sometimes put on, where roles were reversed and it was the teachers' turn to compete. Even the amplified voice might belong to an adolescent boy, since Fraith heard it crack as it enthused about a game of catch.

Sunlight poked jagged holes in the hedge as he came abreast of the front of the school. A drive led through the woods to the gates, but it was blocked by fallen trees. In any case the gap between the spiky wrought-iron gates was too cramped for any vehicle to pass through. Twigs were entangled around the hinges, and the ground was stained rusty where the gates had settled into the mud. Fraith was wondering if he'd chanced upon a reunion at a defunct school, in which case the spectators might well be the children of the pupils, when he was distracted by a rhythmic clatter and a terse shriek that resounded across the field.

It had to be the railway. So it was beyond the far side of the playing field, but he still didn't know the way to the station. Someone must, and Fraith hurried through the lockjawed gates and up the weedy gravel drive. The low sunlight met him with such a fierce glare that all the windows through which it was shining looked unglazed. Once he was past the front of the school he had to fend off the light with his hand. Even shading his eyes didn't give him much of his sight back. He blinked like an animal just rousted from its lair as he stumbled alongside the school.

He could almost have fancied the commentator was talking about trains—about laying the track. Perhaps his confusion had lent the voice a mocking quality unless, since it was speaking of teachers now, that was how it actually sounded. Fraith dabbed at his eyes and then held the hand in front of them, but had to raise it to see the field, where another isolated runner was sprinting across the grass. He was heading for a gap between the spectators, some of whom appeared to be edging towards it; no doubt they were preparing to welcome the competitor. Fraith raised his hand beside his face and turned to peer along the schoolyard edge of the field.

He couldn't see a single adult among the spectators, insofar as he could make them out at all. The large sacks tied up with frayed cord and propped against the schoolyard wall were continuing to twitch, although he couldn't feel a wind. Not just the sacks but the untended turf around them were stained a colour that he did his best to find autumnal, and he was surprised if not uneasy that the watchers hadn't moved away from them. He was straining his eyes to distinguish even one face when all the onlookers leaned forward to gaze across the field.

Fraith peered under his hand into the sunlight and still had to narrow his eyes. There was no longer a gap in the mass of spectators along the far side of the field. At first he couldn't locate the runner, and then he saw a figure sprawled on the muddy grass, apparently having veered towards one corner of the hedge. In a moment several onlookers converged to haul him to his feet and march him out of competition, so enthusiastically that Fraith thought he glimpsed the man's feet attempting to run in the air.

Were they presenting him with a trophy just for joining in? Someone by the distant hedge stepped forward, holding up a slim item against the sun. A dismayingly familiar sound greeted the gesture—a rhythmic clatter somewhere in the audience. Fraith had to peer about to locate a group of boys who were knocking cricket stumps together in a salute that seemed not merely improvised but primitive. The clatter continued as the pointed object rose high and parted its hefty blades before swooping at the figure held by spectators. The savage drumming ceased, isolating another sound—an exhausted shriek that was cut off at once. Spectators closed around the activity, which appeared to involve a good deal of exertion and repetition. Perhaps Fraith hadn't been wholly mistaken in thinking of a trophy, because in a while a group of boys darted away, lobbing their prize to one another. It was about as rounded as the other ragged ball had been.

Fraith tried to concentrate on just one thought in the hope it was the truth: that all the onlookers were so intent on the spectacle they hadn't noticed him. His mouth tasted sour and dusty, every heartbeat seemed to make his entire body quiver, but as two boys dragged a limp incomplete shape to join several more beside the far hedge he managed to free himself of his appalled fascination and set about backing towards the school. He was still in the open when he saw movement by the schoolyard wall.

The metal object glinted as it rose to shoulder height and higher. It was an old loudspeaker held by someone halfway along the line of figures beside the wall. The sunlight must be interfering with Fraith's vision, since the face behind the built-in microphone had a distinctly makeshift look. Its words were plain enough, despite a shrillness that sounded no less senile than childish. "Teach them," it screeched while the megaphone added a rusty distortion. "Pay them back."

At once too much else that Fraith had heard it saying became clearer. Perhaps it was the school rather than the day that was special, though he would rather not learn how. If he'd chanced upon some kind of reunion or revival, it was best left uninvestigated until he could alert the authorities. The sun had started to hide its face behind a forest mound beyond the playing field, and he could have wished it weren't restoring his eyesight as the figures by the schoolyard grew more distinct. He even had the grotesque fancy that the harsh shrill voice belonged to the megaphone itself, give how temporary the commentator's mouth looked. As if provoked by the thought, the figure swung the megaphone towards him. "There's another," it cried in a voice that seemed to scrape the loudspeaker.

All the spectators along the wall turned to find Fraith, who struggled not to see their ramshackle faces clear, because he had a sense that doing so would leave him unable to move. "I'm not," he protested, having understood too much. "I'm like you. I was, I promise."

This earned him a response, not just from all the onlookers beside the wall. He'd never heard anyone laugh in unison before, a piercing noise that sounded as much like a chant as mirth. It almost blotted out the answer of the megaphone. "Aren't now," the strident voice said.

Fraith thought he had one chance to run for it, and swung around. Half a dozen former pupils of the school had made their stealthy way behind him. Whoever used to look after the grounds must have had quite a collection of implements, from which the figures waiting for Fraith had brought an impressive selection. If this wasn't daunting enough, he could see the figures in detail now—their torn muddy clothes, their toothless childish faces that put him in mind of rotten fruit. They weren't simply in danger of wizening; wrinkles kept appearing and being swallowed up like ripples in a pool, along with patches of discolouration. He backed away, almost falling in his haste not merely to keep his distance but to make a last appeal to the organiser of the events. "I'm only looking for the train," he pleaded.

He was afraid to hear the laughter again, but silence answered him—how eager or expectant he couldn't tell. The figure lifted the megaphone without speaking and thrust it forward, indicating the farther left-hand corner of the field. Perhaps that concealed a short cut to the station, invisible at such a distance. Fraith knew only that he mustn't run, or they might think he was like all those who had. He took a breath that pumped up his heartbeat and parched his mouth, and then he set off along the trampled course across the field. He mustn't look at the spectators—mustn't meet whatever they might have for eyes—but he found himself wondering whether Carla's daughters would have cheered him on if he'd given in to running. If he'd ever been too harsh with them, he prayed he could take it back, supposing that would save him. Then the sun went out, and he felt as if the world had.

RECENTLY USED

Tunstall thought he hadn't slept when the phone rang. He clutched it and sat up on the bed, which felt too bare and wide by half. On the bedside table the photograph of him with Gwyneth in the sunlit mountains far away was waiting to be seen once more, and beyond it the curtains framed a solitary feeble midnight star. He rubbed his aching eyes to help them focus on the mobile as he thumbed the keypad. "Hello?" he said before he'd finished lifting the phone to his face.

"Forgive me, is this Charlie?"

The sight of Gwyneth's name on the midget screen had raised his hopes, but the voice belonged to somebody he'd never met. "Charles Tunstall," he had to say, "yes."

"Excuse me, Mr Tunstall. Your name is showing up on this phone as the last person called."

"I know." He couldn't leave it at that, and he said "It's my wife's."

"We hoped so." While the pause after the first word was close to imperceptible, the woman seemed to have to get ready to add "I'm afraid Mrs Tunstall—"

"What? Go on, for God's sake."

Why did he need to interrupt? It only delayed her saying "Your wife has had an accident, Mr Tunstall."

He felt as if they were rehearsing a script whose triteness simply made it more painful. "What's happened?" he said and was unable to go on.

"We believe she missed her footing on the escalator at the shopping precinct."

He knew it all too well. He'd always stood in front of her or held her hand to keep her steady as the metal steps bore them eighty feet down. Why couldn't the friends with whom she'd been dining have looked after her as he did? If she'd wanted to demonstrate her independence by setting off home on her own, why couldn't she at least have held tight to the banisters? Tunstall tried to take a breath before saying his next overused line. "How is she?"

"She's on her way to the hospital. Do you know where that is?"

He resented the question almost as much as the lack of information. "Of course I know."

"You might want to make your way over as soon as possible. Can you drive, or is there somebody who can?"

"I'm not that far gone yet. I can drive myself."

"How close are you?"

Though he was desperate to reduce the answer, he had to say "Fifteen minutes."

"That should do it, Mr Tunstall."

Tunstall struggled not to demand what she meant. "I'm on my way," he said.

He was. As he'd dashed across the bedroom Gwyneth's wardrobe had crept open with a jangle of hangers like the sound of a deadened alarm. Her bathrobe had slipped from the hook on the bathroom door to lie white and motionless beside the shower. The dormant beds in the next room had put him in mind of goodnights, of Gwyneth stooping to kiss the grandchildren. He'd taken the stairs two precarious treads at a time, so clumsily the house had seemed to shake. The kitchen calendar was scrawled with notes by him and Gwyneth, reminders large enough to read along the hall if their handwriting hadn't grown so vague. The dining-table was set for the weekend's family dinner, utensils glimmering in the dimness, and in the front room he might have glimpsed a crossword Gwyneth had begun, frowning at the clues or at fitting the letters into their boxes. As he ended the phone call he lurched out of the house.

The terraced side street was as deserted as his mind was attempting to be. He didn't need to think, he only had to drive. Beyond the bijou front gardens all the houses were silent enough for a stage set awaiting a performance. On both sides of the road parked cars glittered with November frost like a hint of Christmas. At least it hadn't blotted out his windscreen. Tunstall hauled the door open and jabbed the key into the ignition, and felt as if crouching into the driver's seat had shrunk or even crippled him. When he swung the car out of the meagre space between its neighbours, Gwyneth's water bottle from the gym trundled across the floor beside him.

He was driving almost faster than he dared, especially once he turned along the promenade. Now that the summer illuminations had been taken down, the seafront felt like a reminiscence of a holiday resort—the lightless fairground, the shuttered arcades, the hotels closed for the winter. Although a few faint stars glittered intermittently above the flat black sea, the darkness stretching to the horizon looked capable of going on for ever. He mustn't think about that—mustn't think anything other than that he would be in time, which made him tread on the accelerator as if he could outrun the dark.

Beyond the last hotels the buildings dwindled. The road left the side streets behind as it bent inland, where it was flanked by fields darker than the sky. No doubt they helped ice crawl over his windscreen, which made him feel as if his eyes were growing cataracts. Even once he turned the heater up to maximum and raised the headlight beams, he appeared to be speeding into blurred emptiness, defined only by a strip of illuminated tarmac so uniform it mightn't have been moving. When he saw an indistinct light ahead he braked for fear of an oncoming vehicle. He had to scrape the windscreen with his nails to be sure he was seeing the hospital.

He was praying, although wordlessly, by the time it came

into focus. Clumps of floodlights towered above the concrete grounds, blanching flowers around scattered patches of turf, so that the vegetation looked artificial if not dead. The light robbed the long low unadorned buildings not just of any colour but of depth. As the car sped through the gates with a slither of tyres he was desperately tempted to leave it outside the main block, in one of the spaces for ambulances. He would only have to come back and move it before he went to Gwyneth, and he drove fast to the car park.

The metal arm at the entrance must have repeated its actions so often that it was practically lifeless. The hospital buildings were no longer in his mirrors when he found a space among the inert vehicles. Every windscreen was a white slab, and every roof sparkled like a festive decoration. As Tunstall limped breathlessly back to the reception area, he saw the breath he was leaving behind, an ephemeral ghost in the icy air. "Why can't I know where to go?" he pleaded without wishing for an answer, and tried to put all of himself into tramping faster to the hospital.

Before the automatic doors succeeded in crawling apart he was close to digging his fingers between them. Beyond them a glassed-in counter faced several dozen chairs, in some of which figures sat as if they feared any movement would disturb their injuries or ailments. As Tunstall hastened to the reception counter he heard an ambulance reiterate, probably to nobody, that it was reversing. "Excuse me," he said louder than the mechanical voice and tapped on the glass.

The receptionist took some moments to raise her round smooth nondescript face, but not enough to find much of an expression. "You've just brought my wife in," Tunstall was already saying. "She fell on an escalator."

The woman gazed at his lips as if to make certain he'd finished. He couldn't help parting them again, which only silenced her. At last she said "Did we tell you we had?"

"Not you. Whoever rang me did." The need to go through all this brought Tunstall close to clawing at the window. "The name's Tunstall," he blurted. "Hers and mine. It has been since before you were thought of."

"Tunstall." The receptionist's head sank, reminding Tunstall of the sight of her close-cropped turfy blonde coiffure. As she peered at her computer screen she murmured "What first name?"

"Gwyneth," Tunstall said and was compelled to add "Gwyn."

"Gwyneth Tunstall." The receptionist set about typing, not nearly sufficiently fast for him. When she leaned towards the monitor he had the grotesque notion that she was about to nod off, having spent too long at her repetitive job. "She's in a block," she appeared to tell him.

"A Block," Tunstall had to repeat.

"Block A, that's right."

Her deliberateness might have been rebuking his urgency, and made him more nervous. "Where's that again?" he yearned not to need to ask.

"Along there." Raising her left hand just enough to indicate that corridor, she said "You'll see the signs."

He was lurching past the seated patients, none of whom might have stirred, when she called "Mr Tunstall..."

He swung around so violently it seemed to leave his vision behind. Once his eyes cleared he managed to distinguish her through the glass, which the glare of the overhead lights had iced almost opaque. "I was going to say," she said, "when you get there you may have to wait to see her."

"I already have," Tunstall almost retorted. Surely all that mattered was being told where to find Gwyneth, and he made for the corridor as the receptionist began to page a Timmy Sawyer.

The passage was the colour of moonlit fog and nearly as featureless. A few doors bearing words he didn't need to focus on did very little to relieve the blankness of the walls. At the end he saw a sign, apparently too far away to read. He was panting by the time he came close enough to identify the first few letters of the alphabet, as if he were rediscovering how. It was a list of the hospital blocks, and A was Intensive Care.

He couldn't pretend not to have known as much, but mightn't it just mean that somebody cared about Gwyneth—cared enough to keep her alive? Tunstall squeezed his raw eyes shut while he breathed a plea, and opened them at once for fear of losing his sense of where he was. The sign pointed left to all the blocks, and he hurried into a corridor he couldn't have distinguished from the one he'd just left, except for the sight of a nurse wheeling a prone form on a trolley, receding so fast that the sheets flapped as if a wind had invaded the hospital. In another moment nurse and trolley vanished through a pair of doors at the end of the corridor, and at once he couldn't hear them.

Her urgency had brought him close to panic. The doors led to a walkway made of thick translucent plastic, which merged the light above the grounds into a generalised radiance like the glow of a befogged moon. The chill of the night fastened on Tunstall as he blundered through the walkway into the next block. The sign that met his eyes might have been designed for if not by someone close to blindness, but he had to strain them to distinguish that the large ill-preserved letter stencilled on both walls was E, not A at all.

Perhaps there had been a more direct route, but he mustn't think of retracing his steps; it would feel too much like giving up. He could only hasten past the side wards, glimpsing twin ranks of supine sheeted figures with a nurse on watch beyond each pair of doors, an illuminated face like a mask in some kind of shrine. He had to fend off an impression that the corridor was leading him into fog. The pallid surface in the distance was a wall, which stopped retreating once he concentrated on it, and soon he came close enough to see it wasn't even blank. There was a list of blocks, divested of one letter. The arrow sent him left again, and he did his best to run.

His haste seemed to lodge shadowy blotches where the walls met the roof. Beyond another corridor of silent twilit wards a walkway was darkened by fallen leaves, which scraped and scuttled like beetles on the plastic. Tunstall hugged himself and rubbed his shivering arms as he dashed through the passage, which felt entirely too exposed to the wind. The double doors thumped behind him like a faltering heartbeat as he saw the letter that identified the next block. For a panicky moment he feared he'd lost more than his way, and then he realised that the letter wasn't E again, even if the Bs on both walls looked as if a vandal had tried to erase them. What sense did the arrangement of the buildings make? He just had to believe he was heading for the right one, but he clamped a shaky hand over his lips so as not to call Gwyneth's name.

As he hurried down a corridor not at all unlike the ones he was trying to leave behind, a crumbling voice followed him. It was still paging Timmy Sawyer, who was apparently needed in E Block. The address system must be overdue for maintenance; the receptionist's voice was so splintered that the last words could almost have been the harsh cry of a night bird. Tunstall might have imagined the nurses in the wards took him to be responding to the summons. More likely they weren't sure what he was doing, a solitary wanderer in the hospital so late at night, although the frozen glowing faces owned up to no thoughts at all.

He was more than halfway down the corridor before the wall at the end gave up its likeness to fog. His head was aching as much as his eyes by the time the sign came into focus. It was almost the same as the previous list, though in a different order, and where could the arrow have pointed except left? An uneven section of linoleum snagged his feet as he dashed around the corner, and he supported himself on the wall. He thought he felt the chilly plaster crack, but he hadn't time to look.

The next walkway was damaged. Slits in the plastic admitted the wind, and dead leaves were crawling on the grubby floor. Grit had strayed in too, and its grinding underfoot felt like a symptom of fever. Gusts of wind sent shudders through the tunnel. They seemed more threatening than Tunstall cared to understand, so that he hurried along it fast enough to outrun his breath.

He faltered as the double doors ground shut behind him. The letter on each wall was nearly a B, though even closer to an E. Until he controlled his vision the sight put him in mind of a digital display reassembling its fragments. Identifying the letter as an F wasn't reassuring; had whoever laid out the hospital been as confused as Tunstall felt? He had to be grateful to see somebody else in the corridor.

The woman wasn't digging up the floor at the far end; she was nuzzling the wall with a vacuum cleaner. "Excuse me," Tunstall called and hurried towards her, trailing sodden gritty leaves that he hoped she wouldn't notice. "Am I right for Intensive Care?"

She turned with a finger to her lips. The gesture was more distinct than her face, which he could have imagined her holding still with the finger. She pointed left with the silent vacuum cleaner—that must be what the jerky movements meant, however much they looked like an attempt to drive a pest away. Tunstall wasn't anxious to speak again, since his shout had brought dim heads rearing up from beneath sheets beyond the doors on either side of him, though surely not in unison. Before he had a chance to overtake the thin woman she disappeared as if the machine had towed her around the corner. When he reached it she was nowhere to be seen.

He might have concluded she didn't want to be blamed for the state of the corridor. Perhaps the walls were stained just by his blotchy vision, and she couldn't do much about the incompleteness of the linoleum. He mustn't let any of this distract him; he just had to remember that Gwyneth was here in the hospital. The sign in front of him displayed another rearrangement of the letters and sent him left as usual. How often had he turned that way? Would it bring him back where he'd started from? He could only follow the arrow, not quite fast or breathlessly enough to be unable to think.

He did his best not to glance into the wards, where his glimpses of the solitary illuminated faces seemed increasingly similar. They no longer looked enshrined; they reminded him more of waxworks in a museum. The voice in the air sounded synthetic enough to belong to one if not to all. Was Timmy Sawyer needed in the hallway of E Block? Being unable to grasp the last words made Tunstall feel threatened with losing a sense. Ahead of him the double doors shook with the wind, and so did the walkway beyond them. It was quaking so violently he couldn't focus on the tunnel.

Tunstall blundered through the doors and saw there was no tunnel. Where it might have been was a cracked concrete path, enclosed by fog so thick he couldn't see the grounds. He stumbled at a run along the path, shivering as the fog seeped into him. His breaths tasted like a fever by the time he saw a pair of doors ahead. The pallid surface framing them wasn't fog, but the face of the figure beyond the small glass panels might have been. It was a blank white patch.

When he saw the eyes above the erased blotch Tunstall realised it was a surgical mask. The windows in the doors were so befogged that he could have thought a blurred face was forming from the mask rather than concealed by it. Before Tunstall could read any expression in the eyes, the surgeon darted out of sight. Was it the disappearance or the urgency that brought Tunstall to the edge of panic? He only knew he had to be quick. He was even repeating the word, which emerged as one gasp of fog after another. He used both hands to thump the doors, and they lumbered inwards.

The whitish light seemed to flare up, illuminating one more corridor. Leaves scrabbled along it like insects retreating into their nest. Only the letter on the wall should count, an A with its left leg crippled by a fall of plaster. The right-hand line appeared to be pointing to the nearest side ward, and why couldn't that be an omen? As Tunstall lurched in that direction, the voice that had followed him through the hospital reiterated its message. "Timmy Sawyer E hallway—" He didn't need to understand that—indeed, he didn't want to—or how the light had changed as the doors staggered shut. He sprinted to the entrance to the ward as if he could outdistance the voice and peered through the nearest window.

Gwyneth was in the first bed on the left. Her face was upturned on the pillow, and she looked peacefully asleep. Wires and slim tubes led from various parts of her. In the pale foggy light they put Tunstall in mind of a cobweb, and he could imagine wisps of mist floating from them. He eased the left-hand door open and advanced into the ward.

139

He was trying to see only Gwyneth and above all not to blink. It didn't have to matter that the message in the air was growing clearer. As he gazed at her luminous face he was able to believe that her peace was the only message for him. That wasn't quite enough, and he felt his lips part as if they were yearning for a kiss. When he spoke it felt more like a gasp, a breath he couldn't hold in any longer. "Gwyneth."

"Charlie."

He might have mistaken the sound for a whisper of dead leaves, except that her eyelids fluttered as well. He was struggling not to hear the other voice, which had grown less fragmented. He'd just remembered he could block his ears when the words came into focus. "Time he saw where he always goes... Time he saw where he always goes..." All the memories he'd succeeded in keeping at bay overwhelmed him, and he stumbled to reach for Gwyneth's hand. Before he could touch her his eyes gave way to strain, and he blinked.

In a breath he saw the light again, streaming through the broken windows and holes in the roof. It illuminated the remains of the solitary bed leaning on one splintered leg, the rusty springs strewn with fallen plaster. His entire being strove to see what had been there, but once more it was too late. He trudged out of the ward and dragged the doors at the end of the corridor open on their rusty twisted hinges. The moonlit fog was still so thick he wondered if he would be able to locate his car. He found it soon enough—it was alone in the middle of the waste ground—and drove home. He knew it was useless to loiter at or even near the hospital.

The fog stayed among the fields, allowing him to drive faster along the promenade. He parked the car and let himself into the house and plodded upstairs to sit on the bed, where he brought up Gwyneth's last text message on his phone, the goodnight she'd sent while dining with her friends. It wasn't the same as hearing her voice. How old was the message now? Not old enough for him to forget—never that—and he held onto the phone when he lay down.

He thought he hadn't slept when it rang. He clutched it and sat up on the bed, which felt too bare and wide by half. On the bedside table the photograph of him with Gwyneth in the sunlit mountains far away was waiting to be seen once more, and beyond it the curtains framed a solitary feeble midnight star. He rubbed his aching eyes to help them focus on the mobile as he thumbed the keypad. "Hello?" he said before he'd finished lifting the phone to his face.

"Forgive me, is this Charlie?"

Long ago he'd learned he had no option but to go through it all again. Perhaps this time Gwyneth would open her eyes—perhaps she would even see him. "Charles Tunstall," he had to say, "yes."

Chucky Comes to Liverpool

As Robbie watched his mother he felt ten years old, but it wasn't unwelcome for once. She looked as she used to when they played board games together; her eyes would calm down while her face hid its lines until she seemed no older than she was, hardly twice the age he'd racked up now. She'd been happy to concentrate on just one thing, and it included him. He was buoyed up by the memory until she glanced away from the computer screen in the front room and saw him.

Did she think he was spying on her through the window, the way his father had after they'd split up? Her head jerked back as if her frown had pinched her face hard, and Robbie hurried to let himself into the house. Her bicycle and rucksack had narrowed the already narrow hall. As he dumped his schoolbag on the stairs she was snatching pages from the printer, so hastily that one sailed out of her grasp. "Leave it, Robbie," she said.

"I'm only getting it for you."

It was a cinema poster headed **CHUCK IN THE DOCK**. Most of it consisted of a doll's wickedly gleeful round young face, which was held together with stitches that looked bloody even in black and white. Whatever it was advertising would be shown over the weekend at the Merseyscreen multiplex as part of the Liberating Liverpool arts festival, which was all Robbie had time to learn before his mother reached for the sheet. "Well, now you've had a good look after you were told not to," she said.

"What's all that for?"

"Something you mustn't see."

"I just did."

"That isn't clever. That's nothing but sly." Once she'd finished giving him a disappointed look she said "It's about films I don't want you ever to watch."

There were so many of those he'd lost count, if he was counting—any with fights or guns or knives, which could make him behave like boys did, or bombs, though mostly grownups used those, or language, which didn't seem to leave him much. "More of them," he said.

"I won't have you turning into a man like your father. Too many of you think it's your right to bully women and do a lot worse to them." Before Robbie dared to ask what she was leaving unsaid, which was very little where his father was concerned, she added "I'm not saying you're like that yet. Just don't be ever."

"Why did you print all that out? What's it for?"

"It's time we took more of a stand." He guessed she meant Mothers Against Mayhem as she said "They're evil films that should never be shown. They were supposed to be banned everywhere in Liverpool. They get inside children and make them act like that."

"Like what?"

"Like that thing," she said and poked the pages she'd laid face down on the table. "Now that's all. You're bullying me." She gazed harder at him while she said "Promise me you'll never watch any of those films."

"Promise."

"Let's see your hands."

He felt younger again, accused of being unclean. While he hadn't crossed his fingers behind his back, he didn't think he had quite promised either. Eventually she said "You'd better put dinner on. We've a meeting at Midge's."

Midge was the tutor on her assertiveness course and the founder of Mothers Against Mayhem. Robbie sidled past the bicycle to the kitchen, which was even smaller than the front room, and switched on the oven. He still felt proud of learning to cook, though he would never have said so at school. He only wished his mother wouldn't keep reminding him that his father was unable or unwilling even to boil an egg. He watched bubbles pop on the surface of the casserole of scouse, a spectacle that put him in mind of a monster in another sort of film he wasn't meant to view. Gloves too fat for a killer in a film to wear helped him transfer the casserole to the stained mat the table always sported. "Mmm," his mother said and "Yum," despite eating less and faster than Robbie. "Enough for dinner tomorrow," she declared. "Have you got plenty of homework?"

"A bit. A lot really."

"Give it all you've got." She was already shrugging her rucksack on. "I don't know how late I'll be," she said as she wheeled her bicycle to the front door. "If I'm not here you know when to go to bed."

He left the stagnant casserole squatting on its mat while he washed up the dinner items before making for the front room. Like the television, the computer was inhibited by all the parental locks his mother could find. He logged on to find an essay about Liverpool poets, and changed words as he copied it into his English homework book. He was altering the last paragraph when his mobile rang.

It no longer had a Star Wars ringtone since his mother decided that was about war. Robbie didn't give peace much of a chance—he silenced the chorus before they had time to chant all they were saying. "Is that Duncan Donuts?" he said.

"If that's Robin Banks."

His father had named Robbie for a Liverpool footballer, but now his mother told people he was called after a singer. "My mam's with your mam," Duncan said. "All mams together."

"The midge got them."

"More like the minge did."

This went too far for Robbie's tastes. "What are you doing tonight?"

"What do you think? I'm in the park."

"Just finishing my homework."

"Wha?" Duncan improved on this by adding "Doing your housework?"

"Homework," Robbie said, not without resentment. "I'm on the last lap."

"Whose?" Duncan didn't wait for an answer. "Hurry up or I'll of smoked it all."

Robbie found some words to change as he transcribed the paragraph. Shutting the computer down, he hurried out of the house. Across the road Laburnum Place was just a pair of stubby terraces of houses almost as compressed as his, but the next street—Waterworks Street—led to the park. A wind urged clouds across the black October sky while another brought a thick stink up from the grain silos at the Seaforth docks. Robbie heard explosions and saw violent glares along the cross streets, but war hadn't broken out yet; they were premature fireworks, and the huge prolonged crash behind him wasn't the work of a bomb—it was another delivery of scrap at the yard beyond the Strand shopping mall.

A pedestrian crossing guarded by nervous amber beacons ended at the park gates. Shadows of bushes sprawled across the concrete path leading to a disused bandstand. Sleepy pigeons fluttered on the cupola as if waiting to compete for a position on the birdless weathervane. There was no sign of Duncan inside the railings that encircled the bandstand, but Robbie located him by the smell of skunk.

The other thirteen-year-old was sitting on the balustrade at the top of a wide flight of steps that climbed beside a bowling green. Above him a noseless whitish statue on a pedestal brandished the stump of a wrist like the victim of a maniac with a cleaver. Behind the statue a deserted basketball court was overlooked by houses at least twice the size of Robbie's. Duncan must have watched him search around the bandstand, since the vantage point commanded a view in every direction. Robbie ran up the steps two at a time as leaves slithered underfoot, crunching like a baby's bones. "Give us some," he said.

Though Duncan hadn't finished the fat joint, perhaps he had already smoked one. He took a drag before passing Robbie the remains. "It's fucking special, that," he gasped as he laboured to contain the smoke.

Robbie inhaled as much as he could and held it until he had to let some of it out through his nose. More emerged in a series of belches while Duncan had another toke. "You're right," Robbie said, or someone using his voice did.

"Wha?"

"It's special."

"Fucking special."

"Fucking," Robbie had to agree as, with a rumble, the world started to collapse. It was another crash of scrap down by the river, but he could barely hold on to that sense of it. The statue pointed the gun barrel of its arm at a silhouetted tree, bits of which swelled up to flap across the park. Fallen leaves cawed as a tree took them back, and he was afraid he'd smoked too much too soon. In a bid to recover control of the teeming interior of his skull he said "Do you know what they're talking about?"

"The crows? They's saying they's black. Respect, man," Duncan called to them.

"Not them." Robbie laughed, but it didn't help much. "The mams," he said.

"Can't hear them. Can you?"

"Course I can't," Robbie said, hoping their voices wouldn't invade the cavern above his eyes. "I know what they're disgusting, though."

He wasn't sure if he'd intended to use the wrong word. "Wha?" Duncan said.

"The most evillest film anyone's ever made anywhere ever."

Duncan passed him the smouldering roach. As the tip reddened like a warning light he said "Bet I know which."

Robbie exhaled the token toke as if he were anxious to discover "Which?"

"Chucky. One of his."

The idea lit Duncan's face up. It glared pale as plastic, and lines like stitches pinched his red eyes narrow while his teeth gleamed unnaturally white. The jagged lines were shadows of twigs cast by a firework in the sky, however much they lingered, and Robbie tried to erase them by asking "How did you know that?"

"Give us that if you're not having it." Duncan sucked the roach down to his fingertips and doused it on his tongue and threw his head back to swallow it. At last he said "I know everything, that's why. You turn into a puppet if you watch those films."

"Films can't do that. They're just films."

"Those ones can. It started round here."

Robbie had a notion that he already knew all this, and yet he had to ask "What did?"

"Two kids killed a littler one like Chucky does. It was up the road when my mam was living with my real dad before they had me. And then some bigger kids tortured some girl and they were listening to Chucky when they did. A man that had a shop with Chucky videos by the Strand, someone smashed the window and stabbed him with the glass. Chucky does that to people, and a kid in Liverpool stabbed his mam's friend and said Chucky made him. And there was a Paki shop up the road they set fire to because he had magazines with Chucky in them."

Robbie was distracted by a sense of being spied upon. The watchful face was on a screen. He glanced towards it and saw curtains bring the film to an end—no, fall shut at the window of a house beyond the basketball court. "Want to see him?" Duncan said.

Robbie saw shadows clawing their way up through the concrete paths. Pigeons shivered as they strutted across the dim stage of the bandstand like the opening act of a show whose star performer was about to appear. Surely their feathers were only trembling in the wind. "Where?" he risked asking.

"At mine next time they have a meeting."

"You've never got those films."

"I can get them whenever I want them, and lots of others she doesn't like too."

"Why don't we get some of those? Can you get—"

"You're not scared of Chucky, are you?" Duncan's grin widened as if stitches were about to split his cheeks. "Godzillions of kids have watched him and they haven't done anything. Even girls," he said and let his grin drop. "If we smoke enough we'll be too stoned for him to make us." His gaze strayed past Robbie, and he slipped down from the balustrade. "Time we went," he said.

Robbie twisted around to see red and blue fireworks in the gateway beyond the basketball court. They were the roof lights of a police car, and Duncan had already dodged behind the cleaver victim's plinth. "Don't go that way," Robbie had to whisper in case the crows raised the alarm. "Someone in those houses called the police."

"I'm not going. I'm gone," Duncan said and crouched lower. "You go somewhere else."

Robbie was sure that if he encountered the police his face would betray him, grinning too much while he struggled not to grin. He retreated down the steps and showed Duncan his severed head. "Catch you at school. Me, not the police."

"They won't bother much about kids having a smoke. Wait till they've gone and we'll skin up again."

"You can," Robbie said and ran down the steps, desperate to leave behind the swarms of beetles that crunched underfoot. The police might hear that, or the applause his sprint past the bandstand earned from his pigeon audience. He skidded to a halt at the gates that framed the pedestrian crossing, where the beacons were trying to measure his pulse, and then he dashed across the road. Lights flared down the cross streets, but they were fireworks, not police speeding to cut him off. Nobody grabbed him from behind as his key scrabbled to let him into the house.

How long did he have to spend at perfecting the use of the toothbrush on the teeth a face was baring in the mirror? Only the fear that his mother would see that he'd changed sent him to bed. The bed was a boat in which he was floating away from explosions on a beach, and then he was brought home by the soundtrack—the thud of the front door, the trundling of the bicycle along the hall, the thump of the dropped rucksack. Other noises followed—some that he was embarrassed to overhear—but the impact of the rucksack left an echo in his skull. It brought him out of his room once he believed his mother was asleep.

A streetlamp lowered its bulbous head to watch him through the window over the front door. Suppose his mother had left the pages with Midge? They were in the rucksack, and he took them into the front room. Since he couldn't risk switching the light on, he tiptoed to the window and unfolded the crumpled wad in the glare from the street. Except for the poster for a showing of all five Chucky films and a talk about them, the sheets were copies of newspaper reports. Fifteen years ago but less than a mile away, two boys not even his age had tortured a toddler to death. Several newspapers blamed a Chucky film, and one said **For the sake of ALL our kids … BURN YOUR VIDEO NASTY.** The bold letters seemed to glisten like the stitches on Chucky's face. He wasn't so easily destroyed, even if the cinemas in Liverpool had banned him. He'd made some young kidnappers use his voice while they were torturing a girl, and it had been Chucky's idea for a seven-year-old Liverpool boy to stab his mother's friend twenty-one times with a kitchen knife. Newspapers had tried to have him stopped, but two more films had been made about him, though they hadn't been shown in Liverpool. Now he was getting his way there too. No wonder he was grinning, and as Robbie stared into the gleeful eyes the expression tugged at his own mouth.

It must be all right to watch the films when you were old enough—otherwise the dockland cinema wouldn't be allowed to show them. The showing was for adults only, but videos didn't need to be. If Duncan could watch them, Robbie could; he wasn't going to let his mother make his friend despise him. He was years older than any of the boys Chucky had manipulated. Maybe they'd all been young enough to play with dolls and believe in them along with Christmas and fathers and the other things that went away as you grew up. Being frightened of films must do, and it was time it did. Robbie folded the pages and stowed them in the rucksack and took his grin to bed.

He always felt dull the morning after he'd had a smoke, but his mother brightened him. "Good job we've got that dinner," she said over breakfast. "We're at Midge's again. They have to be stopped, those films."

She was on her way to work at Frugo in the mall by the time he left the house. He joined the parade of boys and girls in black and white, which seemed to lead to a funeral for the past—a Liverpool history lesson where most of his classmates were silent as mourners. He didn't have a chance to speak to Duncan until the morning break. As they emerged into the corridor Duncan said "I've got them."

"Chucky."

As Duncan's grin confirmed this, a girl they didn't even know demanded "What about him?"

"We're going to see him," Robbie said.

"My mother says nobody should out of respect."

"That's what crows get," said Duncan.

She and her friend blinked blankly in unison. "They'll bring him back," the other girl said with an extravagant shudder.

"Who will?" Robbie protested in case he was being accused.

"Anyone that watches him."

"Anyone that does when they know they shouldn't," said her friend. "That's like trying to call him up."

"It's like calling up a demon so you'll get possessed," the first girl said.

"These won't, though."

Their scorn provoked Robbie to blurt "Why won't we?"

"They'll never let you in to see those films."

"We don't care. We—"

"We'll get in anyway," Duncan interrupted. "Chucky'll let us in so we can see him."

He mustn't want the girls to know about the viewing session at his house. He wasn't quite as reckless as he liked Robbie to think. The girls scoffed at him and ran into the schoolyard as Duncan muttered "I've got two for tonight. I'll text you when."

For the rest of the day Robbie was dry-mouthed and brittle-skulled and barely able to sit still. He had to at dinner so that his mother wouldn't notice. "Lots of homework again?" she said.

"Like last night."

This was cleverer than usual, because she didn't realise. He must be growing up. "Never mind, you've got all evening," she told him.

He was altering an article about the slums of Victorian Liverpool when his mobile took a message. **shes gon cum ruond**, it said.

Comming, Robbie responded. His head tingled and throbbed while he searched for words to change so that he could leave the house. Televisions relayed images from room to room all the way along the street to the Jawbone Tavern. Duncan and his mother lived in a house as small as Robbie's almost opposite the pub. His friend and a smell of skunk met Robbie at the front door. "Better be ready for this," Duncan said.

Robbie hesitated, only to see several men emerging from the pub for presumably another kind of smoke. Duncan raised two fingers, displaying the joint and gesturing at the men. "Get some of that. Last night's was for wimps."

"Not out here. Someone might see."

"I don't want her smelling it in the house." With a protracted red-eyed look Duncan said "Go out the back."

He needn't make it seem as if Robbie's caution were the problem. Robbie followed him along the hall, which at least was free of bicycles, and through a kitchen cluttered with furniture into the yard. He had a manly toke that made him thoroughly aware of the spectators—upstairs windows, all of them lifeless except for the wailing of a child somewhere he couldn't locate. Before he and Duncan finished the joint he'd had enough of the windowless cell above which fireworks clawed at the sky on his behalf. "Where's Chucky, then?" he said.

"Waiting for you."

Duncan meant for both of them, of course. He led Robbie to the front room, where a plump couch and two undernourished chairs were miming patience at a blank television. The chair that had been on less of a diet was occupied by a romance of the Liverpool slums, while a woman's orange cardigan sprawled across half of the couch. Duncan slipped a disc into the player and lounged beside the cardigan. "Chuck that," he said.

Robbie laid the rumpled paperback on the carpet and propped his spine—more especially the cumbersome head it was sprouting—against the chair as child's play started on the screen. That was the name of the film and, he supposed, what you called the mischief that the Chucky doll got up to once a killer's spirit hid inside it. Why did everyone blame the boy who owned the doll? Why couldn't they see that the doll was pretending to be him? They even took him to a psychiatrist for the doll to kill. At last the boy's mother caught Chucky misbehaving and the boy helped throw him on a fire, burning him for the sake of all the kids as the paper said you should, though the mother still had to blow him to bits with a gun. Robbie was relieved she'd seen the truth at last. As he let go of the bony arms of the chair, which had apparently been bruising his hands for some time, Duncan said "Wimp."

"Who is?"

"Him, going crying to his mam. Hope the other one's better."

How could the doll come back? It had grown its stitches now, but this wasn't even its second film, and so Robbie couldn't tell what had revived it. It killed a woman who used to go with the killer, and then it put her inside a girl doll. As that one began to speak, a noise crept into the room—giggling that ballooned into shrieks. "What's so funny?" Robbie was panicked into asking.

"It's Marge out of the Simpsons."

At once Robbie recognised the croaky female voice from his mother's favourite cartoon show. He felt isolated with the sight of Marge Simpson disguised as a doll that helped Chucky kill people. Eventually she was burned alive, which didn't finish her off, and Chucky was exhaustively shot once again despite shouting "I'll be back." Didn't someone else say that? How many films had Chucky and his partner taken over? A baby or a bloody doll popped out of her to end the film. Duncan ejected the disc and set about searching the cable channels, which fluttered past like slides snatching at the chance to move until Robbie cried "He's there."

Duncan jumped up, and the cardigan cowered away from him, flailing an armless arm. "Who?" he snarled, dashing to the window.

"Chucky. Not out there."

Duncan shut the curtains and glared at Robbie, whether for unnerving him or because he hadn't pointed out that passers-by could see what they were watching. "That's not him."

"It's one of him," Robbie protested, but as the grinning doll sprang from under a boy's bed Duncan poked the information button to reveal it was a Spielberg film. It was meant to be about a poltergeist, which didn't reassure Robbie. "I'd better get home before she does," he said.

Duncan grinned like Chucky. "You're never scared of your mam."

"I'm not scared of any fucker or any fucking thing."

"Better believe I'm not. My dad tried to make me scared of stupid fucking Chucky. Not my real dad, the one I got for my birthday when I was four."

"What did he do?"

"Never mind what he done." Having stared at Robbie, Duncan added "Said Chucky would get me if I was bad. That's what they used to tell kids."

Had someone once told Robbie that? It seemed uneasily familiar. "They didn't know what they were on about," Duncan said. "That's not how Chucky works."

He meant in the films, of course—he couldn't mean anything else. "See you at school," Robbie said.

"Shut it on your way out. I'm going to watch him give the doctor shocks again."

The street was deserted. Lamps patched the pavements with

light, which mouldered on the roofs of parked cars. If Robbie were a girl or in a film he might be daunted by the gaps between the vehicles, where a small jerky figure could dart out as its victim reached one of the stretches of pavement the lamps didn't entirely illuminate. The only place he had to look for Chucky was on all the televisions, and he was lingering outside a window to see that no doll attacked the young couple in bed on the screen when a woman in an armchair caught sight of him. As she sprang to her feet he fled home. She didn't chase him, but did she know where he lived? Suppose she told his mother? She couldn't say he'd been looking for Chucky; nobody knew that, not even Duncan. Chucky was safe in his head where nobody would notice him.

The house was unlit, which meant that Robbie's mother wouldn't see him until he had a chance to sleep off any guilt that might escape onto his face. It didn't look guilty in the bathroom mirror, where it foamed at the mouth while the toothbrush polished its grin. He was in bed well before his mother came home, though he couldn't sleep. If he'd been allowed a computer in his room he would have played on it, but the games might have been too violent for his mother's taste; she'd decided even board games were aggressive. He slept once the grinning doll subsided inside the jack-in-the-box of his head.

He thought he was behaving normally at breakfast, however dull his head felt, until his mother said "What's the matter, Robbie? Why are you looking like that?"

"I'm not looking like anything."

"Your eyes are. Aren't you sleeping?"

"It's all the stuff you've been saying about Chucky."

"I won't again. Don't worry, we'll be getting rid of him." As a further comfort she said "My turn to make dinner."

So there wasn't a meeting. Perhaps that was why Duncan didn't seek him out but only gave him a grin across the classroom. He joined him at the morning break, when the girl who'd accosted them yesterday caught up with them in the schoolyard. "Hope you're happy now," she said.

Robbie grinned, though it felt inadvertent if not meaningless.

155

"Why?" Duncan demanded.

"Someone's brought your Chucky back."

"We haven't lost him," Robbie blurted as Duncan said louder "Who's brought what where?"

"They've got him in a shop down by the Strand, in the window where everyone can see him."

"They've got no respect," her friend said.

"Nobody can stop him. He'll get everywhere," Duncan said, baring his teeth.

He kept the grin up until the girls left them alone. If he seemed to find it hard to abandon, that was just a joke. He made the face at any girls who looked at him and Robbie as they slouched around the yard, and the trick amused Robbie so much that he couldn't help joining in, even if it felt as though strings were attached to the corners of his mouth. His lips had grown weary by the time the bell herded everyone into the school.

The history mistress wanted to hear stories of the past that people's families had told them. One boy said how the government had hated Liverpool so much they'd tried to take all the jobs down south, and a girl retorted that the unions hadn't let her dad or anybody do their jobs. "I think those are legends more than they're history," Mrs Picton said, and Robbie took the cue. "What about Chucky?" he said.

"What about…"

"He's a story mams and dads tell, isn't he? How it all started when those kids watched that film."

Before Mrs Picton could respond, Robbie's classmates did. Someone used to dream Chucky was under the bed after she'd read about him in the paper. Someone knew a girl who'd set her dolls on fire in case any of them might be Chucky. Someone else had heard of a boy who'd attacked his sister because he thought Chucky was inside her. Several people confirmed this, but Duncan said nothing at all. "It's only a film," Mrs Picton said, which sounded somehow familiar. "That doesn't mean any of you should watch anything like that at your age."

"Didn't those boys really kill anyone, then?" Robbie said.

"Of course they did. It's history, and now please leave it alone."

Why should he feel accused? He didn't speak for the rest of the lesson, despite the doubtful glances she kept giving him. When the bell jerked him to his feet at last she said "Will you wait, please, Robbie."

He stood like a doll at his desk until she took him to the headmistress. If someone had reported him for being Chucky in the yard, why wasn't Duncan with him? It should be Duncan who was being stared at and whispered girlishly about as he was escorted along the corridor like a killer to the execution chamber. Robbie and his guard were almost at Mrs Todd's office when he realised they couldn't do this to him; his mother had to be there. But she was in the office.

She looked even more disappointed than the other women did, and he turned on Mrs Picton. "You said it was only a film."

"What have you been watching?" his mother said.

"I didn't see them all. Dunk saw more. They haven't done anything to us. Like she says, it's just a legend. Just some wimpy films."

"Have you been too busy watching films," Mrs Todd enquired, "to do your homework?"

"I did it all. Who says I haven't?"

"The school does," Robbie's mother said sadly. "Your teacher found it on the Internet."

Robbie's skull felt close to cracking like plastic. "That's only like looking it up in a book."

"It was practically word for word," said Mrs Picton. "You'd think you wanted to be caught."

"What have you been filling your head with instead?" his mother clearly didn't care to know.

"Try devoting your imagination to your schoolwork. That's what it's for," Mrs Todd said. "I'm letting you off with a warning this time, but I'll treat any further offence much more seriously. Please remember you're letting yourself and your mother down as well as the school."

"And I'll want to see that work from you done properly," Mrs Picton said.

His mother played his silent jailer as far as the schoolyard. She was hardly out of the gate when Duncan came to him. "What did they want?"

"Just about my homework."

"Was it bad?"

Robbie had to imitate his grin, because he didn't know if Duncan meant the homework or the interview. "It was evil."

This widened Duncan's grin, which aggravated Robbie's. It was starting to feel like a contest when a girl said "What do you two think you look like?"

"Chucky," the boys said in chorus, which made them grin until Robbie's cheeks felt in danger of splitting like plastic.

He couldn't keep it up all afternoon, though his lips stirred if any of the teachers even glanced at him. Though the lessons felt interminable, they ended far too soon. Where could he go except home? He wasn't about to be scared of his mother when he wasn't scared of Chucky, especially since she was. Her nagging would just leave his head duller still—and then he thought of somewhere to go on the way home.

The metal benches outside the shopping precinct were crammed with quartets of pensioners, warily eyeing his schoolmates while they fought at bus stops or flung litter at each other. Robbie felt watched by them as he caught sight of the face across the road, in a small shop on the side street opposite a corner of the precinct. He sprinted in front of a bus stuffed with children and gave the driver his best grin, encouraged by the face in the shop window full of skulls and hairy visages and greenish corpse heads. Though the eyeless round rubbery mask was decorated with stitches, Robbie wasn't sure whether they were all where they should be. The longer he gazed at it, the more secretive the grin seemed to grow. He thought of wearing the mask while his mother lectured him, but she wouldn't let him own it, any more than he could buy even one of the fireworks lined up at the foot of the window. Suppose she didn't know?

He could wear it when he went out at night while she was with Midge. He hadn't enough money on him, but there was more in his room, and that was why he hurried home.

His mother came into the hall as he shut the front door. "What have you been doing now?"

"Nothing. Coming home."

"Can't I trust you any more? Whose idea was it to do exactly what I told you not to?"

"Both of ours." Robbie dropped his schoolbag on the stairs, only to feel that it was blocking his way as she and her bicycle were. "You won't tell his mam I said about him, will you? You don't have to. Please don't, please."

"Why, are you frightened how he'll behave now you've watched those films?"

"Course not. That's stupid. Why do you want to stop people seeing them? They aren't that scary, and they only make little kids be bad."

"I wouldn't grin about it. Is that really what you think? You'd better look at this." Grabbing her rucksack, she extracted the crumpled pages and flapped one at him. "What do you call them?" she said.

She was brandishing the report about the girl who'd been tortured in Manchester. Robbie thought he was expected to say that her tormentors were monsters or just men until he saw what he'd overlooked: the people who'd listened to Chucky's voice had been years older than he was now. He would have liked to have the Chucky mask to hide his face. All he could find to say was "Some of them were girls."

"That shows how bad those films are. That's why they have to be stopped, and now I can't leave you on your own."

"Why can't you?"

"I almost wish we had your father back. Are you going to turn into something else for me to worry about? Aren't you ever going to do anything to make me proud?"

Robbie ducked to his schoolbag so that she wouldn't see his face. "My homework," he muttered.

While he was no more eager to do it than usual, rewriting the history essay distracted him intermittently from his fears—that the English teacher would notice he'd copied from the Internet, that Duncan would discover Robbie had told on him, that they weren't as immune to the films as they'd thought, because they weren't old enough after all. His nerves kept jabbing the dull lump of his mind, and he was glad when his mother called him to dinner.

Perhaps she looked reproachful because she'd made turkey burgers, his favourite. Whenever their eyes met he thought it best to grin. The meal ended some time after he'd stopped enjoying it. As she returned the chutney to the refrigerator his mother said "Now look what you've made me do."

She was craning inside, her neck between the doorframe and the edge of the door, as she held the refrigerator open with one hand. "What?" Robbie said.

"I forgot to buy orange and now there's none for breakfast."

As the legs of his chair and the linoleum collaborated on a squeal that a maniac's victim might have been proud of, Robbie said "I'll go."

"Just hurry there and hurry back."

He ran upstairs and made sure she heard him go into the bathroom, and then he dodged into his room. Now his footfalls felt as light as plastic. The money was the only secret in his room, not that it was much of one; less than half was change he'd kept the last time she'd sent him to the shops. Dust squeaked beneath his fingernails as he groped behind the wardrobe for the coins. He flushed the toilet and sprinted downstairs, to be met by his mother. "Remember what I said," she told him.

As he hurried to the shop he felt as if his face was shaping itself so that the mask would fit. What would the mask allow him to do? He thought of peering in the windows at the televisions inside which Chucky might be hiding, and his grin expanded, only to sag when he reached the street that led down to the Strand. The shop with the masks in was dark.

The door didn't budge, and nobody answered however

hard Robbie clattered the letterbox. "What are you grinning at?" he demanded, but the mask didn't seem to hear. It looked entertained by his plight, unless it was amused by its secret thoughts. Suppose he smashed the window and set Chucky free that way? He glanced about to make sure the street was deserted and in search of something he could use. Then, with a shock that turned his mouth so dry it felt raw with skunk, he realised what he was planning to do.

Had the mask put the idea into his mind? What else might Chucky have sneaked in? Robbie remembered wishing he could wear the mask so that he could deal with his mother, and all at once he saw her neck in the guillotine of the refrigerator. Lightning widened the empty eyes as if the mask had been enlivened by the memory. The flash was the explosion of a firework above the houses, and it sent Robbie away from the window, to the grocery around the corner.

Had the flash been an omen too? There were fireworks under the glass counter, and he used the carton of juice to point. "One of them as well."

He thought the shopkeeper was about to refuse, but she must have been waiting for politeness. As she shook her head and laid the firework on the counter Robbie said "And some matches."

She didn't take the second chance to say no. Robbie paid and hurried back to the intersection. If there was anybody in the other street he wouldn't be able to carry out his plan—but the street was deserted even by traffic. He wandered over to the shop as if he were bound somewhere else entirely, and then he lit the firework.

The stitched mask seemed to watch him askance as he inserted the long cardboard barrel through the letterbox and gave it a violent sideways shove. The firework landed inside the window. In a few seconds it spouted fire, and moments later several fireworks were ablaze. Even if Chucky never stayed burned in the films, mightn't this destroy his face? The mask appeared to writhe in fear as detonations shook the window. The glass held, but the masks slithered down it to fall on top of the outbursts of flame.

Gouts of fire spurted from Chucky's eyes, which grew larger and blacker and emptier, and then the helpless upturned face began to split apart as if the stitches had torn open. When the pieces started curling up and bubbling like slugs, Robbie dashed home.

He felt both reckless and justified. His mother should be proud of him, but could he risk telling her? As he inserted the unnecessarily shaky key into the lock he was trying to decide how much he might hint. He'd eased the door shut when he heard a voice croaking somewhere in the house.

It was Chucky's mate. Before Robbie could begin to deal with this, his mother darted like a killer out of the front room. "Where have you been this time? How long does it take to buy juice?"

He was distracted by the film she'd been watching—the Simpsons film. "There was a shop on fire," he said.

"I suppose I can't blame you for that."

Robbie didn't grin until he was heading for the kitchen, and managed to suppress the expression on his way back. Once he joined in watching the film he had no idea how to look. He tried only laughing if his mother did, but this was almost always when Marge Simpson spoke in that unnatural voice. He peered at the film as if it might show him what else he could do, and then his mobile clanged. As he brought up the message his mother leaned over to read it. **chuckies burnd shop down**, Duncan wanted him to know. "What does he mean?" Robbie's mother demanded.

Robbie thought it wisest just to shrug, and she was rediscovering how to laugh with Marge when the ringtone interrupted. "Is that Duncan again?" Robbie's mother said and silenced the television. "Put him on the loudspeaker."

Robbie was unnerved by the sight of her dubbing Marge's dialogue. Poking the loudspeaker key seemed to bring an audience into the room. "That shop those girls said about, it's on fire," Duncan shouted over the sounds of the crowd. "You want to come and see."

"I saw."

"Did you see Chucky? He's gone now. Maybe he done it and went."

"No he didn't." Since Robbie's fervour apparently impressed his mother, he added "He's just in his films."

"Till someone lets him out."

"I've got to go now," Robbie said and cut the call off.

He still had to face his mother. "Was he trying to tell you he'd started the fire?" she said.

"It wasn't him."

"How do you know?"

"There was a Chucky mask he'd have wanted. It's all burned up."

Far too many seconds passed before her gaze relented. "Just please don't ever watch any of those films again."

"I won't."

"Don't go anywhere near them."

At once, having realised what else he could do, Robbie was afraid she meant to extract the promise. She picked up the remote control, however, and restored the doll's voice. He kept hearing it and Chucky's even once the film was over, but now he knew how to stop them. When his mother started watching a programme about refuges for women he used it as an excuse to go to bed. "You get your sleep. You've plenty to do tomorrow," she said.

She had no idea. He wasn't sure himself. As he lay in bed he saw Chucky's face bubble and blacken while it struggled to crawl out of the flames. It didn't let him sleep much; he kept jerking awake like a puppet someone was testing. He was afraid his mother might interrogate him at breakfast, but perhaps she was used to his red eyes or too preoccupied to notice. He tried not to grin every time she looked at him, and eventually he was able to stay out of her sight by taking his homework into the front room.

For English he had to write about a film. He was tempted to discuss Chucky but didn't know what he might say. He wrote about the Simpsons film, although the need to avoid mentioning the truth about Marge's voice felt like wearing a mask. As he strove to keep his mind on the essay, the phone in the hall went off like an alarm.

Had someone seen him set fire to the shop? Would the police believe why he'd had to do it? He heard his mother take the receiver to the kitchen, but he couldn't distinguish her words or even her tone. He wrote very few words while he listened for her footsteps in the hall. At last she came back and opened the door. "Midge wants us to picket the films tonight," she said. "What am I going to do with you?"

He was searching for an answer when his mobile tried to crawl across the table. **what you doeing tonit**, Duncan wanted to know. Robbie couldn't say, and he felt his skull grow thin as plastic as he waited for his mother to decide. Neither of them had spoken by the time Duncan rang. "Let me hear," Robbie's mother said.

As Robbie amplified the sound Duncan said "Where have you fucked off to now?"

"Doing my homework."

"Hope it's evil." When Robbie didn't respond Duncan said "My mam's got me picketing Chucky tonight. Should be a laugh. Want to come?"

Robbie's mother shook her head as hard as she was gazing at him. "Can't," he said.

"Why, what'll you be doing?"

"Homework," Robbie said, the only safe answer he could think of. "I've got to do some of it again."

"All right," his mother said as he ended the call, "I'm going to trust you. You don't need to come with me tonight."

She was making sure he wouldn't be with Duncan. Robbie felt as if he were in a film where whatever the plot required was bound to happen. Nothing else had to for the rest of the day, and he stayed in the front room when he wasn't helping his mother shop. He wondered if he was grinning too often over dinner, but she left him to clear up. He waited to be certain she was well on her way to Midge's, and then he left the house.

He might have borrowed the bicycle if she hadn't locked it. As he hurried to the bus stops, the smell from the grain silos hovered in the cold dark air like the stench of melted plastic.

Burning claws reared up to sear black prints on the sky or on his eyes, and he heard the mound of Chucky's grave collapse as the doll fumbled its way out, but that was scrap being dumped beside the river. A bus took him into Liverpool, where he alighted just short of the dockland multiplex.

People were converging on it—students, older couples, solitary characters carrying *Gorehound* magazine with Chucky's face on it. All of them were met outside the cinema by pickets waving placards—CHILDREN NOT CHUCKY, HORROR ISN'T HEALTHY, CARE FOR KIDS INSTEAD OF FILMS, SAVE OUR BABES FROM SADISM... Whichever Robbie's mother might be wielding, he ran behind an apartment block without locating her.

The luxury block was guarded by an electrified fence, the outside of which led him parallel to the river. He didn't think anyone saw him sprint from the corner of the fence to the rear of the multiplex, where the plot he was enacting seemed to abandon him. All the back doors of the cinemas were locked, and the side doors were just as immovable. As he faltered in the recess of the exit closest to the pickets, they began to chant "Chuck Chucky out" and drum the staves of their placards on the concrete. Somebody was remonstrating with them, and when Robbie peeked around the corner he saw it was the manager, supported by quite a few of the cinema personnel. Among the pickets growing louder in response were Duncan and Robbie's mother, but nobody appeared to see him dodge through the nearest front door into the multiplex.

Nearly all the staff must be confronting the pickets, and the girls in the box office were dealing with a queue. There wasn't even anyone to take tickets at the entrance to the screens. While the staff at the popcorn counter might have, they were serving customers. Robbie walked not too quickly or too surreptitiously past them into a corridor where posters indicated which door led to which film. He hadn't found the poster he was looking for when he heard Chucky's voice.

It was beyond a door marked STAFF ONLY. Robbie glanced

around to see that the corridor was deserted. He hauled the door open and slipped past as it began to close behind him. He felt as if he were not merely in a film but in a dream he'd had, unless he was having it now. He was where he would have hoped to be—in a projection room.

The projectionist was elsewhere. Six projectors—half the number of screens—were casting images through dwarfish windows on the far side of the room. The mocking gleeful voice led Robbie to the second machine from the left. A window next to the one the projector was using showed him Chucky's face swollen larger than any of the audience beneath it in the darkened auditorium. They were watching a documentary about the films, all five of which were stacked in cans beside the projector.

Robbie lifted both fire extinguishers out of their cradles on the walls and laid them alongside the projector. A film magazine was lying on a table by the door, and he tore it up to pile the pages between the extinguishers. Prising the lid off the topmost can of film, he tipped out the contents, which unwound across the heap of paper. The chant of the pickets and the drumming of sticks urged him on. By the time he'd emptied all the cans his fingernails twinged from opening the lids, and his arms ached with his efforts. None of this mattered, because the extinguishers had prevented the tangle of celluloid from burying all the paper. Perhaps Chucky wanted to be caught—to be stopped. Robbie took out the matchbox and struck a match.

The paper flamed at once, blazing up beneath the pile of film. In a moment the celluloid was on fire. Chucky was still ranting in the shaky darkness, but he wouldn't be for long. Robbie would have liked to see the flames reach the film in the projector, except that the fire or the projectionist might trap him. As the room began to fill with a plastic stench he retreated into the corridor. He was loitering outside the toilets near an exit—he would look as if he were waiting for someone if anybody noticed him—when a man appeared at the far end of the corridor and made for the projection room.

For just an instant Robbie wanted to warn him, and then he

realised that the projectionist must have watched Chucky while checking all the films. Robbie observed him as he pulled the door open and uttered a syllable and lurched into the room. The door shut behind him, puffing out thick smoke, and then there was silence apart from the noise of the pickets. Robbie was at the side exit when a figure covered with flames and partly composed of them staggered into the corridor.

Was it a doll? Bits of plastic were peeling away from it, unless they were pieces of film. It wasn't making much noise; a clogged rising groan was the best it could do for a scream. Perhaps its face was melting. As it pranced away it looked more than ever like a puppet, growing smaller while its hands clutched at and flinched away from its blazing skull. It had almost reached the far end of the corridor when a woman and her children came out of a cinema to scream on its behalf. Robbie had to cover his grin with a hand as if he was overcome by their emotion; he might have been putting on a mask. As the family retreated screaming into the cinema and the puppet fell on any face it had left, he let himself out of the multiplex.

The pickets were still chanting and thumping their sticks. He would have told them there was no longer any need, but however necessary his actions had been, suppose he was misunderstood? He sprinted behind another apartment block while fireworks in the sky celebrated his success. The top deck of a bus from the stop beyond the multiplex gave him a view of people streaming out of all the exits, and just a few signs sprouting from the crowd. A placard sank out of sight as he watched, and he thought it was acknowledging him.

He had to shut a smell of melted plastic out of the house. He felt hollow, but in the best way—emptied of the need to intervene. He drowsed in bed until he heard his mother come home, and then he fell asleep. He didn't dream or waken, even when a church started ringing its bells. Perhaps they were for Chucky's funeral, but there must have been a phone as well, because Robbie opened his eyes at last to see his mother in the doorway of his room. "You had a long one," she said. "My nan used to say you only sleep well if you've been good."

Could he tell her how good he'd been? As he tested the mechanism of his lips she said "You missed it all."

His lips parted, but she headed off whatever he might have said. "It's a good job you weren't there, though."

"Why?"

"There was a fire at the cinema. The police think it was deliberate. They want to talk to us."

Would they understand? She ought to hear before they did, and Robbie was about to tell his secret when she said "One of the staff was in the fire. Midge just called to say he died. We're all going over to hers for a while. I've left your breakfast."

So she hadn't meant the police were after him. He should have seen how normal she wanted life to be. She looked sad for the projectionist, and perhaps he hadn't deserved to be burned, but he'd had to be. All at once she looked sadder. "I forgot your juice again."

"I can get some."

"You're a good boy really. Stay like that," she said and hurried downstairs.

As soon as the bicycle trundled out of the house Robbie headed for the bathroom. He still had work to do. Perhaps he could be sad about it, if you needed to be sad about people who'd turned into dolls. He didn't look sad in the mirror; he could see no expression at all—his ordinary face was the only mask he needed. He was contemplating it when his phone struck up its slogan.

There wouldn't be peace yet, but there might be soon. "You should of been there last night," Duncan told him.

"What happened?"

"My mam and yours nearly got in a fight with the cinema. And somebody started a fire and half of it's burned down, and a feller was in it. I'll tell you all about it when I see you. I've got some stuff that'll do your head in."

Watching so much Chucky had done that to Duncan, Robbie thought. "Where?" he said.

"In the park. I found somewhere nobody'll know we're there. Are you coming now?"

"I've got to go to the shop first."

"Being your mam's good boy again, are you?"

"You'll see." Robbie knew Duncan was grinning, and imagined how they both would when they met. His grin wouldn't be the same as Duncan's; it was a mask, because he was the opposite of Chucky. "I won't be long," he said. "I'll be back."

With the Angels

A s Cynthia drove between the massive mossy posts where the gates used to be, Karen said "Were you little when you lived here, Auntie Jackie?"

"Not as little as I was," Cynthia said.

"That's right," Jacqueline said while the poplars alongside the high walls darkened the car, "I'm even older than your grandmother."

Karen and Valerie giggled and then looked for other amusement. "What's this house called, Brian?" Valerie enquired.

"The Populars," the four-year-old declared and set about punching his sisters almost before they began to laugh.

"Now, you three," Cynthia intervened. "You said you'd show Jackie how good you can be."

No doubt she meant her sister to feel more included. "Can't we play?" said Brian as if Jacqueline were a disapproving bystander.

"I expect you may," Jacqueline said, having glanced at Cynthia. "Just don't get yourselves dirty or do any damage or go anywhere you shouldn't or that's dangerous."

Brian and the eight-year-old twins barely waited for Cynthia to haul two-handed at the brake before they piled out of the Volvo and chased across the forecourt into the weedy garden. "Do try and let them be children," Cynthia murmured.

"I wasn't aware I could change them." Jacqueline managed

not to groan while she unbent her stiff limbs and clambered out of the car. "I shouldn't think they would take much notice of me," she said, supporting herself on the hot roof as she turned to the house.

Despite the August sunlight, it seemed darker than its neighbours, not just because of the shadows of the trees, which still put her in mind of a graveyard. More than a century's worth of winds across the moors outside the Yorkshire town had plastered the large house with grime. The windows on the topmost floor were half the size of those on the other two storeys, one reason why she'd striven in her childhood not to think they resembled the eyes of a spider, any more than the porch between the downstairs rooms looked like a voracious vertical mouth. She was far from a child now, and she strode or at any rate limped to the porch, only to have to wait for her sister to bring the keys. As Cynthia thrust one into the first rusty lock the twins scampered over, pursued by their brother. "Throw me up again," he cried.

"Where did he get that from?"

"From being a child, I should think," Cynthia said. "Don't you remember what it was like?"

Jacqueline did, not least because of Brian's demand. She found some breath as she watched the girls take their brother by the arms and swing him into the air. "Again," he cried.

"We're tired now," Karen told him. "We want to see in the house."

"Maybe grandma and auntie will give you a throw if you're good," Valerie said.

"Not just now," Jacqueline said at once.

Cynthia raised her eyebrows high enough to turn her eyes blank as she twisted the second key. The door lumbered inwards a few inches and then baulked. She was trying to nudge the obstruction aside with the door when Brian made for the gap. "Don't," Jacqueline blurted, catching him by the shoulder.

"Good heavens, Jackie, what's the matter now?"

"We don't want the children in there until we know what state it's in, do we?"

172

"Just see if you can squeeze past and shift whatever's there, Brian."

Jacqueline felt unworthy of consideration. She could only watch the boy wriggle around the edge of the door and vanish into the gloom. She heard fumbling and rustling, but of course this didn't mean some desiccated presence was at large in the vestibule. Why didn't Brian speak? She was about to prompt him until he called "It's just some old letters and papers."

When he reappeared with several free newspapers that looked as dusty as their news, Cynthia eased the door past him. A handful of brown envelopes contained electricity bills that grew redder as they came up to date, which made Jacqueline wonder "Won't the lights work?"

"I expect so if we really need them." Cynthia advanced into the wide hall beyond the vestibule and poked at the nearest switch. Grit ground inside the mechanism, but the bulbs in the hall chandelier stayed as dull as the mass of crystal teardrops. "Never mind," Cynthia said, having tested every switch in the column on the wall without result. "As I say, we won't need them."

The grimy skylight above the stairwell illuminated the hall enough to show that the dark wallpaper was even hairier than Jacqueline remembered. It had always made her think of the fur of a great spider, and now it was blotchy with damp. The children were already running up the left-hand staircase and across the first-floor landing, under which the chandelier dangled like a spider on a thread. "Don't go out of sight," Cynthia told them, "until we see what's what."

"Chase me." Brian ran down the other stairs, one of which rattled like a lid beneath the heavy carpet. "Chase," he cried and dashed across the hall to race upstairs again.

"Don't keep running up and down unless you want to make me ill," Jacqueline's grandmother would have said. The incessant rumble of footsteps might have presaged a storm on the way to turning the hall even gloomier, so that Jacqueline strode as steadily as she could towards the nearest room. She had to pass one of the hall mirrors, which appeared to show a dark blotch hovering in wait for the children. The shapeless sagging darkness at the top of the grimy oval was a stain, and she needn't have waited to see the children run downstairs out of its reach. "Do you want the mirror?" Cynthia said. "I expect it would clean up."

"I don't know what I want from this house," Jacqueline said.

She mustn't say she would prefer the children not to be in it. She couldn't even suggest sending them outside in case the garden concealed dangers—broken glass, rusty metal, holes in the ground. The children were staying with Cynthia while her son and his partner holidayed in Morocco, but couldn't she have chosen a better time to go through the house before it was put up for sale? She frowned at Jacqueline and then followed her into the dining-room.

Although the heavy curtains were tied back from the large windows, the room wasn't much brighter than the hall. It was steeped in the shadows of the poplars, and the tall panes were spotted with earth. A spider's nest of a chandelier loomed above the long table set for an elaborate dinner for six. That had been Cynthia's idea when they'd moved their parents to the rest home; she'd meant to convince any thieves that the house was still occupied, but to Jacqueline it felt like preserving a past that she'd hoped to outgrow. She remembered being made to sit up stiffly at the table, to hold her utensils just so, to cover her lap nicely with her napkin, not to speak or to make the slightest noise with any of her food. Too much of this upbringing had lodged inside her, but was that why she felt uneasy with the children in the house? "Are you taking anything out of here?" Cynthia said.

"There's nothing here for me, Cynthia. You have whatever you want and don't worry about me."

Cynthia gazed at her as they headed for the breakfast room. The chandelier stirred as the children ran above it once again, but Jacqueline told herself that was nothing like her nightmares—at least, not very like. She was unnerved to hear Cynthia exclaim "There it is."

The breakfast room was borrowing light from the large

back garden, but not much, since the overgrown expanse lay in the shadow of the house. The weighty table had spread its wings and was attended by six straight-backed ponderous chairs, but Cynthia was holding out her hands to the high chair in the darkest corner of the room. "Do you remember sitting in that?" she apparently hoped. "I think I do."

"I wouldn't," Jacqueline said.

She hadn't needed it to make her feel restricted at the table, where breakfast with her grandparents had been as formal as dinner. "Nothing here either," she declared and limped into the hall.

The mirror on the far side was discoloured too. She glimpsed the children's blurred shapes streaming up into a pendulous darkness and heard the agitated jangle of the chandelier as she made for the lounge. The leather suite looked immovable with age, and only the television went some way towards bringing the room up to date, though the screen was as blank as an uninscribed stone. She remembered having to sit silent for hours while her parents and grandparents listened to the radio for news about the war—her grandmother hadn't liked children out of her sight in the house. The dresser was still full of china she'd been forbidden to venture near, which was grey with dust and the dimness. Cynthia had been allowed to crawl around the room— indulged for being younger or because their grandmother liked babies in the house. "I'll leave you to it," she said as Cynthia followed her in.

She was hoping to find more light in the kitchen, but it didn't show her much that she wanted to see. While the refrigerator was relatively modern, not to mention tall enough for somebody to stand in, it felt out of place. The black iron range still occupied most of one wall, and the old stained marble sink projected from another. Massive cabinets and heavy chests of drawers helped box in the hulking table scored by knives. It used to remind her of an operating table, even though she hadn't known she would grow up to be a nurse. She was distracted by the children as they ran into the kitchen. "Can we have a drink?" Karen said for all of them.

175

"May we?" Valerie amended.

"Please." Once she'd been echoed Jacqueline said "I'll find you some glasses. Let the tap run."

When she opened a cupboard she thought for a moment that the stack of plates was covered by a greyish doily. Several objects as long as a baby's fingers but thinner even than their bones flinched out of sight, and she saw the plates were draped with a mass of cobwebs. She slammed the door as Karen used both hands to twist the cold tap. It uttered a dry gurgle rather too reminiscent of sounds she used to hear while working in the geriatric ward, and she wondered if the supply had been turned off. Then a gout of dark liquid spattered the sink, and a gush of rusty water darkened the marble. As Karen struggled to shut it off Valerie enquired "Did you have to drink that, auntie?"

"I had to put up with a lot you wouldn't be expected to."

"We won't, then. Aren't there any other drinks?"

"And things to eat," Brian said at once.

"I'm sure there's nothing." When the children gazed at her with various degrees of patience Jacqueline opened the refrigerator, trying not to think that the compartments could harbour bodies smaller than Brian's. All she found were a bottle of mouldering milk and half a loaf as hard as a rusk. "I'm afraid you'll have to do without," she said.

How often had her grandmother said that? Supposedly she'd been just as parsimonious before the war. Jacqueline didn't want to sound like her, but when Brian took hold of the handle of a drawer that was level with his head she couldn't help blurting "Stay away from there."

At least she didn't add "We've lost enough children." As the boy stepped back Cynthia hurried into the kitchen. "What are you doing now?"

"We don't want them playing with knives, do we?" Jacqueline said.

"I know you're too sensible, Brian."

Was that aimed just at him? As Cynthia opened the cupboards the children resumed chasing up the stairs. Presumably the creature Jacqueline had glimpsed was staying out of sight, and so were any more like it. When Cynthia made for the hall Jacqueline said "I'll be up in a minute."

Although she didn't linger in the kitchen, she couldn't leave her memories behind. How many children had her grandmother lost that she'd been so afraid of losing any more? By pestering her mother Jacqueline had learned they'd been stillborn, which had reminded her how often her grandmother told her to keep still. More than once today Jacqueline had refrained from saying that to the twins and to Brian in particular. Their clamour seemed to fill the hall and resonate all the way up the house, so that she could have thought the reverberations were shaking the mirrors, disturbing the suspended mass of darkness like a web in which a spider had come to life. "Can we go up to the top now?" Brian said.

"Please don't," Jacqueline called.

It took Cynthia's stare to establish that the boy hadn't been asking Jacqueline. "Why can't we?" Karen protested, and Valerie contributed "We only want to see."

"I'm sure you can," Cynthia said. "Just wait till we're all up there."

Before tramping into the nearest bedroom she gave her sister one more look, and Jacqueline felt as blameworthy as their grandmother used to make her feel. Why couldn't she watch over the children from the hall? She tilted her head back on her shaky neck to gaze up the stairwell. Sometimes her grandfather would raise his eyes ceilingwards as his wife found yet another reason to rebuke Jacqueline, only for the woman to say "If you look like that you'll see where you're going." Presumably she'd meant heaven, and perhaps she was there now, if there was such a place. Jacqueline imagined her sailing upwards like a husk on a wind; she'd already seemed withered all those years ago, and not just physically either. Was that why Jacqueline had thought the stillbirths must be shrivelled too? They would have ended up like that, but she needn't think about it now, if ever. She glanced towards the children and saw movement above them.

177

She must have seen the shadows of the treetops—thin shapes that appeared to start out of the corners under the roof before darting back into the gloom. As she tried to grasp how those shadows could reach so far beyond the confines of the skylight, Cynthia peered out of the nearest bedroom. "Jackie, aren't you coming to look?"

Jacqueline couldn't think for all the noise. "If you three will give us some peace for a while," she said louder than she liked. "And stay with us. We don't want you going anywhere that isn't safe."

"You heard your aunt," Cynthia said, sounding unnecessarily like a resentful child.

As Brian trudged after the twins to follow Cynthia into her grandmother's bedroom Jacqueline remembered never being let in there. Later her parents had made it their room—had tried, at any rate. While they'd doubled the size of the bed, the rest of the furniture was still her grandmother's, and she could have fancied that all the swarthy wood was helping the room glower at the intrusion. She couldn't imagine her parents sharing a bed there, let alone performing any activity in it, but she didn't want to think about such things at all. "Not for me," she said and made for the next room.

Not much had changed since it had been her grandfather's, which meant it still seemed to belong to his wife. It felt like her disapproval rendered solid by not just the narrow single bed but the rest of the dark furniture that duplicated hers, having been her choice. She'd disapproved of almost anything related to Jacqueline, not least her husband playing with their granddaughter. Jacqueline avoided glancing up at any restlessness under the roof while she crossed the landing to the other front bedroom. As she gazed at the two single beds that remained since the cot had been disposed of, the children ran to cluster around her in the doorway. "This was your room, wasn't it?" Valerie said.

"Yours and our grandma's," Karen amended.

"No," Jacqueline said, "it was hers and our mother's and father's."

In fact she hadn't been sent to the top floor until Cynthia was born. Their grandfather had told her she was going to stay with the angels, though his wife frowned at the idea. Jacqueline would have found it more appealing if she hadn't already been led to believe that all the stillbirths were living with the angels. She hardly knew why she was continuing to explore the house. Though the cast-iron bath had been replaced by a fibreglass tub as blue as the toilet and sink, she still remembered flinching from the chilly metal. After Cynthia's birth their grandmother had taken over bathing Jacqueline, scrubbing her with such relentless harshness that it had felt like a penance. When it was over at last, her grandfather would do his best to raise her spirits. "Now you're clean enough for the angels," he would say and throw her up in the air.

"If you're good the angels will catch you"—but of course he did, which had always made her wonder what would happen to her if she wasn't good enough. She'd seemed to glimpse that thought in her grandmother's eyes, or had it been a wish? What would have caught her if she'd failed to live up to requirements? As she tried to forget the conclusion she'd reached Brian said "Where did they put you, then?"

"They kept me right up at the top."

"Can we see?"

"Yes, let's," said Valerie, and Karen ran after him as well.

Jacqueline was opening her mouth to delay them when Cynthia said "You'll be going up there now, won't you? You can keep an eye on them."

It was a rebuke for not helping enough with the children, or for interfering too much, or perhaps for Jacqueline's growing nervousness. Anger at her childish fancies sent her stumping halfway up the topmost flight of stairs before she faltered. Clouds had gathered like a lifetime's worth of dust above the skylight, and perhaps that was why the top floor seemed to darken as she climbed towards it, so that all the corners were even harder to distinguish—she could almost have thought the mass of dimness was solidifying. "Where were you, auntie?" Karen said.

"In there," said Jacqueline and hurried to join them outside the nearest room.

It wasn't as vast as she remembered, though certainly large enough to daunt a small child. The ceiling stooped to the front wall, squashing the window, from which the shadows of the poplars seemed to creep up the gloomy incline to acquire more substance under the roof at the back of the room. The grimy window smudged the premature twilight, which had very little to illuminate, since the room was bare of furniture and even of a carpet. "Did you have to sleep on the floor?" Valerie said. "Were you very bad?"

"Of course not," Jacqueline declared. It felt as if her memories had been thrown out—as if she hadn't experienced them—but she knew better. She'd lain on the cramped bed hemmed in by dour furniture and cut off from everyone else in the house by the dark that occupied the stairs. She would have prayed if that mightn't have roused what she dreaded. If the babies were with the angels, mustn't that imply they weren't angels themselves? Being stillbirths needn't mean they would keep still—Jacqueline never could when she was told. Suppose they were what caught you if you weren't good? She'd felt as if she had been sent away from her family for bad behaviour. All too soon she'd heard noises that suggested tiny withered limbs were stirring, and glimpsed movements in the highest corners of the room.

She must have been hearing the poplars and seeing their shadows. As she turned away from the emptied bedroom she caught sight of the room opposite, which was full of items covered with dustsheets. Had she ever known what the sheets concealed? She'd imagined they hid some secret that children weren't supposed to learn, but they'd also reminded her of enormous masses of cobweb. She could have thought the denizens of the webs were liable to crawl out of the dimness, and she was absurdly relieved to see Cynthia coming upstairs. "I'll leave you to it," Jacqueline said. "I'll be waiting down below."

It wasn't only the top floor she wanted to leave behind. She'd remembered what she'd once done to her sister. The war had been over at last, and she'd been trusted to look after Cynthia while the adults planned the future. The sisters had only been allowed to play with their toys in the hall, where Jacqueline had done her best to distract the toddler from straying into any of the rooms they weren't supposed to enter by themselves— in fact, every room. At last she'd grown impatient with her sister's mischief, and in a wicked moment she'd wondered what would catch Cynthia if she tossed her high. As she'd thrown her sister into the air with all her strength she'd realised that she didn't want to know, certainly not at Cynthia's expense—as she'd seen dwarfish shrivelled figures darting out of every corner in the dark above the stairwell and scuttling down to seize their prize. They'd come head first, so that she'd seen their bald scalps wrinkled like walnuts before she glimpsed their hungry withered faces. Then Cynthia had fallen back into her arms, though Jacqueline had barely managed to keep hold of her. Squeezing her eyes shut, she'd hugged her sister until she'd felt able to risk seeing they were alone in the vault of the hall.

There was no use telling herself that she'd taken back her unforgivable wish. She might have injured the toddler even by catching her—she might have broken her frail neck. She ought to have known that, and perhaps she had. Being expected to behave badly had made her act that way, but she felt as if all the nightmares that were stored in the house had festered and gained strength over the years. When she reached the foot of the stairs at last she carried on out of the house.

The poplars stooped to greet her with a wordless murmur. A wind was rising under the sunless sky. It was gentle on her face—it seemed to promise tenderness she couldn't recall having experienced, certainly not once Cynthia was born. Perhaps it could soothe away her memories, and she was raising her face to it when Brian appeared in the porch. "What are you doing, auntie?"

"Just being by myself."

She thought that was pointed enough until he skipped out of the house. "Is it time now?"

Why couldn't Cynthia have kept him with her? No doubt she thought it was Jacqueline's turn. "Time for what?" Jacqueline couldn't avoid asking.

"You said you'd give me a throw."

She'd said she wouldn't then, not that she would sometime. Just the same, perhaps she could. It might be a way of leaving the house behind and all it represented to her. It would prove she deserved to be trusted with him, as she ought not to have been trusted with little Cynthia. "Come on then," she said.

As soon as she held out her arms he ran and leapt into them. "Careful," she gasped, laughing as she recovered her balance. "Are you ready?" she said and threw the small body into the air.

She was surprised how light he was, or how much strength she had at her disposal. He came down giggling, and she caught him. "Again," he cried.

"Just once more," Jacqueline said. She threw him higher this time, and he giggled louder. Cynthia often said that children kept you young, and Jacqueline thought it was true after all. Brian fell into her arms and she hugged him. "Again," he could hardly beg for giggling.

"Now what did I just say?" Nevertheless she threw him so high that her arms trembled with the effort, and the poplars nodded as if they were approving her accomplishment. She clutched at Brian as he came down with an impact that made her shoulders ache. "Higher," he pleaded almost incoherently. "Higher."

"This really is the last time, Brian." She crouched as if the stooping poplars had pushed her down. Tensing her whole body, she reared up to fling him into the pendulous gloom with all her strength.

For a moment she thought only the wind was reaching for him as it bowed the trees and dislodged objects from the foliage— leaves that rustled, twigs that scraped and rattled. But the thin shapes weren't falling, they were scurrying head first down the tree-trunks at a speed that seemed to leave time behind. Some of them had no shape they could have lived with, and some might never have had any skin. She saw their shrivelled eyes glimmer eagerly and their toothless mouths gape with an identical infantile hunger. Their combined weight bowed the lowest branches while they extended arms like withered sticks to snatch the child.

In that helpless instant Jacqueline was overwhelmed by a feeling she would never have admitted—a rush of childish glee, of utter irresponsibility. For a moment she was no longer a nurse, not even a retired one as old as some of her patients had been. She shouldn't have put Brian at risk, but now he was beyond saving. Then he fell out of the dark beneath the poplars, in which there was no longer any sign of life, and she made a grab at him. The strength had left her arms, and he struck the hard earth with a thud that put her in mind of the fall of a lid.

"Brian?" she said and bent groaning to him. "Brian," she repeated, apparently loud enough to be audible all the way up the house. She heard her old window rumble open, and Cynthia's cry: "What have you done now?" She heard footsteps thunder down the stairs, and turned away from the small still body beneath the uninhabited trees as her sister dashed out of the porch. Jacqueline had just one thought, but surely it must make a difference. "Nothing caught him," she said.

BEHIND THE DOORS

As Adam ran to the school gates he cried "Look what the teacher gave me, grandad."

It was an Advent calendar, too large to fit in his satchel. Each of the little cardboard doors had the same jolly bearded countenance, with a bigger one for Christmas Day. "Well," Summers said as the mid-December air turned his breath pale, "that's a bit late."

The ten-year-old's small plump face flushed while his eyes grew wider and moister. "He gave me it because I did best in the class."

"Then hurrah for you, Adam." Summers would have ruffled the boy's hair if it hadn't been too clipped to respond. "Don't scoff all the chocolates you should have had already," he said as Adam poked at a door with an inky finger. "We don't want your mum and dad telling me off for letting you spoil your dinner."

"I was going to give you one," the boy protested, shoving the calendar under one arm before he tramped across the road.

Summers kept a sigh to himself as he followed Adam into the park opposite Park Junior. He didn't want to upset the boy, especially when he recalled how sensitive he'd been at Adam's age. He caught up with him on the gravel path along an avenue of leafless trees, above which the sky resembled an untrodden snowfield. "How did you earn the prize, Adam?"

"The maths teacher says I should be called Add 'Em."

"Ha," said Summers. "Who's the witty teacher?"

"Mr Smart," Adam said and glanced back to see why Summers had fallen behind. "He's come to our school because Miss Logan's having a baby."

Summers overtook him beside the playground, a rubbery expanse where swings hung inert above abandoned cans of lager. "What else can you tell me about him?"

"I expect he was teaching when you were at school." With some pride in the observation Adam said "He must be as older than you than I'm old."

"Does he always give his pupils calendars like that?"

"I don't know. Shall I ask him?"

"No, don't do that. Don't mention me, that's to say anything I said."

"Didn't you ever get one?"

Summers attempted to swallow a sour stale taste. "Not that I could tell you."

Adam considered this while his expression grew more sympathetic, and then he said "You can have mine if you like."

Summers was touched by the offer but disconcerted by the prospect. "I tell you what," he said, "you give me that and I'll buy you another."

He was glad for Adam as soon as the boy handed him the calendar. Even if only the winter day made the cardboard feel cold and damp, the corners were scuffed and the colours looked faded. The jovial faces were almost as white as their beards, and the floppy red hats had turned so brown that they resembled mounds of earth perched on the heads. Summers thrust the calendar under his arm to avoid handling it further. "Let's get you home," he said.

Beyond a bowling green torn up by bicycles a Frugo Corner supermarket had replaced a small parade of shops that used to face the park. As the automatic doors let out the thin strains of a carol from the overhead loudspeakers, Summers wondered if it was too late for Advent calendars to be on sale. He couldn't bring the date to mind, and trying to add up the spent days of

December made his head feel raw. But there were calendars beside the tills, and Adam chose one swarming with creatures from outer space, though Summers was unclear what this had to do with Christmas.

His old house was half a mile away across the suburb. Along the wide quiet streets the trees looked frozen to the sky. He saw Adam to the antique door that Paul and Tina had installed within their stained-glass wrought-iron porch. "Will you be all right now?"

The boy gave the elderly formula an old-fashioned look. "I always am," he reminded Summers and slipped his key into the lock.

The streets narrowed as Summers made his way home. The houses grew shabbier and their doorbells multiplied, while the gardens were occupied by seedy cars and parts of cars. Each floor of the concrete block where he lived was six apartments long, with a view of an identical block. Once Elaine left him he'd found the house too large, and might have given it to his son even if Paul hadn't moved in with a partner.

The apartment was something like halfway along the middle balcony, two doors distant from the only other number with a tail, but Summers knew it by the green door between the red pair. He marched down the hall to the kitchen, where he stopped short of the bin. If the sweets in the calendar weren't past their edible date, why shouldn't he finish them off?

He stood it on the mantelpiece in the main room, beneath Christmas cards pinned to the nondescript wallpaper. As he searched for the first cardboard door he heard an object shift within the calendar, a sound emphasised by the silence of the hi-fi and the television and the empty suite that faced them. At last he located the door in the midst of the haphazard dates and pried it open with a fingernail. The dark chocolate behind the door was shaped like the number. "One up for me," he declared, biting it in half.

The sweet wasn't stale after all. He levered the second door open as soon as he found it, remarking "Two's not for you" as he put the number in his mouth. How many did he mean to see off? He ought to heed the warning he'd given Adam about dinner. "Three's a crowd," he commented once he managed to locate the number. That had certainly felt like the case when, having decided that Paul was old enough for her to own up, Elaine had told Summers about the other man. The taste in his mouth was growing bitter yet sickly as well, and any more of it might put him off his dinner. Perhaps it already had, but since taking early retirement he'd gained weight that he could do with losing. There was no point in eating much when he was by himself.

For a while he watched the teachers' channel, which seemed to be the only sign of intelligence on television. An hour or two of folk music on the hi-fi with the sound turned low out of consideration for the neighbours left him readier for bed. He brushed his teeth until the only flavour in his mouth was toothpaste, and then he did his best to be amused by having to count a multitude of Santas in the dark before he could fall asleep.

At least his skull wasn't crawling with thoughts of tomorrow's lessons and more lessons yet to plan, and tests to set, and conflicts to resolve or at any rate address, both among the children and within themselves. However badly he might sleep, he no longer had to set the alarm clock, never mind lying awake for hours before it went off or struggling to doze until it did. Since it was Friday he needn't bother with breakfast; he would be meeting some of his old colleagues from Dockside Primary—and then he realised he'd lost count of the weeks. His friends would be preparing for tonight's Christmas play at the school, and they'd cancelled their usual Friday lunch.

He could still do without breakfast, given the stale sweetish taste in his mouth. He brushed his teeth at length and used mouthwash before swallowing his various pills. Once he was dressed heavily enough to switch off the heating he wandered into the living-room to feed himself today's date from the Advent calendar. When at last he put his finger on the eighteenth he felt he'd earned a walk in the park.

In spring he'd liked to take his classes to the one near Dockside Primary—to imagine that their minds were budding like the trees. That was before teaching had turned into a business of filling in forms and conforming to prescribed notions as narrow as the boxes on the documents. Now he could think that the children in the schoolyard of Park Junior were caged not just by the railings but by the educational system. He couldn't see Adam, but if he ventured closer the boy might be embarrassed by his presence. What was Summers doing there at all? The children's uninhibited shouts must prove that Smart was nowhere near.

Summers watched the school until he saw teachers trooping back from lunch, but none of them looked familiar. Once the yard was empty he stood up from the bench. Ambling around the park used up some time, and then he strolled to the Dockside library, where he might have found work if the job had involved fewer numbers. People even older than he was or just as unemployed were reading the papers, and he had to content himself with a tabloid. Perhaps the prose as terse as the bitten-off headlines was all that some people could read. That was a failure of education, like the young and even younger criminals who figured in many of the reports. The paper took him a very few minutes to read, and then he hurried back to the school. He wanted to be there before anyone emerged.

Some teachers did in the midst of the flood of children, but he recognised none of them, and Adam was impatient to question him. "How many did you have?"

Summers was thrown by the irrational notion that it could have been a problem set by Smart. "Not as many as you, I expect," he retorted.

"I just had one and then we had some after dinner."

"Good boy." Summers felt a little sly for adding "Did your teacher say anything about it?"

"He wanted me to add up all the days till today in my head."

"Just this month, you mean. And did you?"

"I got it right. He said everyone should be like me."

"It wouldn't be much of a world if we were all the same, do

189

you think?" Summers sensed that the boy had more to tell. "Is that all he did?"

"Jimmy was next to top in class but he got the answer wrong."

"What happened, Adam?"

"Mr Smart gave him a calendar as well but now Jimmy has to give it back."

"I knew he couldn't change. He's the shit he always was."

Summers had done his best to lower his voice, but Adam giggled with delight. "What did you say, grandad?"

"You didn't hear it, and don't tell your parents, all right? There's no need for language like that."

"I don't mind. Some of the boys in my class say worse, and the girls."

"Then they shouldn't, even about—" Although Summers had already said too much, his nerves were prompting him. "Just so long as your teacher never tries anything like that with you," he said. "He'll have me to deal with. I've got the calendar."

"He won't, grandad. He says he wishes all the summers were like me."

Summers recalled Smart's jokes about his name, but they'd been vicious. "So long as you are, Adam," he said, and nothing more until they reached the house. "I'll see you all tomorrow," he said, which meant once a week.

He brought dinner home from the Donner Burger Pizzeria, and ate nearly half of the fish and some of the chips before thoughts of Smart stole his appetite. He'd prove he deserved to have the prize. He cleared the kitchen table and laid the calendar face up on it. The open doors stood more or less erect, and he totted up their numbers while he looked for the fourth. There it eventually was, and he rewarded himself with the contents as he added to the total in his head and carried on the search. Ten became fifteen, and he swallowed to make room for the five in his mouth. He needn't eat any more chocolates; he certainly shouldn't see off however many led to today's, even if it would feel like saving Adam from any reason to be grateful to the teacher. Twenty-what, twenty-one, twenty-more... At the eighth he lost count and had to start again. The relentless glare of the fluorescent tube overhead intensified his sense of sitting an examination, but it was only a mock one. One, three, six, ten… This time he progressed as far as the eleventh, and then searching through the numerical maze drove the total out of his head. He did his best to add up the numbers without looking for them, but he'd tallied fewer than many when he found he had to see them. He tried saying them aloud as he found them and repeating the latest total over and over while he searched for the next number, though he had to keep raising his voice to hold the count in his head. At last he arrived at the date and shouted the total, not loud enough to bother the neighbours, he hoped. He was about to feed himself one more sweet when he wondered if he'd arrived at the right answer.

He added all the numbers up again, and the total was even louder than the process. It was a shout of frustration, because the amount was twenty-two less than his previous answer, which couldn't even mean he'd missed a number out. He tried another count, though his throat was raw with shouting before he came to the end. Figuring out the difference aggravated the headache that was already making his vision throb. The total was nineteen more than the last one, which meant it was three less than he'd added up in the first place, but why did he need to know any of this? His head felt as if it was hatching numbers, a sensation that exacerbated a greasy sweetish sickness in his mouth. He stumbled to the bathroom to gulp water and splash some on his face. When none of this seemed to help he groped his way into the bedroom, but his thoughts came to bed with him. The year Smart had taken him for mathematics had been one of the worst of his life.

"I'm here to make you smart like me," the teacher had informed the class. "If I don't do it one way I'll do it another." With his plump petulant constantly flushed face he'd resembled an overgrown schoolboy, and he'd revealed a schoolboy's ingenuity at inventing tortures, tweaking a tuft of hair at the nape of the neck to lift his victim on tiptoe and hold them there until he'd delivered a lecture to them or about them. He'd called his favourite victim Summer because, he'd said in anything but praise, the boy was so singular. Before long Summers had spent every school night lying awake in terror of the next day, but he'd been too ashamed to tell his parents and afraid that any intervention would only make the situation worse. He'd lost count of how often he'd been singled out before the first of December, when Smart asked him to add up the days of the month.

Everyone had found his bewilderment hilarious. He'd had to risk answering at last, and Smart had given him a round of dry applause. When he'd produced an advent calendar from his briefcase Summers had felt encouraged until he was called to the front of the class to find the date. Long before he did, the teacher was declaring "Summer means to keep us all here till next summer." After that every mathematics lesson began with Summers on his feet to announce the total to date. He'd succeeded for over a week, having lost even more sleep to be sure of the answers, but he'd gone wrong on the ninth and on every school day for the rest of December. He'd still had to find the day's sweet as he stood on tiptoe, raised ever higher by the agonising drag at his neck, and then he'd had to drop the chocolate into the bin.

His anger at the memory kept him awake. Counting Father Christmases no longer helped, and he tried adding up punches to Smart's cruel smug face. That was satisfying enough to let Summers doze, only to waken in a rage, having realised that he didn't need to find the numbers on the calendar to count them. He turned it on its face and listed all the dates in a column on a pad—if he hadn't felt that mobile phones involved too many numbers he would have had a calculator to use now. He tapped each date with the pen as he picked his way down the column. A smell of paint threatened to revive his headache, but eventually he had a number to write at the foot of the last row and another to add at the top of the next one. At last he had the full amount, and muttered something like a prayer before adding up the dates again. He did the sum a third time to be certain, and then he rewarded himself with a bath. Three times in a row he'd arrived at the same answer.

He oughtn't to have tried to prove he could repeat the calculation in his head. By the time he succeeded, the water was too cold to stay in. He meant only to glance at the bedside clock to see how soon he ought to leave for Paul's and Tina's, but he was already late. He almost snagged the padding of his jacket with the zip as he hurried out, to be hindered by tins of paint on the balcony. His left-hand neighbour's door had turned green. "Just brightening the place up for you," the overalled workman said, sounding rather too much like a nurse in a sickroom.

Summers had scarcely rung the bell in the wrought-iron porch when Adam ran to open the door. "I said grandad said he was coming."

Paul emerged in a chef's apron from the kitchen as Tina appeared from the dining-room with an electric corkscrew. "I didn't mean to keep you waiting," Summers said.

"Don't give it a thought." To his wife Paul said "I told you he'd never mistake the date."

"He's just being silly, Teddy," Tina assured Summers, which only made him wonder what else she'd said about him. "Take your grandfather's coat, Adam," she said and blinked at Summers. "Haven't you been well?"

"Perfectly," Summers said, feeling too defensive to be truthful. "What makes you ask?"

"You look as if you could do with feeding," Paul said.

"You can have one of my chocolates if you like," said Adam.

"I hope you thanked grandpa for the calendar," Paul said. "I never had one at your age."

"I gave grandad one as well."

"Poor mite," Tina said to Paul, and less satirically "That was kind of you, Adam."

"He gave me mine so he could have the one the teacher gave me."

"I don't think I understand."

She was gazing at Paul, but Summers felt interrogated.

"Perhaps we could discuss it later," he said.

"Adam, you can set the table," Tina said as if it were a treat, and gestured the adults into the lounge. Once the door was shut she said "What's the situation?"

"I shouldn't really think there is one," Summers tried saying.

"It sounds like one to us," Tina said without glancing at Paul. "Why did you want Adam's present?"

"I just took it off him because it looked a bit ancient. Exactly like his grandfather, you could say."

"You mean you binned it."

Summers might have said so, but suppose Adam learned of it? "I didn't do that, no. I've still got most of it."

"Most," Paul said like some kind of rebuke.

"I ate a few chocolates." Summers felt driven to come up with the number. "Five of them," he said with an effort. "I'm sure they're nowhere near as good as the ones I gave Adam."

"They can't be so bad," Tina said, "if you saw five of them off."

"All right, it wasn't only that. I just didn't want Adam taking anything from that man."

"Which man?" Tina demanded as Paul said even more sharply "Why?"

"The maths man. I hope he won't be there much longer. Smart," Summers made himself add and wiped his lips. "I wouldn't trust him with a dog, never mind children."

"What are you saying?" Tina cried as Paul opened his mouth.

"I had him for a year at Adam's age. It felt like the rest of my life." Summers saw he had to be specific so that they wouldn't imagine worse. "He loved hurting people," he said.

"He'd never get away with that these days at school," Paul protested.

"There are more ways than physical. Let's just hope Adam stays his favourite."

Tina gave Summers a long look before enquiring "Have you said any of this to Adam?"

"I wouldn't put him under any pressure, but I do think you

should keep a close eye on the situation."

"I thought you said there wasn't one," Tina said and opened the door to the hall. "We'll be discussing it further."

Summers gathered that he wouldn't be involved, and couldn't argue while Adam might hear. He offered to help but was sent into the dining-room, where Tina served him a glass of wine while his son and grandson brought in dinner. He saw they meant to make him feel at home, but every Saturday he felt as if he'd returned to find the house almost wholly unfamiliar, scattered with a few token items to remind him he'd once lived there—mostly photographs with Elaine in them. At least he could enthuse about Paul's casserole, but this gave Adam an excuse to ask "Do you know what it's called, grandad?"

"Adam," his mother warned him.

"It's not called Adam." Perhaps the boy was misbehaving because he'd been excluded from the conversation in the lounge. "It's cock off, Ann," he said.

"That's very rude," Tina said, "and not at all clever."

"Maybe it's cocker fan."

"That's rude too." Apparently in case it wasn't, Tina insisted "And silly as well."

"Then I expect it's cock—"

"Now, Adam, you've already impressed us with your schoolwork," Summers said as he thought a grandparent should. "You're an example to us all. You're even one to me."

"How am I, grandad?"

"I've been doing some sums of my own. I can tell you what the month adds up to so far." When nobody asked for the answer Summers felt not much better than distrusted, but he'd repeated the amount to himself all the way to the house. "One hundred and eighty-one," he said with some defiance.

Adam squeezed his eyes shut for a moment. "No it isn't, grandad."

"I'm sure it is, you know." On the way to growing desperate Summers said "Hang on, I've left today out, haven't I?"

"That's not it, grandad. One hundred and ninety, you should

have said."

"I don't think that can be right," Summers said to the boy's parents as well. "That's ten times whatever it's ten times, nineteen, isn't it, of course."

"I should have thought the last thing you'd want to do," Tina said, "is undermine his confidence."

"He's undermining mine," Summers complained, but not aloud. He was silent while he tried to make the days add up to Adam's total. They either fell short or overshot it, and the need to carry on some sort of conversation didn't help, any more than the drinks during and after the meal did.

The streets were full of numbers—on the doors of houses and the gates, on the front and back of every car and, if they were for sale, in their windows too. There were just three digits to each registration plate, and he tried to add up each group as it came in sight. He was absurdly grateful to reach home, although the orange lights on the balcony had turned his door and its neighbours identically black. "Nine," he repeated, "nine, nine," and felt as if he were calling for aid by the time he managed to identify the door.

The Advent calendar was still lying on its numbers, and he hoped that would keep them out of his head—but they were only waiting for him to try to sleep, and started awake whenever he did. They got out of bed with him in the morning and followed him into the bath. Couldn't he just add today to Adam's total? That seemed too much like copying an answer in an examination, and in any case he wanted to learn how Adam had arrived at the result. When it continued to elude him he floundered out of the bath.

He did his best to linger over dressing, then listed all the numbers on a new sheet of the pad, pronouncing them aloud to make certain he missed none. Today's date could be added once he'd written down the total. He poked each number with the ballpoint as the amount swelled in his head, only for the pen to hover above the space beneath the line he'd drawn at the foot of the column. He went down the list of figures again and again, jabbing at them until they looked as though they'd contracted a disease. He announced every amount on the way to the total—he might almost have been uttering some kind of Sunday prayer—but none of this was much use. One hundred and seventy-nine, one hundred and ninety-three, one hundred and eighty seven... He hadn't hit upon the same amount twice, let alone the one Adam had told him, when somebody rang the raucous doorbell.

He thought they might have come to complain about his noise, especially once he noticed it was dark. He couldn't leave the table until the sum was done. "One hundred and ninety," he said, but that wasn't the whole of the total. "Seven," he yelled in a rage, "one hundred and ninety-seven," and shoved back his chair to tramp along the hall.

He was preparing to apologise, if hardly to explain, but Tina was outside. "Well, this is a surprise," he said. "Come in."

"I won't, thanks, Teddy. I just came to tell you—" With a frown that Summers felt was aimed to some extent at him, she turned to say "Adam, I told you to wait in the car."

"I wanted to say goodbye to grandad."

"Why," Summers said in bewilderment, "where's anybody going?"

"Adam will be going home with a friend next week." Apparently in recompense, Tina added "You'll still be coming to us for Christmas."

"You mean I'm not wanted for picking up Adam from school."

"I've explained the situation."

As Summers managed not to retort that he suspected the opposite, Adam said "Grandad, did you go to school when you were a baby?"

"I wasn't quite that young. Why do you ask?"

"Grandma said you were a baby when Mr Smart had you at school."

Elaine had been in the same class—Summers used to thank their schooldays for bringing them together. Now he was almost too enraged to ask "What else did she say about me?"

"We won't talk about it now if you don't mind," Tina said,

"and I hope it won't spoil Christmas either. Just say goodbye to your grandfather till then, Adam."

"Bye, grandad," the boy said. "You got something nice from Mr Smart, didn't you? All the chocolates."

"I won't argue," Summers said and watched Tina shoo Adam back to the car. When he returned to the kitchen the clamour of numbers and emotions in his head robbed him of the ability to think. Turning the calendar over didn't help, especially since every open door had been flattened shut. He stared at however many identical idiotically grinning faces there were, and the pad swarming with diseased amounts, and all at once his mind seemed to clear. Had Tina freed him? Now that he wouldn't be associated with Adam, surely he could deal with the teacher.

He didn't feel beset by numbers once he went to bed. He slept, and in the morning he was able to ignore the calculations on the pad. He listened to symphonies on the radio until it was time to head for Park Junior, and was in a shelter with a view of the school several minutes before the last bell. When the children streamed out under the grey sky, the explosion of colours and chatter felt like a promise of spring. He was cut off from it, skulking in a corner so that Adam wouldn't notice him. Soon he saw his grandson with another boy, and they set about kicking a ball as they followed a young woman into the park.

As Summers turned his face to the wall to make sure he wasn't recognised, he felt like a schoolboy sent to stand in the corner. Surely Adam hadn't looked happier than he did when his grandfather met him. As soon as the thumps of the football passed the shelter Summers peered towards the school. Suppose the teacher had sneaked away unobserved? Summers hurried to the railings opposite the school but could see nobody he knew. The doors let out some teachers and then even more he didn't recognise, and he was clenching his shaky fists in frustration by the time a man emerged into the deserted schoolyard.

He was thin and bent, and as grey as the sky—his suit, his thinning hair, the smoke of the cigarette he lit before stalking to the gates. For a moment Summers wondered if the teacher was too old to bother with—even old enough to be given some grudging respect—and then he saw that Smart had become the vicious old man he'd resembled forty years ago. Any hesitation felt too much like fear, and he barely managed to unclench his fists as he strode out of the park. "Mr Smart," he said in triumph. "Can I ask you a question?"

The teacher stared at him with no more interest than emotion. "Are you a parent?"

"That and a lot more." Summers was determined to relish the confrontation. "Can you tell me what December adds up to so far?" he said.

"Are you asking for one of my pupils?"

"No, I'm speaking for myself. I've learned to do that." Summers struggled to contain his rage as he enquired "Can you do it in your head?"

"Quite obviously I can." Smart took a measured puff at the cigarette and exhaled smoke, disturbing a stained hair in his left nostril. "It's two hundred and thirty-one," he said, "if that's of any consequence to you."

"Not so sure of yourself for a bit there, were you? That's a taste of what it feels like."

"I fear you have the advantage of me," Smart said and made to step around him.

"You bet I have. It's taken long enough but it was worth the wait." Summers sidestepped to block his way. "Don't you know me yet?" he demanded. "Tortured so many youngsters you've lost count, have you?"

"What on earth do you imagine you're referring to?" Smart narrowed his already pinched eyes at a clatter of cans in the park, where Summers had seen teenagers drinking lager on the swings. "That's what comes of undermining discipline in school," Smart said. "They'd never behave like that if we were still allowed to touch them."

"It's your sort who undermined it. Made everyone who suffered from the likes of you want to make sure nobody ever does again. It's your fault it's so hard to keep discipline now. It's swine like you that lost teachers their respect."

Smart lifted the cigarette towards his face but seemed uncertain where his mouth was. "Did I have you at school?"

"Recognised one of your victims at last, have you? One of the ones you could touch. Do you dream about touching children, you filthy shit? I've often thought that's what your sort wanted to get up to. You took it out on children because they made you want to fiddle with them. I bet having them at your mercy worked you up as well." Was Smart's face turning grey just with the winter twilight? "Just remember I know where you are now," Summers murmured. "If I even think you're mistreating anyone I'll make it my business to lose you your job. What are you going to do with your fag? Thinking of using it on me, are you? Just try and I'll stick it somewhere that'll make you scream."

Smart's mouth had begun to work soundlessly, and Summers was reminded of a masticating animal. The cigarette looked close to dropping from the man's fingers, which were shaking the ash loose. Had Summers gone too far? Not unless Smart could identify him, and surely the man would have done so aloud. "Have the Christmas you deserve," Summers told him and turned away from him.

When he glanced back from the park he saw the teacher standing just where he'd left him. Smart raised his hand as though bidding him some kind of farewell, but he was finding his mouth with the cigarette. "Who's the baby now?" Summers muttered. "Go on, suck your dummy. Suck yourself to death."

He felt exhilarated as a schoolboy who'd got away with a prank. He might almost have boasted to the teenage drinkers on the swings. If he had any doubts about how he'd spoken to the teacher, they left him as soon as he saw his old house. It was Smart's fault that he wasn't trusted to bring Adam home, and when he reached the apartment block he might have thought the teacher had played another trick. The glare of the declining sun showed him that both doors flanking his had turned green, so that every door on the balcony was the same colour.

"It's nine, you swine," he said, he hoped not too loud, and let himself in once he was sure of the number on the door. Smart couldn't undermine his confidence any longer, and so he tore the calculations off the pad and flung the spotty wad of paper in the bin. The calendar was a trophy, all the more so since Smart didn't know he had it. He microwaved a cottage pie and a packet of vegetables, and gobbled the lot like a growing boy. He could have thought he was growing up at last, having dealt with the teacher.

How many doors had he already opened on the calendar? He wasn't going to reopen them; taking chocolates at random was one more way to taunt the teacher. "Unlucky for you," he mumbled as he crunched the thirteenth sweet, and "That's how old you like them, is it?" on prising open the tenth door. He might have finished all the chocolates except for not wanting to make himself sick. The best celebration would be a good night's sleep.

At first he didn't understand why it kept being interrupted. Whenever he jerked awake he felt as if he'd heard a sound, unless he'd had a thought. He stayed in bed late; he couldn't be seen with Adam at the school in case Smart took some revenge. What if he'd simply made the teacher even more vindictive? Suppose Smart had recognised him after all and meant to take it out on Adam? A sour stale taste urged Summers to the bathroom. Water didn't rid him of the taste, and he stumbled to the kitchen, only to falter in the doorway. More compartments than he'd opened on the calendar last night stood open now—six doors, no, seven. Those that had reopened were the five he'd previously emptied. With its upright tabs the calendar resembled a miniature graveyard.

"I wish it was yours, you swine," Summers muttered. He was growing more anxious, and once he was dressed he headed for Park Junior. Soon he saw Adam, though not soon enough for his nerves. The boy was chasing other boys in the schoolyard and being chased, and looked entirely carefree, but had he encountered Smart yet? For a moment Summers had the irrational notion that the teacher was not merely hiding like himself but skulking at his back. There was nothing in the corner of the shelter except a scattering of cigarette butts on the floor and on the end of the bench.

Once the schoolyard was deserted Summers lingered in the shelter, listening for Smart's cold high voice—straining his ears so hard that he thought he heard it amid the scrape of windblown leaves on gravel. The idea that Smart was still at large in the school made him want to storm into the school and report the swine to the headmistress—to say whatever would get rid of him. To overcome the compulsion he had to retreat out of sight of the school. Long before the final bell he was back in the shelter. He hadn't counted the cigarette ends, and so he couldn't tell if they'd multiplied or even whether they'd been rearranged like an aid to a child's arithmetic. He spied on the schoolyard until he saw Adam, who looked happier than ever. Summers hid his face in the corner while the boys and their football clamoured past, and then he turned back to the school. He watched until the doors finished swinging at last, but there was no sign of Smart in the secretive dusk.

Had he been moved to another school? "So long as you're safe, Adam," Summers murmured, but the comment seemed to sum up how little he'd achieved. He was so preoccupied that he nearly tried to let himself into the wrong flat. Of course the number on the door was upside down. He shut his door and tramped along the hall to stare at the Advent calendar as if it might inspire him. The shadows of the cardboard markers appeared to deepen the empty compartments, and he was seeing them as trenches when the doorbell rang.

Paul's expression was oddly constrained. "Well, you'll be pleased," he said.

"You're trusting me with Adam again."

Paul took a breath but didn't speak at once. "The teacher you had trouble with," he said, "you can forget about him."

"Why would I want to do that?"

"He's no longer with us." Since Summers didn't react Paul added "He's dead."

"Good heavens," Summers said, although he hoped those

weren't involved. "When did that come about?"

"He had some kind of stroke when he was driving home yesterday. People saw him lose control and his car went into the front of a bus."

"That's unexpected." Summers did his best to control his face but thought it prudent to admit "I can't say I'm too distressed."

"I wasn't expecting you to be."

"So I'll be collecting Adam from school tomorrow, yes?"

Paul made another breath apparent on the way to saying "Let's leave it for this week, shall we? We'll sort it out after Christmas."

"Is it you who doesn't want me looking after him?" When Paul was silent Summers said "I didn't know I'd raised you not to stand up for yourself."

His son paused but said "Mum makes it sound as if you didn't for yourself at school."

"Then she'd better know I've changed. Just hope you never find out how much, like—" Summers' rage was close to robbing him of discretion. "Go home to your family. I'll leave you all alone till Christmas," he said and shut the door.

Any qualms he might have suffered over causing Smart's demise were swallowed by his fury with Elaine and Tina and, yes, Paul. He stalked into the kitchen to bare his teeth at the calendar. "I wish I'd been there," he said in a voice that wasn't far from Smart's. "Did you count the seconds when you saw what was coming? It'd just about sum you up." Talking wasn't enough, and he poked a door open at random. "Revenge is sweet, don't you think? Revenge is a sweet," he said and shoved the pair of digits he'd uncovered into his mouth.

Perhaps it was too sweet, the chocolate plaque bulging with numbers. He didn't much care for the taste that filled his mouth once the unexpectedly brittle object crumbled like a lump of ash. As the sweetness immediately grew stale he had the impression that it masked a less palatable flavour. He grabbed a bottle of brandy still half full from last Christmas and poured some into the Greatest Granddad mug Adam had given him. A mouthful seared away part of the tastes, and another did more of the job, but he still felt as if some unpleasant sensation lay in wait for him. Perhaps he was exhausted, both emotionally and by insomnia. He could celebrate the end of Smart with a good night's sleep.

His nerves didn't let him. He kept thinking he'd heard a sound, unless he was about to hear one, or was it too stealthy to be audible? He didn't know how often he'd opened his aching eyes to confront the cluttered darkness before he saw a pair of red eyes staring back at him. They were two of the digits on the bedside clock until one pinched into a single line. It was a minute after midnight, and a day closer to Christmas.

The thought sent him out of bed. While he wouldn't be putting any of the contents of the calendar anywhere near his mouth, perhaps he could relax once he'd located the date and opened the door. As the fluorescent tube jittered alight he could have imagined he glimpsed a flap staggering upright on the calendar. He peered at the swarm of identically mirthful faces in search of the date. How many of the doors were open? Seven, or there should be, and he prodded them while counting them aloud. However often he added them up there was one more, and it was today's.

Could he have opened the door and forgotten? Was that a blurred fingerprint on the chocolate? He grabbed the calendar and shook the sweet into the bin. He was tempted to stuff the calendar in as well, if that wouldn't have felt too much like continuing to fear the teacher. "Do your worst," he mumbled, still not entirely awake. Throwing the calendar on the table, he sat down to watch.

Before long the lids of some of the compartments began to twitch. It was his debilitated vision or the shaking of the table, if not both. Whenever his head lurched more or less upright, having slid off his fists that were propping it up, he had to force his eyes wide and count the open doors afresh. "Eight," he kept declaring, even when someone thumped on the wall of the kitchen. "Had enough for one day, have you?" he retorted, though he wasn't sure to whom. He didn't notice when the fluorescent glow merged with pallid sunlight, but it seemed to be an excuse for retreating into bed.

It was almost dark by the time he gave up dozing. He had enough food to last until Christmas—enough that he needn't be troubled by the identical doors on the balcony. He ate some of a bowl of cereal while he glared a raw-eyed challenge at the calendar, and then he listened to a carol concert on the radio—it was many years since he'd heard carollers at his or anybody's door. The music lulled him almost to sleep until the choir set about amassing the twelve days of Christmas and all that they brought. Even after he switched off the radio, the numbers kept demanding to be totalled in his head.

Well before midnight he was at the kitchen table, where he stood the bedside clock next to the calendar. The digits twitched into various shapes on their way to turning into eyes, which he could have imagined were refusing to blink because they were determined to watch him, even without pupils. At last—it seemed much longer than a minute—the final digit shrank, but nothing else moved. Didn't that last number look more like an I than a 1? Summers was attempting to ignore it when it crumbled into segments, but he mustn't feel compelled to count them; he had to catch the calendar opening today's door, or see whatever happened. He gripped his temples and dug his thumbs into his cheeks, feeling the bones of his skull. His face began to ache, but not enough to keep him alert, though he didn't know he'd dozed until his head jerked up. "Eight," he said when at last he thought he was sure of the number. He oughtn't to start bothering the neighbours again, and there was a way to avoid it—by tearing all the open doors off the calendar. They and the boxy holes they left put him in mind of a vandalised graveyard, an idea that felt capable of shrinking Smart no larger than an insect. "That's all you are. That's all you ever were," Summers muttered as his head drooped.

When had he eaten last? No wonder he was weak. At least he didn't need to leave the table to find food. He dragged the calendar to him and fumbled a door open. Some instinct must have guided him, since it was the first unopened one—the number of his flat. As he bit the chocolate, the coiled object on the little slab writhed into life. Its tail slithered from between his teeth, and it wormed down his throat as though it had rediscovered its burrow in the earth.

His head wavered up, and he clapped a hand over his mouth. No more doors were open after all—only eight, he was able to believe once he'd counted the gaping compartments several times. The calendar wasn't as close to him as he'd imagined, and he might have been sure he'd dreamed the grisly incident except for an odd taste in his mouth. Perhaps it was merely stale and sweetish, or was there an underlying earthiness? It sent him to gulp brandy straight from the bottle, and he turned back to the table just in time to glimpse a movement. A lid had been lifted, although it was instantly still.

"Caught you," Summers cried. It bore today's date. The prize it had exposed was marked with scratches, as if someone had been clawing at it for want of a better victim. He shook the chocolate into the bin and tore off the date. "Finished for today?" he demanded, but couldn't interpret the lack of an answer. He was sinking shakily onto the chair when he glanced at the clock. The number beside the blind red eyes was his apartment's. No, it was upside down with its tail in the air, but it still showed he'd spent the night in front of the calendar.

He felt as if Smart had robbed him of all sense of time as well as any confidence about numbers. He would be no fun on Christmas Day if he'd had so little sleep. "You won't spoil this Christmas as well," he vowed. Suppose the presents for his family and Tina were ruined somehow? He threw the calendar on its face and pinned it down with a saucepan so heavy that his arms shook. Once he'd returned the clock to the bedside table he fetched the presents from the living-room and lined them up in bed before he joined them.

He had to keep reminding himself that the muffled rustling came from the presents, especially whenever it wakened him after dark. His lurches into consciousness were too reminiscent of the Christmas he'd spent dreading next year's days with Smart, far too many to count—shivering awake to realise the worst nightmare wasn't in his sleep. The nights leading up to his retirement had been just as bad, and Smart's fault too. He saw the eyes blink wide to stare towards him, and managed to name the digits next to them. "One and two, that's three to you," he mouthed, and "Happy Christmas" when the right eye narrowed to a slit. He didn't need to go and look at the calendar; surely he would hear if anything happened. He lay awake listening, and tried not to move in case that disturbed the wrappings of the presents, though why should he fear being heard? It was almost dawn by the time he went to look.

The light in the fluorescent tube buzzed and fluttered like an insect and eventually grew still. Summers used both hands to remove the saucepan and then turned over the calendar. It put him in mind of lifting a slab—one from beneath which something might scuttle or crawl. Nothing else stirred, however. That wasn't why he let the calendar fall on its back with a hollow flimsy sound. All the numbers on the remaining doors were blurred beyond any possibility of recognition, while the festive faces were no more than blotches with misshapen blobs for eyes. Had age overtaken the calendar? Summers only needed to open today's door to finish celebrating his triumph. He could open all of them to find it if he had to—but prising one open revealed that the sweet was as unrecognisably deformed as the number on the door. The next was the same, and its neighbour, and he felt as if they were showing how deranged Smart had always been or was now. At last Summers wakened enough to realise that he didn't have to try every door; today's was larger. As soon as he located it he dug his fingertip under the lid.

His nail sank into a substance too firm for chocolate but in another way not firm enough, and then the object moved beneath his finger. As he recoiled, the door sprang up, exposing a greyish piebald surface in which a rounded lump bulged. He was trying to grasp the sight when the lump into which he'd poked his finger blinked again and glared at him. Even though it had already begun to wither and grow discoloured, he knew it all too well.

He swept the calendar onto the floor and trampled on it, feeling more than cardboard give way underfoot. He might have been stamping on a mask, but not an empty one. Once it was crushed absolutely flat he watched to be sure that nothing crept from beneath it, not even a stain, and then he retreated to the bedroom.

Suppose he'd set the madness free? He didn't like to keep the presents so close to the remains of the calendar. In any case it might be wise to set off for his old house—he was afraid it could take him some time to find. At least he hadn't undressed for bed. He clutched the presents to his chest and hurried onto the balcony, beyond which a greyish light was starting to take hold of the world. He gazed at his door until he succeeded in fixing at least the shape of the number in his mind. "You're the one with your tail hanging down," he said.

It was daylight now, however grey, and he did his best to hasten through the streets. He shouldn't be distracted by trying to count Christmas trees in windows, let alone Christmas lights. Today's date ought to be enough for him. "Two and five and you're alive," he told some children before they fled across the road. He mustn't frighten anyone. Among the reasons he'd retired had been the fear of needing to resemble Smart so as to teach.

He came to his old road at last, only to feel as if someone had gone ahead of him to jumble all the numbers. He just had to locate his old home, not remember which number it was. He didn't have to count his way to it, and he was surprised how soon he found the wrought-iron porch. He hugged the presents—one, two and another—as he thumbed the bellpush. "Two and five and you're alive," he carolled until the boy ran to open the door. Summers was about to hand him the presents when the boy turned his back. "I don't know what he wants," he called. "It's some old man."

HOLDING THE LIGHT

A s his cousin followed him into the Frugoplex lobby Tom saw two girls from school. Out of uniform and in startlingly short skirts they looked several years older. He hoped his leather jacket performed that trick for him, in contrast to the duffle coat Lucas was wearing. Since the girls were giggling at the cinema staff dressed as Halloween characters, he let them see him laugh too. "Hey, Lezly," he said in his deepest voice. "Hey, Dianne."

"Don't come near us if you've got a cold," Lezly protested, waving a hand that was bony with rings in front of her face.

"It's just how boys his age talk," Dianne said far too much like a sympathetic adult and blinked her sparkly purple eyelids. "Who's your friend, Tom?"

"It's my cousin Lucas."

"Hey, Luke."

Lezly said it too and held out her skull-ringed hand, at which Lucas stared as if it were an inappropriate present. "He's like that," Tom mumbled but refrained from pointing at his own head. "Don't mind him."

"Maybe he doesn't want to give you his germs, Lezly." To the boys Dianne said "What are you going to see?"

"*Vampire Dating Agency,*" Lucas said before Tom could make a choice.

"That's for kids," Lezly objected. "We're not seeing any films with them."

"We don't have to either, do we, Lucas?" Tom said in a bid to stop his face from growing hotter. "What are you two seeing?"

"*Cheerleaders with Guts,*" Dianne said with another quick glittery blink.

"We can't," Lucas informed everyone. "Nobody under fifteen's allowed."

Tom glared at him as the girls did. At least none of the staff dealing with the noisy queues appeared to have heard the remark. Until that moment Tom had been able to prefer visiting the cinema to any of the other activities their parents had arranged for the boys over the years—begging for sweets at neighbours' houses, ducking for apples and a noseful of water, carving pumpkins when Lucas's received most of the praise despite being so grotesque only out of clumsiness. Now that the parents had reluctantly let them outgrow all this Tom seemed to be expected to take even more care of his cousin. Perhaps Lucas sensed his resentment for once, because he said "We don't have to go to a film."

"Who doesn't?" said Dianne.

Tom wanted to say her and Lezly too, but first he had to learn "Where, then?"

"The haunted place." When nobody admitted to recognising it Lucas said "Grinfields."

"Where the boy and girl killed themselves together, you mean," Lezly said.

"No, he did first," Dianne said, "and she couldn't live without him."

It was clear that Lucas wasn't interested in these details, and he barely let her finish. "My mum and dad say they did it because they watched films you aren't supposed to watch."

"My parents heard they were always shopping," Tom made haste to contribute. "Them and their families spent lots of money they didn't have and all it did was leave them thinking nothing was worth anything."

That was his father's version. Perhaps it sounded more like a gibe at the girls than he was afraid Lucas's comment had. "Why do you want us to go there, Luke?" Dianne said.

"Who's Luke?"

"I told you," Tom said in some desperation, "he's like that."

"No I'm not, I'm like Lucas."

At such times Tom understood all too well why his cousin was bullied at school. There was also the way Lucas stared at anybody unfamiliar as if they had to wait for him to make up his mind about them, and just now his pasty face—far spottier than Tom's and topped with unruly red hair—was a further drawback. Nevertheless Dianne said "Are you sure you don't want to see our film?"

She was speaking to Tom, but Lucas responded. "We can't. We've been told."

"I haven't," Tom muttered. He watched the girls join the queue for the ticket desk manned by a tastefully drooling vampire in a cloak, and then he turned on Lucas. "We need to switch our phones off. We're in the cinema."

Accuracy mattered most to Lucas. Once he'd done as he was told Tom said "Let's go, and not to the kids' film either."

A frown creased Lucas's pudgy forehead. "Which one, then?"

"None of them. We'll go where you wanted," Tom said, leading the way out into the Frugall retail park.

More vehicles than he thought he could count in a weekend were lined up beneath towering lamps as white as the moon. In that light people's faces looked as pallid as Lucas's, but took on colour once they reached the shops, half a mile of which surrounded the perimeter. As Tom came abreast of a Frugelectric store he said "We'll need a light."

Lucas peered at the lanky lamps, and yet again Tom wondered what went on inside his cousin's head. "A torch," he resented having to elucidate.

"There's one at home."

"That's too far." Before Lucas could suspect he didn't want their parents learning where the boys would be Tom said "You'll have to buy one."

He was determined his cousin would pay, not least for putting the girls off. He watched Lucas select the cheapest flashlight and load it with batteries, then drop a ten-pound note beside the till so as to avoid touching the checkout girl's hand. He made her place his change there for him to scoop up while Tom took the flashlight wrapped in a flimsy plastic bag. "That's mine. I bought it," Lucas said at once.

"You hold it then, baby." Tom stopped just short of uttering the last word, though his face was hot again. "Look after it," he said and stalked out of the shop.

They were on the far side of Frugall from their houses and the school. An alley between a Frugranary baker's and a Frugolé tapas bar led to a path around the perimeter. A twelve-foot wall behind the shops and restaurants cut off most of the light and the blurred vague clamour of the retail park. The path was deserted apart from a few misshapen skeletal loiterers nuzzling the wall or propped against the chain-link fence alongside Grinfields Woods. They were abandoned shopping trolleys, and the only sound apart from the boys' padded footsteps was the rustle of the plastic bag.

Tom thought they might have to follow the path all the way to the housing estate between Grinfields and the retail park, but soon they came to a gap in the fence. Lucas dodged through it so fast that he might have forgotten he wasn't alone. As Tom followed he saw his own shadow emerge from a block of darkness fringed with outlines of wire mesh. The elongated shadows of trees were reaching for the larger dark. By the time the boys found the official path through the woods they were almost beyond the glare from the retail park, and Lucas switched on the flashlight. "That isn't scary," he declared as Tom's shadow brandished its arms.

Tom was simply frustrated that Lucas hadn't bothered to remove the flashlight from the bag. He watched his cousin peer both ways along the dim path like a child showing how much care he took about crossing a road, and then head along the stretch that vanished into darkness. The sight of Lucas swaggering off as though he didn't care whether he was followed did away with any qualms Tom might have over scaring him more than he would like. He tramped after Lucas through the woods that looked as if the dark had formed itself into a cage, and almost collided with him as the blurred jerky light swerved off the path to flutter across the trees to the left. "What's pulling something along?" Lucas seemed to feel entitled to be told.

"It's got a rope," Tom said, but didn't want to scare Lucas too much too soon. "No, it's only water."

He'd located it in the dried-up channel out of sight below the slope beyond the trees. It must be a lingering trickle of rain, which had stopped before dark, unless it was an animal or bird among the fallen leaves. "Make your mind up," Lucas complained and swung the light back to the path.

The noise ceased as Tom tramped after him. Perhaps it had gone underground through the abandoned irrigation channel. Without warning—certainly with none from Lucas—the flashlight beam sprang off the ragged stony path and flew into the treetops. "Is it laughing at us?" Lucas said.

Tom gave the harsh shrill sound somewhere ahead time to make itself heard. "What do you think?".

"Of course it's not," Lucas said as if his cousin needed to be put right. "Birds can't laugh."

Once more Tom suspected Lucas wasn't quite as odd as he liked everyone to think, although that was odd in itself. When the darkness creaked again he said "That's not a bird, it's a tree."

Lucas might have been challenging someone by striding up the path to jab the beam at the treetops. As he disappeared over a ridge the creaking of the solitary branch fell silent. Though he'd taken the light with him, Tom wasn't about to be driven to chase it. He hadn't quite reached the top of the path when he said "No wonder aunt and uncle say you can't make any friends."

He hadn't necessarily intended his cousin to hear, but Lucas retorted "I've got one."

Tom was tempted to suggest that Lucas should have brought this unlikely person instead of him. His cousin was taking the light away as though to punish Tom for his remark. Having left the path, he halted under an outstretched branch. "You can see where they did it," he said.

The flashlight beam plunged into the earth—into a circular shaft that led down to the middle of the irrigation tunnel. At some point the entrance had been boarded over, but now the rotten wood was strewn among the trees. Tom peered into the opening, from which a rusty ladder descended into utter darkness. "You can't see if you don't take the bag off."

As darkness raced up the ladder, chasing the light out of the shaft, Lucas said "What do you think is laughing now?"

"Maybe you should go down and find out."

Another hollow liquid giggle rose out of the unlit depths, and Tom thought of convincing his cousin it wasn't water they were hearing. Lucas crumpled the bag in his hand and sent the light down the shaft again. The beam just reached the foot of the ladder, below which Tom seemed to glimpse a dim sinuous movement before Lucas snatched the beam out of the shaft and aimed it at the branch overhead. "He hung himself on that, didn't he, and then she threw herself down there."

He sounded little more than distantly interested, which wasn't enough for Tom. "Aren't you going down, then? I thought you wanted a Halloween adventure."

The glowing leafless branch went out as Lucas swung the light back to the path. "All right," he said and made for the opposite side of the ridge.

Did he really need absolute precision or just demand it? As Tom trudged after him he heard a rustling somewhere near the open shaft. "I thought you never left litter," he called. "How about that bag?"

"It's here," Lucas said and tugged it half out of his trouser pocket before stuffing it back in.

When Tom glanced behind him the Frugall floodlights glared in his eyes, and he couldn't locate what he'd heard—perhaps leaves stirring in a wind, although he hadn't felt one. Of course there must be wildlife in the woods, even if he'd yet to see any. He followed Lucas down the increasingly steep path and saw the flashlight beam snag on the curve of a stone arch protruding from the earth beside the track. It was the end of the tunnel, which had once helped irrigate the fields beyond the ridge. Now the fields were overgrown and the tunnel was barricaded, or rather it had been until somebody tore the boards down. As Lucas poked the flashlight beam into the entrance he said "Where's the bell?"

Tom thought the slow dull metallic notes came from a car radio in the distance, but said "Is it in the tunnel?"

Lucas stooped under the arch, which wasn't quite as tall as either of the boys. "Listen," he said. "That's where."

Tom heard a last reverberation as he stepped off the path. Surely it was just his cousin's gaze that made him wonder if the noise had indeed come from the tunnel, unless someone was playing a Halloween joke. Suppose the girls had followed them from the cinema and were sending the sound down from the ridge? In his hopelessly limited experience this didn't seem the kind of thing girls did, especially while keeping quiet as well. The thought of them revived his discontent, and he said "Better go and see."

Lucas advanced into the tunnel at once. His silhouette blotted out most of the way ahead, the stone floor scattered with sodden leaves, the walls and curved roof glistening with moss, a few weeds drooping out of cracks. The low passage was barely wider than his elbows as he held them at his sides—so narrow that the flashlight bumped against one wall with a soft moist thud as he turned to point the beam at Tom. "What are you doing?"

"Get that out of my face, can you?" As the light sank into the cramped space between them Tom said "I'm coming too."

"I don't want you to."

Tom backed out, almost scraping his scalp on the arch. "Now you've got what you want as usual. Just you remember you did."

"It won't be scary if we both go in." This might have been an effort to placate his cousin—as much of one as Lucas was likely to make—but Tom suspected it was just a stubborn statement of fact. "I'm not scared yet," Lucas complained. "It's Halloween."

"Want me to make sure?"

"I know it is." Before Tom could explain, if simply out of frustration, Lucas said "You've got nothing to do."

He sounded intolerably like a teacher rebuking an idle pupil. As Tom vowed to prove him wrong in ways his cousin wouldn't care for, Lucas ducked out of the tunnel and thrust the flashlight at him. "You can hold this while I'm in there."

Tom sent the beam along the tunnel. It fell short of the ladder, which was a couple of hundred yards in. Once Lucas returned to the tunnel the light wouldn't even reach past him. Tom was waiting to watch his reaction to this when Lucas said "I don't mean here."

He might have been criticising Tom's ability to understand, a notion that was close to more than Tom could take. "Where?" he demanded without at all wanting to know.

"Go up and shine it down the hole, then I can see where halfway is. Shout when you get to the hole."

"And you answer." In case this wasn't plain enough Tom added "So I can hear."

"Course I will."

Tom could have done without the haughtiness. He made off with the flashlight, swinging it from side to side of the deserted woods. As he reached the top of the path the lights above the distant retail park glared in his eyes, and he had a momentary impression that a rounded object was protruding just above the shaft at the midpoint of the tunnel. He squeezed his eyes shut, widening them as he stepped onto the ridge. Perhaps he'd seen an exposed root beyond the shaft, but he couldn't see it now. He marched to the opening and sent the beam down to the tunnel, where he seemed to glimpse movement—a dim shape like a scrawny limb or an even thinner item retreating at speed into the dark. It must have been a shadow cast by the ladder. "Come on," he called. "I'm here."

"I'm coming."

Tom was disconcerted to hear his cousin's shout resound along the tunnel while it also came from beyond the ridge. Despite straining his eyes he couldn't judge how far the flashlight beam reached; the glare from the retail park was still hindering his vision. He dodged around the shaft to turn his back on the problem, and saw that the beam of the cheap flashlight fell short of illuminating the tunnel itself. "Can you see the light?" he called.

"I see something."

Tom found this wilfully vague. "What?" he yelled.

"Must be you."

This was vaguer still, particularly for Lucas. Was he trying to unnerve his cousin? Tom peered into the shaft, waiting for Lucas to dart into view in a feeble attempt to alarm him. Or did Lucas mean to worry him by staying out of sight? Tom vowed not to call out again, but he was on the edge of yielding to the compulsion when an ill-defined figure appeared at the bottom of the shaft. He didn't really need it to turn its dim face upwards to show it was Lucas. "What am I doing now?" Tom grudged having to ask.

"Holding the light."

"I'm saying," Tom said more bitterly still, "what do you want me to do?"

"Stay there till I say," Lucas told him and stooped into the other section of the tunnel.

Tom tried to listen to his receding footsteps but soon could hear nothing at all—or rather, just the sound he'd previously ascribed to plastic. Perhaps the bag in his cousin's pocket was brushing against the wall, except that Tom seemed to hear the noise behind him. Had Lucas sneaked out of the far end of the tunnel to creep up and pounce on him? Surely his shadow would give him away, and when Tom swung around, only the trees were silhouetted against the glare from the retail park. He'd kept the flashlight beam trained down the shaft on the basis that he might have misjudged Lucas, but how long would he have to wait to hear from him? He had a sudden furious idea that, having left the tunnel, Lucas was on his way home. "Where are you now?" he shouted.

"Here," Lucas declared, appearing at the foot of the shaft.

So he'd been playing a different trick—staying out of sight until Tom grew nervous. "Finished with the light?" Tom only just bothered to ask.

"Go and meet me at the end," Lucas said before ducking into the dark.

Tom felt juvenile for using the flashlight to search among the trees around him—he wasn't the one who was meant to be scared—and switched it off as he hurried down the path. He was waiting at the mouth of the tunnel by the time his cousin emerged. Lucas looked dully untroubled, unless the darkness was obscuring his expression, and Tom wished he'd hidden long enough to make his cousin nervous. "What's it like?" he tried asking.

"Like I wasn't alone."

"You weren't."

"That's scary."

Tom thought he'd been more than sufficiently clear. He was feeling heavy with resentment when Lucas said "Now it's your turn."

As Tom switched on the flashlight, darkness shrank into the tunnel. "You can't do that," Lucas protested. "I'm supposed to go on top with it so you'll be in the dark."

Was he planning some trick of the kind Tom had spared him? When Tom hesitated while the unsteady shadows of weeds fingered the moss on the walls of the tunnel, Lucas said "I have to say what we do with it. It's mine."

Tom was so disgusted that he almost dropped the flashlight because of his haste to be rid of it. "I'll have to shout," Lucas told him. "You won't see."

He hadn't extinguished the light, which scrambled up the path ahead of him, leaving Tom to wonder if Lucas was uneasy after all. Suppose that distracted him from keeping the beam down the shaft? Once his cousin vanished over the ridge Tom peered along the tunnel, but it might as well have been stuffed with earth. He hadn't distinguished even a hint of light when Lucas called "It's waiting."

His voice was in more than one place again—somewhere down the tunnel and on the ridge as well. It occurred to Tom that he should have extracted a promise, and he cupped his hands around his mouth to yell "Say you'll wait there for me."

"That's what I'm doing."

Tom could have fancied he was hearing another voice imitate Lucas. "Say you will," he insisted, "as long as I want the light."

"I will as long as you want the light."

This had to be precise enough, and surely Lucas was incapable of acting other than he'd said he would. Wasn't his saying it in more than one voice like a double promise? Tom had no reason to hesitate, even if he wished Dianne were with him to be scared and then comforted. He wouldn't be comforting Lucas, and he ducked into the tunnel.

The darkness fastened on his eyes at once. They felt coated with it, a substance like the blackest paint. It hindered his feet too, as if they had to wade through it, shuffling forward an inch at a time, which was all he felt able to risk. He extended his arms in front of him to avoid touching the slimy walls, though he could have imagined his fingertips were about to bump into the dark. Of course there was nothing solid in front of him. Lucas hadn't switched off the flashlight and sneaked down the ladder to stand in the blackness until Tom's outstretched fingers found him. Just the same, the thought made Tom bring his hands back and lower his arms. "Are you really up there?" he shouted.

"You'll see."

His cousin's voice was somewhere ahead and above the tunnel. Otherwise the exchange didn't reassure Tom as much as he would have hoped if he'd needed reassurance. It wasn't simply that his shout had been boxed in by the walls and the roof that forced his head down; his voice had seemed muffled by some obstacle in front of him. Was he about to see it? There appeared to be a hint of pallor in the blackness, if that wasn't just an effect of straining his eyes or of hoping to locate the flashlight beam. When he edged forward the impression didn't shift, and he kept his gaze fixed on the promise of light until his foot nudged an object on the floor of the tunnel.

He heard it stir and then subside. He had no room to sidle around it, and he didn't care to turn his back. By resting his foot on it and trampling on it he deduced that it was a mass of twigs and dead leaves. He trod hard on it on his way past, and worked out that the material must have fallen down the shaft, which was just visible ahead by the light that nearly reached down to the tunnel roof. He could scarcely believe how long he'd taken to walk halfway; it felt as if the darkness had weighed down the passing of time. A few waterlogged leaves slithered underfoot as he reached the shaft and was able to raise his head. "See me?" he called.

Lucas was an indefinite silhouette against the night sky beyond the flashlight, which almost blinded Tom even though the beam on the wall opposite the ladder was so dim. "You were a long time," Lucas protested.

An acoustic quirk made versions of his voice mutter in both sections of the tunnel. Before Tom could reply, less irately than the complaint deserved, Lucas said "When you've been through the rest you have to come back this way."

That he had needn't mean Tom should. Lucas wasn't frightened yet, which was among the reasons why Tom intended to leave the tunnel by the far end so as to tiptoe up behind him. He shut his eyes to ready them for the darkness as far as he could. He hadn't opened them when Lucas enraged him by calling "Are you scared to go in?"

Tom lowered his head as if he meant to butt the dark and advanced into the tunnel. He wouldn't have believed the blackness could grow thicker, but now it didn't just smother his eyes—it filled them to the limit. He'd taken a very few steps, which felt shackled by his wariness, when his foot collided with another heap of leaves. He heard twigs if not small branches snap as he trod several times on the yielding heap, which must be almost as long as he was tall. Once he was past it the floor seemed clear, but how far did he have to shuffle to catch his first glimpse of the night outside? It couldn't be so dark out there that it was indistinguishable from the underground passage. He was stretching his eyes wide, which only served to let more of the darkness into them, when his foot struck a hindrance more solid than leaves—an object that his groping fingers found to be as high and wide as the tunnel. The entrance was boarded up.

So Lucas hadn't just been setting out the rules of the game. Perhaps he'd believed he was making it plain that Tom couldn't leave the tunnel at this end. Tom thumped the boards with his fists and tried a few kicks as well, but the barrier didn't give. When he turned away at last he had to touch the cold fur of the wall with his knuckles to be certain he was facing down the tunnel. He shuffled forward as if he were being dragged by his bent head, and his blacked-out eyes were straining to find the light when his toe poked the mass of leaves and wood on the floor. If he was so close to the shaft, why couldn't he make out even a hint of the flashlight beam? "What are you playing at?" he shouted.

There was no response of any kind. Perhaps Lucas had decided to alarm him. He dealt the supine heap a kick, but it held more or less together. He tramped on it a number of times while edging forward. It was behind him, though not far, when something moved under his feet—a large worm, he thought, or a snake. As he stumbled clear of it he heard scattered leaves rustle with its movement, and recognised the sound he'd attributed to plastic on his way to the tunnel. He needn't think about it further—he only wanted to reach the light. That still wasn't visible, and he wasn't eager to shout into the dark again, surely just because Lucas might think he was scared. He had no idea how many timid paces he'd taken before he was able to lift his head.

For a moment this felt like nothing but relief, and then he saw that the top of the shaft was deserted. "Lucas," he yelled. "Lucas." He was trying just to feel furious, but the repetition unnerved him—it seemed too close to doing his best to ensure that only his cousin would respond. He was about to call once more when Lucas appeared above him, at least fifty feet away, and sent the flashlight beam down the highest rungs of the ladder. Tom would have shouted at him except for being assailed by a sudden unwelcome thought. He knew why he'd seemed to take too long to return to the shaft: because the supine mass on which he'd trodden was further from it than before. While he'd been

221

trying to find his way out, it had crawled after him in the dark.

He twisted around to peer behind him, but the blackness was impenetrable. Although he was afraid to see, not seeing might be worse. "Lucas," he blurted, and then forced himself to raise his voice. "Send the light down here."

The response was a noise very much like one he'd previously heard—a clang like the note of a dull bell. Now he realised it had been the sound of an object swinging against the ladder, repeatedly colliding with the upper rungs. This time the flashlight was making the noise, and struck another rung as it plummeted down the shaft. The lens smashed on the tunnel floor, and the light went out at once.

"What have you done now," Tom almost screamed, "you stupid useless retard?" He dropped into a crouch that felt as if a pain in his guts had doubled him over. His fingers groped over the cold wet stone and eventually closed around the flashlight. He pushed the switch back and forth, but the bulb must be broken too. When he jerked his head back to yell at Lucas he saw that the dim round hole at the top of the shaft was empty once more. He staggered to his feet and threw out a hand to help him keep his balance, and clutched an object that was dangling beside him in the tunnel. It was the rope he'd wanted to think was a worm or a snake.

A mindless panic made him haul at the bedraggled rope, and an object nuzzled the back of his hand. It was a face, though not much of one, and as he recoiled with a cry he felt it sag away from the bone. He was backing away so fast he almost overbalanced when he heard sounds in the other section of the tunnel. Between him and the way out, someone was running through the absolute blackness as if they had no need of light—as if they welcomed its absence.

For a moment that seemed endless Tom felt the darkness claim him, and then he shied the flashlight in the direction of the sodden flopping footsteps. He clutched at the ladder and hauled himself desperately upwards. He mustn't think about climbing towards the outstretched branch that had creaked as the boys made for the ridge. Perhaps nobody had killed themselves—perhaps that was just a story made up by adults to scare children away from any danger. He could no longer hear the loose footsteps for all the noise he was making on the shaky ladder. Lucas must be waiting by the shaft—he'd promised to—and of course he'd turned the light away when he'd heard Tom thumping the boards that blocked the tunnel. The thought gave Tom the chance to realise who the friend Lucas said he had must be. "I'm still your friend," he called, surely not too late, as he clambered up the rusty ladder. He didn't dare to look down, and he was just a few rungs from the top when he lost his footing. His foot flailed in the air and then trod on the head of whatever was climbing after him.

It moved under his foot—moved more than any scalp ought to be able—as he kicked it away. He was terrified what else he might tread on, but he only found the rung again. His head was nearly level with the exit from the shaft before a pulpy grasp closed around his ankle. However soft they were, the swollen fingers felt capable of dragging him down into the blackness to share it with its residents. He thrust his free hand above the shaft in a desperate appeal. Surely Lucas hadn't felt so insulted that he'd abandoned his cousin—surely only he was out there. "Get hold of me," Tom pleaded, and at once he had his answer.

THE LONG WAY

It must have been late autumn. Because everything was bare I saw inside the house.

Dead leaves had been scuttling around me all the way from home. A chill wind kept trying to shrink my face. The sky looked thin with ice, almost as white as the matching houses that made up the estate. Some of the old people who'd been rehoused wouldn't have known where they were on it except for the little wood, where my uncle Philip used to say the council left some trees so they could call it the Greenwood Estate. Nobody was supposed to be living in the three streets around the wood when I used to walk across the estate to help him shop.

So many people in Copse View and Arbour Street and Shady Lane had complained about children climbing from trees and swinging from ropes and playing hide and seek that the council put a fence up, but then teenagers used the wood for sex and drink and drugs. Some dealers moved into Shady Lane, and my uncle said it got shadier, and the next road turned into Cops View. He said the other one should be called A Whore Street, though my parents told him not to let me hear. Then the council moved all the tenants out of the triangle, even the old people who'd complained about the children, and boarded up the houses. By the time I was helping my uncle, people had broken in.

They'd left Copse View alone except for one house in the middle of the terrace. Perhaps they'd gone for that one because the boards they'd strewn around the weedy garden looked rotten. They'd uncovered the front door and the downstairs window, but I could never see in for the reflection of sunlight on leaves. Now there weren't many leaves and the sun had a cataract, and the view into the front room was clear. The only furniture was an easy chair with a fractured arm. The chair had a pattern like shadows of ferns and wore a yellowish circular antimacassar. The pinstriped wallpaper was black and white too. A set of shelves was coming loose from the back wall but still displaying a plate printed with a portrait of the queen. Beside the shelves a door was just about open, framing part of a dimmer room.

I wondered why the door was there. In our house you entered the rooms from the hall. My uncle had an extra door made so he could use his wheelchair, and I supposed whoever had lived in this house might have been disabled too. There was a faint hint of a shape beyond the doorway, and I peered over the low garden wall until my eyes ached. Was it a full-length portrait or a life-size dummy? It looked as if it had been on the kind of diet they warned the girls about at school. As I made out its arms I began to think they could reach not just through the doorway but across far too much of the room, and then I saw that they were sticks on which it was leaning slightly forward—sticks not much thinner than its arms. I couldn't distinguish its gender or how it was dressed or even its face. Perhaps it was keeping so still in the hope of going unnoticed, unless it was challenging me to object to its presence. I was happy to leave it alone and head for my uncle's.

He lived on Pasture Boulevard, where he said the only signs of pasture were the lorries that drove past your bedroom all night. The trees along the central reservation were leafy just with litter. My uncle was sitting in the hall of the house where he lived on the ground floor, and wheeled himself out as soon as he saw me. "Sorry I made you wait, Uncle Philip," I said.

"I'll wait for anything that's worth the wait." Having raised a thumb to show this meant me, he said "And what's my name again, Craig?"

"Phil," I had to say, though my parents said I was too young to.

"That's the man. Don't be shy of speaking up. Ready for the go?"

He might have been starting a race at the school where he'd taught physical education—teaching pee, he called it—until he had his first stroke. When I made to push the chair he brought his eyebrows down and thrust his thick lips forward, which might have frightened his pupils but now made his big square face seem to be trying to shrink as the rest of him had. "Never make it easy, Craig," he said. "You don't want my arms going on strike."

I trotted beside him to the Frugo supermarket that had done for most of the shops that were supposed to make the estate feel like a village. Whenever a Frugo lorry thundered past us he would mutter "There's some petrol for your lungs" or "Hold your breath." In the supermarket he flung a week's supply of healthy food from the Frugorganic section into the trolley and bought me a Frugoat bar, joking as usual about how they'd turned the oats into an animal. I pushed the trolley to his flat and helped him unload it and took it back to Frugo. When I passed his window again he opened it, flapping the sports day posters he'd tacked to the wall of the room, to shout "See you in a week if you haven't got yourself a girlfriend."

I had the books I borrowed from the public library instead, but I didn't need him to announce my deficiency. I knew he disapproved of girls for boys my age—they sapped your energy, he said. "I'll always come," I promised and made for Copse View, where the trees looked eager to wave me on. The wind gave up pushing me as I reached them, and I stopped at the house where the boards had been pulled down. As I peered across the front room, resting my fists on the crumbling wall, my eyes began to ache again. However much I stared, the dim figure with the sticks didn't seem to have moved—not in an hour and a half. It had to be a picture; why shouldn't whoever used to live there have put a poster up? I felt worse than stupid for taking so long to realise. My parents and the English teacher at my school said I had imagination, but I could do without that much.

Ten minutes brought me home to Woody Rise. "Well, would he?" my uncle used to say even after my parents gave up laughing or groaning. The houses on this edge of the estate were as big as his but meant for one family each—they looked as if they were trying to pass for part of the suburb that once had the estate for a park. My father was carrying fistfuls of cutlery along the hall. "Here's the boy who cares," he called, and asked me "How's the wheelie kid?"

"Tom," my mother rebuked him from the kitchen.

I thought he deserved more reproof when I wasn't even supposed to shorten my uncle's name, but all I said was "Good."

As my father repeated this several times my mother said "Let's eat in here. Quick as you like, Craig. We've people coming round for a homewatch meeting."

"I thought you were going out."

"Just put your coat on your chair for now. We've rescheduled our pupils for tomorrow. Didn't we say?"

She always seemed resentful if I forgot whichever extra job they were doing when. "I suppose you must have," I tried pretending.

"Had you found some mischief to get up to, Craig?" my father said. "Has she got a name?"

"I hope not," my mother said. "You can welcome the guests if you like, Craig."

"He's already looked after my brother, Rosie."

"And some of us have done more." In the main this was aimed at my father, and she said more gently "All right, Craig. I expect you want to be on your own for a change."

I would rather have been with them by ourselves—not so much at dinner, where I always felt they were waiting for me to drop cutlery or spill food. I managed to conquer the spaghetti bolognese by cutting up the pasta with my fork, though my mother didn't approve much of that either. Once I'd washed up for everyone I was able to take refuge in my bedroom before all the neighbours came to discuss watching out for burglars and car thieves and door-to-door con people and other types to be afraid of. I needed to be alone to write.

Nobody knew I did. My stories tried to be like the kind of film my parents wouldn't let me watch. That night I wrote about a girl whose car broke down miles from anywhere, and the only place she could ask for help was a house full of people who wouldn't come to her. The house was haunted by a maniac who cut off people's feet with a chainsaw so they couldn't escape. I frightened myself with this more than I enjoyed, and when I went to sleep despite the murmur of neighbours downstairs I dreamed that if I opened my eyes I would see a figure standing absolutely still at the end of the bed. I looked once and saw no silhouette against the glow from the next street, but it took me a while to go back to sleep.

For most of Sunday my parents were out of the house. As if they hadn't had enough of teaching at school all week, my mother did her best to coax adults to read and write while my father educated people about computers. They couldn't help reminding me of my school, where I wasn't too unhappy so long as I wasn't noticed. It was in the suburb next to the estate, and some of the boys liked to punch me for stealing their park even though none of us was alive when the estate was built, while a few of the girls seemed to want me to act as uncouth as they thought people from it should be. I tried to keep out of all their ways and not to attract any questions in class. My work proved I wasn't stupid, which was all that mattered to me. I liked English best, except when the teacher made me read out my work. I would mumble and stammer and squirm and blush until the ordeal was done. I hated her and everyone else who could hear my helplessly unmodulated voice, most of all myself.

I wouldn't have dared admit to anyone at school that I quite liked most homework. I could take my own time with it, and there was nobody to distract me, since my parents were at night school several evenings, either teaching or improving their degrees. It must have been hard to pay the mortgage even with two teachers' salaries, but I also thought they were competing with each other for how much they could achieve, and perhaps with my uncle as well. All this left me feeling I should do more for him, but there

229

was no more he would let me do.

Soon it was Saturday again. I was eager to look at the house on Copse View, but once it was in sight I felt oddly nervous. I wasn't going to avoid it by walking around the triangle. That would make me late for my uncle, and I could imagine what he would think of my behaviour if he knew. The sky had turned to chalk, and the sun was a round lump of it caught in the stripped treetops; in the flat pale light the houses looked brittle as shell. The light lay inert in the front room of the abandoned house. The figure with the sticks was there, in exactly the same stance. It wasn't in the same place, though. It had come into the room.

At least, it was leaning through the doorway. It looked poised to jerk the sticks up at me, unless it was about to use them to spring like a huge insect across the room. While the sunlight didn't spare the meagre furniture—the ferny chair and its discoloured antimacassar, the plate with the queen's face on the askew shelf still clinging to the pinstriped wall—it fell short of illuminating the occupier. I could just distinguish that the emaciated shape was dressed in some tattered material—covered with it, at any rate. While the overall impression was greyish, patches were as yellowed as the antimacassar, though I couldn't tell whether these were part of the clothes or showing through. This was also the case with the head. It appeared to be hairless, but I couldn't make out any of the face. When my eyes began to sting with trying I took a thoughtless step towards the garden wall, and then I took several back, enough to trip over the kerb. The instant I regained my balance I dashed out of Copse View.

Perhaps there was a flaw in the window, or the glass was so grimy that it blurred the person in the room, though not the other contents. Perhaps the occupant was wearing some kind of veil. Once I managed to have these thoughts they slowed me down, but not much, and I was breathing hard when I reached my uncle's. He was sitting in the hall again. "All right, Craig, I wasn't going anywhere," he said. "Training for a race?"

Before I could answer he said "Forget I asked. I know the schools won't let you compete any more."

230

I felt as if he didn't just mean at sports. "I can," I blurted and went red.

"I expect if you think you can that counts."

As we made for Frugo I set out to convince him in a way I thought he would approve of, but he fell behind alongside a lorry not much shorter than a dozen houses. "Don't let me hold you up," he gasped, "if you've got somewhere you'd rather be."

"I thought you liked to go fast. I thought it was how you kept fit."

"That's a lot of past tense. See, you're not the only one that knows his grammar."

I was reminded of a Christmas when my mother told him after some bottles of wine that he was more concerned with muscles than minds. He was still teaching then, and I'd have hoped he would have forgotten by now. He hardly spoke in the supermarket, not even bothering to make his weekly joke as he bought my Frugoat bar. I wondered if I'd exhausted him by forcing him to race, especially when he didn't head for home as fast as I could push the laden trolley. I was dismayed to think he could end up no more mobile than the figure with the sticks.

I helped him unload the shopping and sped the trolley back to Frugo. Did he have a struggle to raise the window as he saw me outside his flat? "Thanks for escorting an old tetch," he called. "Go and make us all proud for a week."

He'd left me feeling ashamed to be timid, which meant not avoiding Copse View. As I marched along the deserted street I thought there was no need to look into the house. I was almost past it when the sense of something eager to be seen dragged my head around. One glimpse was enough to send me fleeing home. The figure was still blurred, though the queen's face on the plate beside the doorway was absolutely clear, but there was no question that the occupant had moved. It was leaning forward on its sticks at least a foot inside the room.

I didn't stop walking very fast until I'd slammed the front door behind me. I wouldn't have been so forceful if I'd realised my parents were home. "That was an entrance," said my father.

"Anything amiss we should know about?"

"We certainly should," said my mother.

"I was just seeing if I could run all the way home."

"Don't take your uncle too much to heart," my mother said. "There are better ways for you to impress."

On impulse I showed them my homework books. My father pointed out where the punctuation in my mathematics work was wrong, and my mother wished I'd written about real life and ordinary people instead of ghosts in my essay on the last book I'd read. "Good try," she told me, and my father added "Better next time, eh?"

I was tempted to show them my stories, but I was sure they wouldn't approve. I stayed away from writing any that weekend, because the only ideas I had were about figures that stayed too still or not still enough. I tried not to think about them after dark, and told myself that by the time I went to my uncle's again, whatever was happening on Copse View might have given up for lack of an audience or been sorted out by someone else. But I was there much sooner than next week.

It was Sunday afternoon. While my mother peeled potatoes I was popping peas out of their pods and relishing their clatter in a saucepan. A piece of beef was defrosting in a pool of blood. My father gazed at it for a while and said "That'd do for four of us. We haven't had Phil over for a while."

"We haven't," said my mother.

Although I wouldn't have taken this for enthusiasm, my father said "I'll give him a tinkle."

Surely my uncle could take a taxi—surely nobody would expect me to collect him and help him back to his flat after dark. I squeezed a pod in my fist while I listened to my father on the phone, but there was silence except for the scraping of my mother's knife. My hand was clammy with vegetable juice by the time my father said "He's not answering. That isn't like him."

"Sometimes he isn't much like him these days," said my mother.

"Can you go over and see what's up, Craig?"

As I rubbed my hands together I wondered whether any more of me had turned as green. "Don't you want me to finish these?" I pleaded.

"I'll take over kitchen duty."

My last hope was that my mother would object, but she said "Wash your hands for heaven's sake, Craig. Just don't be long."

While night wouldn't officially fall for an hour, the overcast sky gave me a preview. I was in sight of the woods when I noticed a gap in the railings on Shady Lane. Hadn't I seen another on Arbour Street? Certainly a path had been made through the shrubs from the opening off Shady Lane. It wound between the trees not too far from Copse View.

As I dodged along it bushes and trees kept blocking my view of the boarded-up houses. I couldn't help glancing at the vandalised house; perhaps I thought the distance made me safe. The scrawny figure hadn't changed its posture or its patchwork appearance. It looked as if it was craning forward to watch me or threatening worse. Overnight it had moved as much closer to the street as it had during the whole of the previous week.

I nearly forced my own way through the undergrowth to leave the sight behind. I was afraid I'd encouraged the figure to advance by trying to see it, perhaps even by thinking about it. Had the vandals fled once they'd seen inside the house? No wonder they'd left the rest of the street alone. I fancied the occupant might especially dislike people of my age, even though I hadn't been among those who'd rampaged in the woods. I was almost blind with panic and the early twilight by the time I fought off the last twigs and found the unofficial exit onto Arbour Street.

I was trying to be calmer when I arrived at my uncle's. He seemed to be watching television, which lent its flicker to the front room. I thought he couldn't hear me tapping on the pane for the cheers of the crowd. When I knocked harder he didn't respond, and I was nervous of calling to him. I was remembering a horror film I'd watched on television once until my mother had come home to find me watching. I'd seen enough to know you should be apprehensive if anyone was sitting with his back to you in that kind of film. "Uncle Philip," I said with very little voice.

The wheelchair twisted around, bumping into a sofa scattered with magazines. At first he seemed not to see me, then not to recognise me, and finally not to be pleased that he did. "What are you playing at?" he demanded. "What are you trying to do?"

He waved away my answer as if it were an insect and propelled the chair across the room less expertly than usual. He struggled to shove the lower half of the window up, and his grimace didn't relent once he had. "Speak up for yourself. Weren't you here before?"

"That was yesterday," I mumbled. "Dad sent me. He—"

"Sending an inspector now, is he? You can tell him my mind's as good as ever. I know they don't think that's much."

"He tried to phone you. You didn't answer, so—"

"When did he? Nobody's rung here." My uncle fumbled in his lap and on the chair. "Where is the wretched thing?"

Once he'd finished staring at me as if I'd failed to answer in a class he steered the chair around the room and blundered out of it, muttering more than one word I would never have expected him to use. "Here it is," he said accusingly and reappeared brandishing the cordless phone. "No wonder I couldn't hear it. Can't a man have a nap?"

"I didn't want to wake you. I only did because I was sent."

"Don't put yourself out on my behalf." Before I could deny that he was any trouble he said "So why's Tom checking up on me?"

"They wanted you to come for dinner."

"More like one did if any. I see you're not including yourself."

I don't know why this rather than anything else was too much, but I blurted "Look, I came all this way to find out. Of—"

One reason I was anxious to invite him was the thought of passing the house on Copse View by myself, but he didn't let me finish. "Don't again," he said.

"You'll come, won't you?"

"Tell them no. I'm still up to cooking my own grub."

"Can't you tell them?"

I was hoping that my father would persuade him to change his mind, but he said "I won't be phoning. I'll phone if I want you round."

"I'm sorry," I pleaded. "I didn't mean—"

"I know what you meant," he said and gazed sadly at me. "Never say sorry for telling the truth."

"I wasn't."

I might have tried harder to convince him if I hadn't realised that he'd given me an excuse to stay away from Copse View. "Don't bother," he said and stared at the television. "See, now I've missed a goal."

He dragged the sash down without bothering to glance at me. Even if that hadn't been enough of a dismissal, the night was creeping up on me. I didn't realise how close it was until he switched on the light in the room. That made me feel worse than excluded, and I wasn't slow in heading for home.

Before I reached the woods the streetlamps came on. I began to walk faster until I remembered that most of the lamps around the woods had been smashed. From the corner of the triangle I saw just one was intact—the one outside the house on Copse View. I couldn't help thinking the vandals were scared to go near; they hadn't even broken the window. I couldn't see into the room from the end of the street, but the house looked awakened by the stark light, lent power by the white glare. I wasn't anxious to learn what effect this might have inside the house.

The path would take me too close. I would have detoured through the streets behind Copse View if I hadn't heard the snarl of motorcycles racing up and down them. I didn't want to encounter the riders, who were likely to be my age or younger and protective of their territory. Instead I walked around the woods.

I had my back to the streetlamp all the way down Arbour Street. A few thin shafts of light extended through the trees, but they didn't seem to relieve the growing darkness so much as reach for me on behalf of the house. Now and then I heard wings or litter flapping. When I turned along Shady Lane the light started to jab at my vision, blurring the glimpses the woods let me have of the house. I'd been afraid to see it, but now I was more afraid not to see. I kept having to blink scraps of dazzle out of my eyes, and I waited for my vision to clear when a gap between the trees framed the house.

Was the figure closer to the window? I'd been walking in the road, but I ventured to the pavement alongside the woods. Something besides the stillness of the figure reminded me of the trees on either side of the house. Their cracked bark was grey where it wasn't blackened, and fragments were peeling off, making way for whitish fungus. Far too much of this seemed true of the face beyond the window.

I backed away before I could see anything else and stayed on the far pavement, though the dead houses beside it were no more reassuring than the outstretched shadows of the trees or the secret darkness of the woods, which kept being invaded by glimpses of the house behind the streetlamp. When I reached the corner of the triangle I saw that someone with a spray can had added a letter to the street sign. The first word was no longer just Copse.

Perhaps it was a vandal's idea of a joke, but I ran the rest of the way home, where I had to take time to calm my breath down. As I opened the front door I was nowhere near deciding what to tell my parents. I was sneaking it shut when my mother hurried out of the computer room, waving a pamphlet called Safe Home. "Are you back at last? We were going to phone Philip. Are you by yourself? Where have you been?"

"I had to go a long way. There were boys on bikes."

"Did they do something to you? What did they do?"

"They would have. That's why I went round." I wouldn't have minded some praise for prudence, but apparently I needed to add "They were riding motorbikes. They'd have gone after me."

"We haven't got you thinking there are criminals round every corner, have we?" My father had finished listening none too patiently to the interrogation. "We don't want him afraid to go out, do we, Rosie? It isn't nearly that bad, Craig. What's the problem with my brother?"

"He's already made his dinner."

"He isn't coming." Perhaps my father simply wanted confirmation, but his gaze made me feel responsible. "So why did you have to go over?" he said.

"Because you told me to."

"Sometimes I think you aren't quite with us, Craig," he said, though my mother seemed to feel this was mostly directed at her. "I was asking why he didn't take my call."

"He'd been watching football and—"

I was trying to make sure I didn't give away too much that had happened, but my mother said "He'd rather have his games than us, then."

"He was asleep," I said louder than I was supposed to speak.

"Control yourself, Craig. I won't have a hooligan in my house." Having added a pause, my mother turned her look on my father. "And please don't make it sound as if I've given him a phobia."

"I don't believe anyone said that. Phil's got no reason to call you a sissy, has he, Craig?" When I shook or at least shivered my head my father said "Did he say anything else?"

"Not really."

"Not really or not at all?"

"Not."

"Now who's going on at him?" my mother said in some triumph. "Come and have the dinner there's been so much fuss about."

Throughout the meal I felt as if I were being watched or would be if I even slightly faltered in cutting up my meat and vegetables and inserting forkfuls in my mouth and chewing and chewing and, with an effort that turned my hands clammy, swallowing. I managed to control my intake until dinner was finally done and I'd washed up, and then I was just able not to dash upstairs before flushing the toilet to muffle my sounds. Once I'd disposed of the evidence I lay on my bed for a while and eventually ventured down to watch the end of a programme about gang violence in primary schools. "Why don't you bring whatever you're reading downstairs?" my mother said.

"Maybe it's the kind of thing boys like to read by themselves," said my father.

I went red, not because it was true but on the suspicion that he wanted it to be, and shook my head to placate my mother. She switched off the television in case whatever else it had to offer wasn't suitable for me, and then my parents set about sectioning the Sunday papers, handing me the travel supplements in case those helped with my geography. I would much rather have been helped not to think about the house on Copse View.

Whenever the sight of the ragged discoloured face and the shape crouching over its sticks tried to invade my mind I made myself remember that my uncle didn't want me. I had to remember at night in bed, and in the classroom, and while I struggled not to let my parents see my fear, not to mention any number of situations in between these. I was only wishing to be let off my duty until the occupant of the derelict house somehow went away. My uncle didn't phone during the week, and I was afraid my father might call him and find out the truth, but perhaps he was stubborn as well.

I spent Saturday morning in dread of the phone. It was silent until lunchtime, and while I kept a few mouthfuls of bread and cheese down too. I lingered at the kitchen sink as long as I could, and then my mother said "Better be trotting. You don't want it to be dark."

"I haven't got to go."

"Why not?" my father said before she could.

"Uncle Phil, Uncle Philip said he'd phone when he wanted me."

"Since when has he ever done that?"

"Last week." I was trying to say as little as they would allow. "He really said."

"I think there's more to this than you're telling us," my mother warned me, if she wasn't prompting.

"It doesn't sound like Phil," my father said. "I'm calling him."

My mother watched my father dial and then went upstairs.

"Don't say you've nodded off again," my father told the phone, but it didn't bring him an answer. At last he put the phone down. "You'd better go and see what's up this time," he told me.

"I think we should deal with this first," said my mother.

She was at the top of the stairs, an exercise book in her hand. I hoped it was some of my homework until I saw it had a red cover, not the brown one that went with the school uniform. "I knew it couldn't be our work with the community that's been preying on his nerves," she said.

"Feeling he hasn't got any privacy might do that, Rosie. Was there really any need to—"

"I thought he might have unsuitable reading up there, but this shows he's been involved in worse. Heaven knows what he's been watching or where."

"I haven't watched anything like that," I protested. "It's all out of my head."

"If that's true it's worse still," she said and tramped downstairs to thrust the book at my father. "We've done our best to keep you free of such things."

He was leafing through it, stopping every so often to frown, when the phone rang. I tried to take the book, but my mother recaptured it. I watched nervously in case she harmed it while my father said "It is. He is. When? Where? We will. Where? Thanks." He gazed at me before saying "Your uncle's had a stroke on the way home from shopping. He's back in hospital."

I could think of nothing I dared say except "Are we going to see him?"

"We are now."

"Can I have my book?"

My mother raised her eyebrows and grasped it with both hands, but my father took it from her. "I'll handle it, Rosie. You can have it back when we decide you're old enough, Craig."

I wasn't entirely unhappy with this. Once he'd taken it to their room I felt as if some of the ideas the house in Copse View had put in my head were safely stored away. Now I could worry about how I'd harmed my uncle or let him come to harm. As my father drove us to the hospital he and my mother were so silent that I was sure they thought I had.

My uncle was in bed halfway down a rank of patients with barely a movement between them. He looked shrunken, perhaps by his loose robe that tied at the back, and on the way to adopting its pallor. My parents took a hand each, leaving me to shuffle on the spot in front of his blanketed feet. "They'll be reserving you a bed if you carry on like this, Phil," my father joked or tried to joke.

My uncle blinked at me as if he were trying out his eyes and then worked his loose mouth. "Nod, you fool," he more or less said.

I was obeying and doing my best to laugh in case this was expected of me before I grasped what he'd been labouring to pronounce. I hoped my parents also knew he'd said it wasn't my fault, even if I still believed it was. "God, my shopping," he more or less informed them. "Boy writing on the pavement. Went dafter then." I gathered that someone riding on the pavement had got the bags my uncle had been carrying and that he'd gone after them, but what was he saying I should see as he pointed at his limp left arm with the hand my mother had been holding? He'd mentioned her as well. He was resting from his verbal exertions by the time I caught up with them. "Gave me this," he'd meant to say. "Another attack."

My parents seemed to find interpreting his speech almost as much of an effort as it cost him. I didn't mind it or visiting him, even by myself, since the route took me nowhere near Copse View. Over the weeks he regained his ability to speak. I was pleased for him, and I tried to be equally enthusiastic that he was recovering his strength. The trouble was that it would let him go home.

I couldn't wish he would lose it again. The most I could hope, which left me feeling painfully ashamed, was that he might refuse my help with shopping. I was keeping that thought to myself the last time I saw him in hospital. "I wouldn't mind a hand on Saturday," he said, "if you haven't had enough of this old wreck."

I assured him I hadn't, and my expression didn't let me down while he could see it. I managed to finish my dinner that night and even to some extent to sleep. Next day at school I had to blame my inattention and mistakes on worrying about my uncle, who was ill. Before the week was over I was using that excuse at home as well. I was afraid my parents would notice I was apprehensive about something else, and the fears aggravated each other.

While I didn't want my parents to learn how much of a coward I was, on another level I was willing them to rescue me by noticing. They must have been too concerned about the estate— about making it safe for my uncle and people like him. By the time I was due to go to him my parents were at a police forum, where they would be leading a campaign for police to intervene in schools however young the criminals. I loitered in the house, hoping for a call to say my uncle didn't need my help, until I realised that if I didn't go out soon it would be dark.

December was a week old. The sky was a field of snow. My white breaths led me through the streets past abandoned Frugo trolleys and Frugoburger cartons. I was walking too fast to shiver much, even with the chill that had chalked all the veins of the dead leaves near Copse View. The trees were showing every bone, but what else had changed? I couldn't comprehend the sight ahead, unless I was wary of believing in it, until I reached the end of the street that led to the woods. There wasn't a derelict house to be seen. Shady Lane and Arbour Street and, far better, Copse View had been levelled, surrounding the woods with a triangle of waste land.

I remembered hearing sounds like thunder while my uncle was in hospital. The streets the demolition had exposed looked somehow insecure, unconvinced of their own reality, incomplete with just half an alley alongside the back yards. As I hurried along Copse View, where the pavement and the roadway seemed to be waiting for the terrace to reappear, I stared hard at the waste ground where the house with the occupant had been. I could see no trace of the building apart from the occasional chunk of brick, and none at all of the figure with the sticks.

I found my uncle in his chair outside the front door. I wondered if he'd locked himself out until he said "Thought you weren't coming. I'm not as speedy as I was, you know."

As we made for Frugo I saw he could trundle only as fast as his weaker arm was able to propel him. Whenever he lost patience and tried to go faster the chair went into a spin. "Waltzing and can't even see my partner," he complained but refused to let me push. On the way home he was slower still, and I had to unload most of his groceries, though not my Frugoat bar, which he'd forgotten to buy. When I came back from returning the trolley he was at his window, which was open, perhaps because he hadn't wanted me to watch his struggles to raise the sash. "Thanks for the company," he said.

I thought I'd been more than that. At least there was no need for me to wish for any on the walk home. I believed this until the woods came in sight, as much as they could for the dark. Night had arrived with a vengeance, and the houses beyond the triangle of wasteland cut off nearly all the light from the estate. Just a patch at the edge of the woods was lit by the solitary intact streetlamp.

Its glare seemed starkest on the area of rubbly ground where the house with the watchful occupant had been. The illuminated empty stretch reminded me of a stage awaiting a performer. Suppose the last tenant of the house had refused to move? Where would they have gone now that it was demolished? How resentful, even vengeful, might they be? I was heading for the nearest street when I heard the feral snarl of motorcycles beyond the houses. Without further thought I made for the woods.

Arbour Street and Shady Lane were far too dark. If the path took me past the site of the house, at least it kept me closer to the streetlamp. I sidled through the gap in the railings and followed the track as fast as the low-lying darkness let me. More than once shadows that turned out to be tendrils of undergrowth almost tripped me up. Trees and bushes kept shutting off the light before letting it display me again, though could anyone be watching? As it blazed in my eyes it turned my breaths the colour of fear, but

I didn't need to think that. I was shivering only because much of the chill of the night seemed to have found a home in the woods. The waste ground of Copse View was as deserted as ever. If I glanced at it every time the woods showed it I might collide with something in the dark.

I was concentrating mostly on the path when it brought me alongside the streetlamp. Opposite the ground where the demolished house had been, the glare was so unnaturally pale that it reduced the trees and shrubs and other vegetation to black and white. A stretch of ferns and their shadows beside the path looked more monochrome than alive or real. My shadow ventured past the lamp before I did, and jerked nervously over a discoloured mosaic of dead leaves as I turned my back on the site of the house. Now that the light wasn't in my eyes I could walk faster, even if details of the woods tried to snag my attention: a circular patch of yellowish lichen on a log, lichen so intricate that it resembled embroidery; the vertical pattern on a tree trunk, lines thin and straight as pinstripes; a tangle of branches that put me in mind of collapsed shelves; a fractured branch protruding like a chair arm from a seat in a hollow tree with blanched ferns growing inside the hollow. None of this managed to halt me. It was a glimpse of a face in the darkness that did.

As a shiver held me where I was I saw that the face was peering out of the depths of a bush. It was on the side of the path that was further from Copse View, and some yards away from my route. I was trying to nerve myself to sprint past it when I realised why the face wasn't moving; it was on a piece of litter caught in the bush. I took a step that tried to be casual, and then I faltered again. It wasn't on a piece of paper as I'd thought. It was the queen's portrait on a plate.

At once I felt surrounded by the deserted house or its remains. I swung around to make sure the waste ground was still deserted—that the woods were. Then I stumbled backwards away from the streetlamp and almost sprawled into the undergrowth. No more than half a dozen paces away—perhaps fewer—a figure was leaning on its sticks in the middle of the path.

It was outlined more than illuminated by the light, but I could see how ragged and piebald the scrawny body was. It was crouching forward, as immobile as ever, but I thought it was waiting for me to make the first move, to give it the excuse to hitch itself after me on its sticks. I imagined it coming for me as fast as a spider. I sucked in a breath I might have used to cry for help if any had been remotely likely. Instead I made myself twist around for the fastest sprint of my life, but my legs shuddered to a halt. The figure was ahead of me now, at barely half the distance.

The worst of it was the face, for want of a better word. The eyes and mouth were little more than tattered holes, though just too much more, in a surface that I did my utmost not to see in any detail. Nevertheless they widened, and there was no mistaking their triumph. If I turned away I would find the shape closer to me, but moving forward would bring it closer too. I could only shut my eyes and try to stay absolutely still.

It was too dark inside my eyelids and yet not sufficiently dark. I was terrified to see a silhouette looming on them if I shifted so much as an inch. I didn't dare even open my mouth, but I imagined speaking—imagined it with all the force I could find inside myself. "Go away. Leave me alone. I didn't do anything. Get someone else."

For just an instant I thought of my uncle, to establish that I didn't mean him, and then I concentrated on whoever had robbed him. An icy wind passed through the woods, and a tree creaked like an old door. The wind made me feel alone, and I tried to believe I entirely was. At last I risked looking. There was no sign of the figure ahead or, when I forced myself to turn, behind me or anywhere else.

I no longer felt safe in the woods. I took a few steps along the path before I fought my way through the bushes to the railings. I'd seen a gap left by a single railing, but was it wide enough for me to squeeze through? Once I'd succeeded, scraping my chest and collecting flakes of rust on my prickly skin, I fled home. I slowed and tried to do the same to my breath at the end of my street, and then I made another dash. My mother's car was pulling away from the house.

She halted it beside me, and my father lowered his window. "Where do you think you've been, Craig?"

His grimness and my mother's made me feel more threatened than I understood. "Helping," I said.

"Don't lie to us," said my mother. "Don't start doing that as well."

"I'm not. Why are you saying I am? I was helping Uncle Phil. He's gone slow."

They gazed at me, and my father jerked a hand at the back seat. "Get in."

"Tom, are you sure you want him—"

"Your uncle's been run over."

"He can't have been. I left him in his flat." When this earned no response I demanded "How do you know?"

"They found us in his pocket." Yet more starkly my father added "Next of kin."

I didn't want to enquire any further. When the isolated streetlamp on Copse View came in sight I couldn't tell whether I was more afraid of what else I might see or that my parents should see it as well. I saw nothing to dismay me in the woods or the demolished street, however—nothing all the way to Pasture Boulevard. My mother had to park several hundred yards short of my uncle's flat. The police had put up barriers, beyond which a giant Frugo lorry was skewed across the central strip, uprooting half a dozen trees. In front of and under the cab of the lorry were misshapen pieces of a wheelchair. I tried not to look at the stains on some of them and on the road, but I couldn't avoid noticing the cereal bars strewn across the pavement. "He forgot to buy me one of those and I didn't like to ask," I said. "He must have gone back."

My parents seemed to think I was complaining rather than trying to understand. When I attempted to establish that it hadn't been my fault they acted as if I was making too much of a fuss. Before the funeral the police told them more than one version of the accident. Some witnesses said my uncle had been wheeling his chair so fast that he'd lost control and spun into the road. Some said he'd appeared to be in some kind of panic, others that a gang of cyclists on the pavement had, and he'd swerved out of their way. The cyclists were never identified. As if my parents had achieved one of their aims at last, the streets were free of rogue cyclists for weeks.

I never knew how much my parents blamed me for my uncle's death. When I left school I went into caring for people like him. In due course these included my parents. They're gone now, and while sorting out the contents of our house I found the book with my early teenage stories in it—childish second-hand stuff. I never asked to have it back, and I never wrote stories again. I couldn't shake off the idea that my imagination had somehow caused my uncle's death.

I could easily feel that my imagination has been revived by the exercise book—by the cover embroidered with a cobweb, the paper pinstriped with faded lines, a fern pressed between the yellowed pages and blackened by age. I'm alone with my imagination up here at the top of the stairs leading to the unlit hall. If there's a face at the edge of my vision, it must belong to a picture on the wall, even if I don't remember any there. Night fell while I was leafing through the book, and I have to go over there to switch the light on. Of course I will, although the mere thought of moving seems to make the floorboards creak like sticks. I can certainly move, and there's no reason not to. In a moment—just a moment while I take another breath—I will.

From an anecdote by Kim Greyson. Thanks, Kim!

About the Author

JOHN RAMSEY CAMPBELL (born 4 January 1946 in Liverpool) is an English horror fiction author, editor and critic. Since he first came to prominence in the mid-1960s, critics have cited Campbell as one of the leading writers in his field: T. E. D. Klein has written that "Campbell reigns supreme in the field today", while S. T. Joshi stated, "future generations will regard him as the leading horror writer of our generation, every bit the equal of Lovecraft or Blackwood."

Acknowledgments

"The Address" first appeared in *Cut Corners,* edited by Shane McKenzie.

"Behind the Doors" first appeared in *Memoryville Blues* [*Postscripts* 30/31], edited by Peter Crowther and Nick Gevers.

"Chucky Comes to Liverpool" first appeared in *Haunted Legends,* edited by Ellen Datlow and Nick Mamatas.

"The Decorations" first appeared as *The Decorations,* Alpenhouse Apparitions, Stockton, 2005.

"Getting It Wrong" first appeared in *A Book of Horrors,* edited by Stephen Jones.

"Holding the Light" first appeared as *Holding the Light,* PS Publishing, Hornsea, 2011.

"The Long Way" first appeared as *The Long Way,* PS Publishing, Hornsea, 2008.

"Passing through Peacehaven" first appeared in *Portents,* edited by Al Sarrantonio.

"Peep" first appeared in *Postscripts* 10, edited by Peter Crowther.

"Recently Used" first appeared in *Black Static* 24, edited by Andy Cox.

"The Room Beyond" first appeared in *The New and Perfect Man* [*Postscripts* 24/25], edited by Peter Crowther and Nick Gevers.

"The Rounds" first appeared in *The End of the Line,* edited by Jonathan Oliver.

"With the Angels" first appeared in *Visitants,* edited by Stephen Jones.

All other stories original to this collection.

Colophon

The text of this book was set in Plantin, a typeface by Frank Hinman Pierpont based on a Granjon design and imitiating the effect of greater ink spread in older printing. Hinesburg was used for titling. The type ornament is from Plants.

4217548R00142

Printed in Great Britain
by Amazon.co.uk, Ltd.,
Marston Gate.